MONSTERLAND

ALSO BY JAMES CROWLEY

✦✦

Starfish

MONSTERLAND

Though my soul may set in darkness,
it will rise in perfect light;
I have loved the stars too fondly
to be fearful of the night.
—Sarah Williams,
"The Old Astronomer to His Pupil"

JAMES CROWLEY

G. P. PUTNAM'S SONS

G. P. Putnam's Sons
an imprint of Penguin Random House LLC
375 Hudson Street
New York, NY 10014

Copyright © 2017 by James Crowley.
Map copyright © 2017 by Richard Amari.
Interior illustrations copyright © 2017 by Morgan Schweitzer.

Library of Congress Cataloging-in-Publication Data is available upon request.

Printed in the United States of America.
ISBN 9780399175893
1 3 5 7 9 10 8 6 4 2

Design by Eileen Savage.
Text set in Chronicle Text G1.

For Leila

CONTENTS

VOLUME III

VOLUME I

— *chapter* 1 —

No Man's Land

CHARLIE WAS THERE again, in this familiar place, with its windswept sand and jagged rocks, its vast emptiness. For a moment, he thought he saw the boy out on the open plain in the distance. He had seen him here before and called to him, but there was never an answer. This left Charlie to wonder if the boy was ever really there, or if instead, he was seeing nothing more than the other shadows that stretched across the horizon. The name he called out to the boy was Billy, and in this place Billy always walked alone, in silhouette, toward a setting sun.

"Charlie, Charlie Cooper."

Charlie opened his eyes. There was a puddle of drool next to his hand on the yellow plastic grain finish of his desk.

"Would you care to join us?"

Charlie's fifth-grade class laughed, and someone—even the teacher, Ms. Hatchet, wasn't sure who—was making cartoonish snoring sounds.

"Come on, Charlie, sit up. You may be surprised. You might actually find this interesting." Ms. Hatchet clapped her hands. "And, class, that goes for the rest of you too. We're almost there. Class!" Another clap. "Class!"

Charlie blinked, slowly focusing on his notebook and the tattered photograph that was propped up against it. The picture was of two boys standing in front of a large barn. Charlie was the smaller of the two, although it was difficult to make out his cousin Billy's face through the sun flares that had dappled the camera's lens that day. Both boys were wearing vampire capes and smiles that exposed pointed, plastic fangs, and surrounding them were pumpkins, piles and piles of pumpkins.

Charlie lifted his head and stared blankly at the map that was pulled down in front of the blackboard. He wasn't ready to be back in Ms. Hatchet's class yet. He was tired and wished he could just keep on sleeping, but he knew that wasn't an option—there had already been plenty of warnings. Charlie folded the photograph and returned it to the pocket of his sweatshirt.

"Now, this area, which would eventually become part of the Oklahoma Territory," Ms. Hatchet was saying, "was known as No Man's Land. It was thought at the time to be the hangout of outlaws and other questionable characters."

Ms. Hatchet paused as the rest of her class sat up slightly. The students, a gruesome assembly of smeared makeup, hooded capes, and rubber-molded masks, were almost all in costume.

"Yes, *outlaws*. I thought that might get your attention. You see this region." Ms. Hatchet pointed at the northwest corner of the map. "When they divided up the land into the Oklahoma, Colorado, and Kansas Territories, they forgot this section."

Charlie studied the faded region of the map. Sure enough, the mapmakers at the time had missed a section.

"But the authorities learned their lesson. Just because a place isn't on an official map doesn't mean it doesn't exist," Ms. Hatchet lectured. "And although this strip certainly *did* exist, it did not formally become part of the United States until the passage of the Organic Act of 1890, which assigned the land to the newly appointed Oklahoma Territory."

"Okay, class, so let's remember, 'Ok-la-homa Territory.' Repeat after me: 'Ok-la-homa Territory.'"

"Ok-la-homa Territory," the class robotically returned.

Charlie's gaze wandered to the window. It had rained on and off all morning, and through the cotton ball cobwebs and rubber spiders that decorated the window's frame, he could see that a heavy gray mist still hung in the treetops surrounding the playground.

"I think there may be a lesson here for all of us," Ms. Hatchet continued. "Could you imagine, a no-man's-land? Hundreds of thousands of forgotten acres that some surveyor failed to include on any maps?"

Charlie looked at the clock. It seemed to be stubbornly hovering a few minutes before the top of the hour.

"Sounds to me like this is the story of one mapmaker who didn't do his homework." Ms. Hatchet glanced at her watch. "Well, looks like All Hallows' Eve is almost upon us!"

Ms. Hatchet turned, concealing her face for a moment, and then spun back around, wearing a wrinkled green witch mask that muffled her voice. "Remember, have fun tonight, but be safe. And please make sure you are home before the clock strikes twelve, for midnight is the bewitching hour, when the monsters, ghouls, and goblins roam our streets looking for girls and boys who do not obey their parents, or teachers, and who refuse to brush their teeth . . ."

The entire class looked at "Stink Mouth" Sam, who conspicuously covered his mouth.

"Oh, come on," Sam called out. "I brushed this morning!"

"That's good, Sam. Lesson learned," Ms. Hatchet continued as the bell rang. "All right, Happy Halloween!"

The class erupted, running for the door.

"Keep the mayhem to a minimum and don't eat all your candy at once!" Ms. Hatchet shouted over her students' exit.

Charlie got up from his desk and slowly pulled on his backpack. His foot had fallen asleep, and he stomped as he stood to shake the pins and needles free.

"Hold on there, Charlie," Ms. Hatchet said. She was still wearing the witch mask, so it was difficult to understand exactly what she was saying. "Aren't you forgetting something?"

"Forgetting something, Ms. Hatchet?"

Ms. Hatchet held out an old pillowcase with *Charlie* scribbled across the front in smeared orange and black Magic Marker. Earlier in the week, they had decorated the trick-or-treat sacks in art class, Charlie with less enthusiasm than his classmates.

"I know it's just the candy from school today, but it's a start, right?"

Charlie took the sack from Ms. Hatchet. "Oh yeah, the candy. Thank you. I must have left it in the cafeteria."

"And, Charlie," Ms. Hatchet said, removing her mask. "About the quiz. A little better, but I know it's not your best. Still having trouble concentrating?"

"A little."

"Well, these things take time, so keep trying, okay?"

Other than a quick look toward the door, Charlie did not respond. While he appreciated Ms. Hatchet's checking in on him, he really just wanted to leave. Charlie always wanted to leave, to be somewhere else, anywhere except for where he was.

"I have something for you." Ms. Hatchet opened her desk and presented a pair of plastic glow-in-the-dark fangs to Charlie. They were taped to a full-size Hershey's chocolate bar.

"I remember you saying you lost yours."

"Thank you, Ms. Hatchet." Charlie peeled the plastic fangs from the Hershey's wrapper and dropped the chocolate into the sack with the other candy he had collected at lunch.

"There will be plenty more candy after trick-or-treating, right?"

"I don't know, Ms. Hatchet. I don't think I'm going trick-or-treating this year."

Ms. Hatchet set the witch mask down on her desk. "You sure?"

"This'll be enough," Charlie said, swinging the sack over his shoulder.

"No trick-or-treating. Well, you are still working in the pumpkin patch tonight, aren't you?"

"Yes, ma'am."

"I doubt Old Joe would have it any other way. It's good having it back, isn't it? The pumpkin patch?"

Charlie shoved the fangs in his mouth and nodded.

"The town—well, everyone—really missed it last year." Ms. Hatchet smiled.

Charlie tried to smile back, but with his mouth full of glow-in-the-dark plastic, it was hard to tell if he was succeeding.

"All right, I will see you there."

"Okay, Ms. Hatchet, see you there." Charlie turned to the door, but stopped just before opening it.

"Yes, Charlie?"

He held up the candy sack.

"Thanks again," Charlie said. Then he bit down on the fangs and walked out the door.

chapter 2

The Orchards

A WHIRLWIND OF LEAVES, red, purple, and gold, swirled around Charlie's sneakers as he walked across the playground, counting his steps home. Usually, counting things made him feel better, but today it was somehow harder to keep track with the plastic fangs in his mouth. He wasn't sure why. He wasn't counting out loud—he was counting to himself—but still he was having trouble concentrating.

Following the cracks in the sidewalk, Charlie passed the other kids from his class, going largely ignored except for a sad, sympathetic smile from a girl named Birdy Fargus. Charlie tried to wave back; however, Birdy did not seem to notice, so he kept on moving, careful to go the long way around the rock outcrop that marked the start of the high school playing fields.

From the cover of the tree line, he could see a group of older kids, some already in costume, lingering on the rocks. *To avoid their teachers and coaches,* Billy used to laugh. But now, Charlie thought, looking out over the open fields, Billy was gone. Charlie glanced back at the older kids and decided to stick to the high trees. Even though it took a little longer, he knew the detour was worth the effort, and was soon on the main street that went through the middle of town anyway.

Charlie's hometown sat at the foot of the mountains, right along the coast, and was said to be "picturesque" with "something to offer tourists year-round." In spring, it was the flowers that clung to the rolling grass hills. Summer, it was the beaches and wild, rambling rivers. In autumn, it was haunted hayrides, cake doughnuts, apple cider, and the colors of the ever-changing trees; and in winter, the mountains' great pine forests were covered with snow—a perfect backdrop for any Christmas card. But of all the holidays that the town celebrated, Halloween was the favorite. No one seemed to know exactly how or why it was so popular, or if they did, they rarely spoke of it, electing instead to point their fingers toward the foot of the mountains and the abandoned military base that was adjacent to the orchards where Charlie's family lived.

Everyone knew Charlie's grandfather as "Old Joe," even Charlie. And for Old Joe, Halloween was more than just a holiday; some even said it was his obsession. For almost every October, as far back as any kid in the town could remember, Old Joe had transformed the orchards and large barn that sat down the hill from his house into a hayride and haunted maze. Visitors loaded into wagons and were taken to the three-story barn and the pumpkin patch that draped up the hill to the dark woods behind it. The pumpkins were only available to those who dared to pass through the haunted structure, taking some of the children years to work up the courage and make the journey.

Charlie turned down a gravel drive, which led up through Old Joe's orchards. The apple trees were spread out between the pines along the foothills, bordered by the mountains and the river. Charlie lived with his mother, father, and Old Joe in the house that was the centerpiece of the property. With its sagging windows and rotting widow's walk, the big Victorian was in a constant state of disrepair and looked almost as haunted as the decorated barn.

"Honey, is that you?"

Charlie passed the jack-o'-lanterns that lined the worn wooden steps to the porch, and threw open the screen door.

"Yeah, it's me," Charlie yelled. There was a scratchy Bobby "Boris" Pickett and the Crypt-Kickers album blaring from an old record player.

"Shut the door, will you?" his mother called to him. "With this front coming in, there's suddenly a real chill in the air."

Charlie did as he was told and crossed the living room's creaky floorboards to the double doors that led into the kitchen.

"How are you? Good day?" Charlie heard his mother say through a thick veil of pasta steam. She was boiling huge pots of spaghetti for the brain and gut bowls that the haunted barn's guests would have to put their hands in to enter.

Charlie shrugged.

"How was school?"

"Ah, it was okay. We learned about a mapmaker who forgot to put things on a map."

"That's interesting." Charlie's mother was preoccupied with the pot of pasta that she was struggling to strain in the sink.

"I guess."

"You should get changed and see if you can help out down at the barn."

"Where's Dad?"

"At work, but he'll be home soon. There's still some time to trick-or-treat before you give Old Joe a hand, though. Knock on a few doors, get some candy . . ."

"Why does everyone keep saying that?"

"Saying what, honey?"

"That I can go trick-or-treating," he mumbled.

"Well, you certainly don't have to go if you don't want to." His mother set the strainer in the sink. "You all right?"

"I don't know."

"Charlie . . ."

"I guess . . . I guess I just wish Billy was going to be here . . ." Charlie was about to say more but stopped.

"Oh, honey." His mother sighed, pulling him into a hug. "I do too."

She kissed him gently on the forehead, and when Charlie looked up, he could see a familiar sadness in her eyes.

"We all miss him. You hang in there, though, and you'll see. The world won't seem so bad someday."

Charlie slipped the plastic vampire teeth Ms. Hatchet had given him into his mouth.

"I better get ready."

"Okay," his mother said, forcing a smile and letting him go. "I know Old Joe will be happy to see you."

"Tell him I'll be down in a bit," Charlie said over his shoulder as he left the kitchen.

In the living room, "Monster Mash" was skipping on the record player, repeating again and again, *"Whatever happened to my Transylvania Twist?"* Charlie ignored it and started up the stairs, counting each one as he climbed.

He passed Old Joe's room at the top of the landing, and his parents', then paused at the room that had been his cousin Billy's. It had become more of a storeroom lately; there were cardboard boxes open with surplus Halloween decorations and discarded bits of costumes strewn about. Charlie took a step into the room to search for his werewolf mask but retreated when he saw Billy's vampire costume neatly folded on top of an open box.

Their first Halloween together, Old Joe had said Billy was tall and thin enough, so he persuaded him to play the haunted barn's resident vampire. With the long black hooded cloak, ghost-white makeup, and specially fitted fangs, Billy made an imposing figure looming in the shadows of the pumpkin patch. But that . . . that was before. Charlie quickly turned away from the dark folded suit and closed the door. He continued down the hall to his room, telling himself that his mask was somewhere else, more than likely under his bed.

Charlie's room was in the corner of the house where the eaves joined the attic to the second floor. The winding bend of a giant oak grew just out the window, giving him the feeling that he lived in a tree house. He sat on the foot of his bed and thought for a moment, then pulled the photograph from his sweatshirt pocket. His mother had taken the photo of the boys with her ancient instamatic camera just last October, a few years after Billy had come to live with them. Billy had been having trouble at home back then, and when he ran away a second time, Old Joe suggested he spend that summer, longer if need be, working in the orchard.

He recalled the talks he'd overheard from the kitchen before his cousin arrived that June. *You'd be amazed,* Old Joe said at dinner one night, *what a little hard work and some fresh air can do for a boy.*

So Billy joined Charlie that summer in the orchard. They worked hard, but when their chores were done, Old Joe let them run free through the apple trees, swim in the river, and camp in the mountains that bordered the property. Then summer turned to fall, and instead of returning home, Billy stayed. He enrolled in school and lived with them. He became a regular part of the family, and after a while, everyone just thought of him as Charlie's older brother.

Charlie put the photograph back in his pocket, lay down on his bed, and looked out the window at the sprawling tree. He was tired and remembered admitting to the school counselor that he was still having trouble sleeping. And even when he managed to fall asleep, strange dreams would wake him in the middle of the night, the old house quiet except for his family's heavy breathing and the groaning moan of the old oak as it swayed in the wind.

On these sleepless nights, Charlie often found himself wandering the house, drifting from room to room, sometimes spending hours staring at the family photos that hung in the hall and down the stairs. Alone and afraid, he would look at Old Joe's medals from the war and occasionally take down the saber that was displayed next to a neatly folded flag. Some nights, Charlie would sit on the front porch and gaze into the darkness, and others he'd wake at the foot of his parents' bed, with his mother or father sleepwalking him back to his room, where he found himself tangled up in his blankets by morning.

Charlie closed his eyes. He could still see the picture. He could still see Billy standing next to him, and he could see that they were smiling.

— *chapter 3* —

Trick or Treat

"CHARLIE," HIS MOTHER called, "they're going to need your help down at the barn."

It was late. He must have fallen asleep. Charlie saw out the window that the approaching storm was now clinging to the top of the mountain and had already darkened the late-afternoon sky. The wind had picked up too, which was giving a cluster of birds some trouble as they fought to seek shelter in the high trees beyond the orchards.

Charlie jumped down to search for his rubber wolf mask under the bed and was relieved to find it buried in a pile of clothes. He pulled it on and paused at his reflection in the mirror, satisfied with his decision to be a werewolf this year instead of a vampire.

Charlie heard his bedroom door creaking open on its rusty hinges and quickly crouched down behind the bed. He knew it was Ringo from the tapping sound of his nails on the floorboards. The dog was a stray, but the day he showed up at the orchards, Old Joe had said he was sure that the mutt was at least part German shepherd. Charlie thought he sort of looked like a wolf and considered them to be the best of friends.

Ringo peered up from the doorway, cocked his head suspiciously, and then barked, which prompted Charlie to jump out at the big dog. Ringo dropped down, baring his teeth in a low growl.

"It's me," Charlie said, laughing and lifting up his mask. "I don't get how you could live here and still be tricked by this old thing."

As Ringo moved closer, Charlie pulled the mask back down and growled. Ringo barked again and whimpered in return, before jumping up and knocking Charlie to the floor.

"Come on, boy," Charlie said, pushing his dog off him.

They took the stairs three at a time and burst into the kitchen, planning to only stop long enough for Charlie to grab his sack of school candy and to zip up his hooded sweatshirt.

"I thought you weren't going trick-or-treating," Charlie's mother said, her ancient instamatic camera already in hand. She was dressed in her mummy costume but had yet to put on her headdress or face makeup. "And what did I tell you about letting Ringo in the kitchen? You know he'll get into those brain bowls, not to mention the spa-*gut*-ti that I just finished making—"

"I'm not going. Just thought I'd bring some of the candy I got at school down to the barn." Charlie went one way around the kitchen table and then the other, but knew that once the instamatic was out, it was going to be difficult getting past her.

"Well, you know Old Joe loves having a few chocolate bars around, that's for sure," she went on, fumbling with the camera. "Now, turn around for me, Charlie, and stand up straight."

Charlie obeyed and faced his mother.

"There," she said, snapping a photo. "But let's try one now without the mask?" Charlie's mother pushed the rubber were-wolf muzzle to the top of his head. "Say boo!"

Charlie sighed and exposed his plastic fangs to the flash. Then he quickly pulled the mask back down.

"Well, there's your Christmas card." Charlie's father entered the kitchen wrapping his head in his mummy linens. "Merry Christmas from the haunted house weirdos and our fanged son, with wishes to you and yours." He half laughed. "How you doing, Charlie?"

"I'm all right."

"Heading down to the barn?"

Charlie nodded.

"I'll be there as soon as I get this wrapped up—get it? Wrapped up? It's mummy humor—"

"Yeah, Dad, I get it, wrapped up," Charlie said flatly.

"Old Joe's going to need some help tying things down. Looks like we're in for some nasty weather," Charlie's father added, looking out the window. "But you know he's not about to let a few storm clouds put a damper on things."

"You two hold still, now," Charlie's mother ordered, taking another picture and winding back the film. "Oh, and, Charlie,

I talked to Ms. Hatchet and she's going to drop by tonight. I'm so glad you're in her class this year. She's been such a dear this past—"

But Charlie was no longer listening. With Ringo at his heels, he pulled his hood over his mask, threw the candy sack on his shoulder, and kicked open the screen door. They jumped to the bottom of the porch stairs and ran down the hill toward the barn until Ringo stopped to bark at the trees lining the gravel driveway.

"Oh no, don't you even think about running off—"

Ringo whimpered, glanced up at Charlie and then back to the woods.

"Leave it alone, Ringo, it's just some old squirrel. He's trying to get ready for winter and doesn't need you bothering him."

Ringo barked again and bolted off into the trees.

"Oh, come on, Ringo!" Charlie shouted after him. He looked toward the barn and the mountains that towered just beyond the tree line. Even with the storm brewing, there were already a few early trick-or-treaters making their way toward the pumpkin patch.

"Ringo!" Charlie called, but the dog was already gone.

IT WAS QUIET AND THE TREES THAT COVERED THE LONG GRAVEL drive seemed eerie now that the sun was setting. Charlie walked, counting his steps as he listened to his sneakers crunching on the crushed stone. He had doubled back through the woods hoping that he would cut Ringo off before he got to the road. But there was no sign of him, so he decided to head to the barn, figuring that Ringo knew the property as well as anyone and would eventually show up—he always did.

Charlie followed the drive toward the edge of the orchards and stopped at a high fence with rolls of loose barbed wire hanging along the top. A faded sign on the rusted chain-link read: WARNING—GOVERNMENT PROPERTY—NO TRESPASSING.

From the road, the fence was almost all that was still visible of the old army base. Tarmacs that were once heavy with military traffic were now overgrown with vegetation. The small garrison had been decommissioned because of "cutbacks," Old Joe said, but that was before Charlie was born. There were stories about the base, from the old days, suspicious rumors, really, of strange projects that the government had kept hidden. Charlie pleaded with Old Joe to tell him what he remembered, but was routinely rebuffed. His parents had made Old Joe promise "not to fill the boy's head with nonsense," and Old Joe was a man of his word.

"Ringo! Ringo, you out there?" Charlie shouted at the shadowy trees around him. "We can throw a few rocks at the old armory if you want to . . ."

But his voice trailed off again, and the only answer was the cawing squawk of a magpie that was perched just above his head on a twisted branch. Magpies drove Old Joe crazy. They were always getting into his workbench back at the barn. He often pointed out that when magpies stole food from his lunch, they usually just went for the cookie. He claimed that showed their intelligence, but they still drove him crazy.

"Hello, Mr. Magpie," Charlie said, addressing the bird. "You haven't seen a dog back here, have you?"

Like Ringo, the bird ignored him. It stared at him briefly, and then flew off into the trees. Charlie looked up again at the darkening sky. He could tell the rain was coming, but he still had a little time before Old Joe would really need him, so he pushed through a hole in the fence and climbed over the pile of crumbled concrete that blocked his path.

Charlie counted his steps until he hit a row of rusted Quonset huts and dilapidated buildings, one of which, the old armory, had large steel-framed windows that still held a few panes of broken glass. He had been here many times, but that was before, with Billy. The boys used to spend hours in these woods together, despite the warning signs and barbed wire. With Billy gone, Charlie still found himself here every now and then, but it was different. Charlie no longer came here to play and explore; nowadays he came here to smash out what little glass was left in the armory's high window frames.

Charlie picked up a hunk of concrete and threw it at the corner of one of the windows. Missing its target, it skipped with an echo across the abandoned building. He tried again and again, rock after rock, each time without success. So Charlie kicked around the rubble until he found a small stone, and with a low, angry grunt, he threw it as hard as he could. It hit the corner of the window, smashing a sliver of the dangling glass, which fell to the ground with a satisfying shattering sound. He smiled. Now he could go.

Charlie turned and called again for Ringo. When the dog

still didn't answer, he had to assume he was already at the barn with Old Joe. He pulled the werewolf mask down, slung the candy over his shoulder, and turned back toward the fence. He counted out a few steps but stopped abruptly when he noticed something standing in the shadows in front of him.

"Ringo? Is that you?"

The shadow was silent.

"Ringo?" Charlie repeated. He could feel the heaviness of his breath on the rubber of his mask.

"*Ringo?*" a voice said.

Charlie spun around. Someone was behind him.

"Boo!" An illuminated skeletal face appeared with the click of a flashlight.

"Yeah, boo," the figure blocking Charlie's path added. The flashlight beam shifted to a mask with ghoulish green features.

"Hey, keep that light out of my face," the boy in the ghoul mask said to the boy in the skeleton mask. There was a third boy, dressed as a mummy, standing on a pile of rubble above them. He was wrapped in rags fashioned from what looked like an old beach towel, which hung around his feet, dragging in dirty strips.

"What are you doing here?" the homemade mummy said. The voice was muffled and a little lost under his costume.

"Looks like he's smashing windows," the ghoul pointed out.

The mummy scratched his bandaged head. "But the sign says no trespassing."

"It sure does," the skeleton agreed. "No trespassing."

"It doesn't matter," Charlie said, trying unsuccessfully

to sound strong. "No one comes back here anymore. No one cares."

"The army does—they must. Doubt they would have that sign up if they didn't," the mummy countered.

"We could call the cops," the boy in the skeleton mask said, walking toward Charlie. "Or you could just hand over your candy and we can let it go. No harm done, right?"

"Candy, candy, we want candyyyy," the ghoul moaned.

Charlie's heart was racing. He pulled his clutched fist from his pocket and held the candy sack firmly with two hands. Back at school, he didn't really care about the candy. Or at least he thought he didn't. But now he suddenly felt different. It was his and he was bringing it to the barn to share with Old Joe.

"Come on, give us the candy," the skeleton said.

"No," Charlie replied, making an effort to steady his voice. He tried to imagine what Billy would do if he were here.

"No?" The ghoul stepped forward. "Let's go, hand it over."

"It's mine." Charlie slowly started to back toward the hole in the fence. The boys were all bigger than him, but Charlie knew he was pretty fast, the second-fastest in his class after Birdy Fargus, actually, so he figured if he could just get to the road that he might be able to make a break for the barn or hide in the pumpkin patch.

"Come on," the mummy said.

"Candy, candy. Me want candyyyy," the ghoul moaned again, swiping at Charlie's candy.

"Go get your own," Charlie said, pulling the candy sack closer.

"Go get my own? Ooooo," the ghoul mocked.

Charlie could feel his fear turning to anger. When the bigger boy reached for the sack a second time, Charlie tried to push him, but the ghoul barely moved.

"All right," the skeleton said, grabbing ahold of the sack from the side. "You asked for it."

"It's mine!" Charlie shouted. "Leave me alone!"

"Ha-ha, that little kid won't give you his candy." The mummy laughed at his friend.

"I said," the skeleton demanded, jerking the bag and Charlie forward, "give me the candy . . ."

Charlie's foot slipped on the wet ground and he fell, hitting his head on a chunk of broken concrete. When he looked up, the only thing he could see was tiny flashes of dancing yellow light.

"Let go!" the skeleton shouted, pulling roughly at the candy sack in Charlie's hands. But Charlie, his head aching, hung on, the older boy dragging him and the sack across what was left of the gravel tarmac.

"This kid is crazy. Just let him keep his stupid candy," the mummy said.

"No way." The boy in the skeleton mask wrestled with the bag until it ripped. "Give it!" he shouted, and kicked at Charlie.

Charlie felt his lip swelling, the pounding in his head worsening, and the candy sack slipping through his fingers. It all seemed to be going in slow motion now, and for a second, just as the Hershey's bar from Ms. Hatchet fell from the hole in the sack and hit Charlie in the head, it was almost like time stood still.

"Just. Let. Go!" With a final tug, the boy in the skeleton mask jerked the bag free and fell back onto the ground, sending the ghoul and the mummy into another fit of laughter.

"What's your problem?" the skeleton spat, climbing back to his feet with Charlie's candy sack in his hand.

"You can barely steal candy from a baby!" the ghoul cried.

"I got it, didn't I?" the skeleton snapped, joining the mummy and the ghoul. They stood above Charlie, riffling through the sack.

"Doesn't look like much," the ghoul complained.

"It's just my school candy." Charlie coughed. He was lying facedown on the wet concrete and could already taste the salty blood on his lip.

"Your school candy?" the mummy repeated. "What's school candy?"

"From school today. We went from classroom to classroom at lunch." Charlie was having trouble catching his breath. "I didn't go trick-or-treating."

"School candy. That's just sad." The mummy laughed. "And what do you mean, you didn't go trick-or-treating? Who doesn't go trick-or-treating?"

"Maybe he means he just hasn't gone yet," the ghoul offered. "You're going later, right?"

"No, I'm not," Charlie declared. It hurt his head to raise his voice. "What's the big deal?"

"What's the big deal? It's free candy, kid. Everybody knows that."

"Forget about him, will you?" The skeleton was hunched

over with his arm buried up to his elbow in the old pillowcase. "May not look like much, but there's some good stuff in here . . . Reese's, jawbreakers . . . Here." The skeleton tossed the mummy some Milk Duds.

"I think you might have hurt him," the mummy said, looking down.

Charlie agreed. Beneath his werewolf mask, he could feel his head pounding and could still see the flecks of dancing light. And for what? Ringo and those stupid squirrels; all he was trying to do was get down to the barn to help Old Joe.

"Serves him right." The skeleton closed the sack and stepped over Charlie.

The mummy followed after the skeleton. "You should have just given us the candy, kid."

"It does appear that way," the ghoul added with a shrug.

"What's a little kid doing out here by himself, anyway? You should try to get some friends next year!" the skeleton called back to Charlie.

"And go trick-or-treating!" the ghoul shouted.

"Ah, leave him alone," the mummy said, having grown bored with the whole ordeal.

"Leave him alone? But it's Halloween. Ooooo, scary!" the skeleton taunted. "Hey, kid, it's gonna be a long night. Hope the ghosts don't get you!" His voice echoed behind him as the boys ran away from the armory.

Charlie sat up and watched them leave—with his candy. The candy he was taking to the barn to share with Old Joe. It was dark now, but he could hear the jingle of the chain-link when they climbed through the hole in the fence, laughing their way back to the road.

Charlie pulled himself to his feet. If Billy were here, he thought, they would be sorry. He was sure of that. But as he stood, Charlie felt dizzy and stumbled out of the armory. A dull ache from the throbbing lump on his forehead was spreading rapidly through the rest of his body and he suddenly felt sick to his stomach. It was colder now and the trees overhead seemed more sinister, prompting Charlie to pull the hood of his sweat-shirt back over his werewolf mask. When he did, the Hershey's bar from Ms. Hatchet fell out and landed with a thud in the road.

At least they didn't get all of it, Charlie thought. He picked up the chocolate, shoved it into his pocket with his photograph and plastic fangs, and walked slowly back to the road that led down to Old Joe's barn.

— *chapter 4* —

Old Joe's Haunted Barn

THE PUMPKIN PATCH was already packed when Charlie came down the hill to the haunted barn. Despite the weather, it looked like the entire town was there. Young and old alike, a variety of witches, other werewolves, and tutued princesses milled about with ghosts, goblins, and all kinds of ghouls. The crowds would continue like this in steady waves, starting with the younger children and their parents, gradually building in age to the older kids. The evening usually wrapped up with Old Joe reminding them to go home, as the event officially ended with the ringing of a bell at the twelfth stroke of midnight.

Charlie pushed open the big bay doors of the haunted barn. Old Joe was up on a ladder near the doorway making a last-minute adjustment to the "spooky pirate" that swung down from a rafter above the exit. He was whistling and singing a song to himself, which he often did.

Though the worst of the throbbing had stopped, Charlie

considered showing Old Joe the lump on his head. It felt like it was still swelling against the side of his mask, and he was suddenly so tired that all he really wanted to do was just go lie down somewhere. Charlie tried to duck past the ladder, but Old Joe stopped singing as soon as he spotted his grandson, whom he recognized immediately, even with the werewolf mask.

"Hold the ladder there, will you, Charlie?" Old Joe called down to him. "This is all fun for the kiddos, you know, but tonight of all nights it pays to be careful."

Charlie steadied the ladder, although with the pounding in his head, he felt that the ladder was really steadying him.

"They say that the ghouls and goblins like to get out tonight and move around among us," Old Joe said with a glimmer in his eye. He was wearing his old military uniform, a mainstay of his famous Halloween celebrations. As the "host of the haunt," he felt that, while he needed to stay on theme, he should still appear as one of the living to serve as guide and gatekeeper to this realm of the unknown.

"But your parents don't like me talking like that," Old Joe continued as he hid the ladder behind one of the plywood partitions that divided the barn into a tight, disorienting maze. "My guess is that it scares them."

Old Joe dropped to a knee and put his big hands on Charlie's shoulders. "How you doing under there, buddy?"

"I'm okay," Charlie mumbled through his werewolf mask.

"Just okay?"

Charlie did not answer. He looked down at his feet instead.

"It won't be the same for any of us tonight, you know." Old Joe threw his arm around his grandson. "But we trudge on, right? Chin up. We've talked about this."

Charlie nodded as Old Joe stood.

"And we have this storm to worry about, right? Should keep things interesting."

"You need a hand?" Charlie asked, fighting back a yawn. "Dad said you might need some help tying things down."

"Naw, we're good until it all really gets going. Run off. Scare some folks in the pumpkin patch. But be careful. Strange goings-on tonight to be sure . . . strange indeed."

"I'll be all right," Charlie said.

"Of course you will, boy," Old Joe stated proudly, punching his grandson in the shoulder. "Now, come on. Remember, chin up."

"Yes, sir. Chin up."

Charlie adjusted his mask as he stepped out of the darkness of the haunted barn and into the shuffle of the lantern-lit pumpkin patch. Still dizzy, he stumbled forward, knocking over a toddler dressed as a bear cub and a scarecrow, before remembering that he had to be careful with his mask on to avoid the pumpkins that dotted his path.

"Get a load of that. It doesn't look like a real gravestone to me," Charlie heard when he stopped to help the bear cub back to its feet. "Just looks like an old piece of plywood."

Despite his aching head, Charlie instantly recognized the voice. It was the older boy in the skeleton mask. There he was, entering the pumpkin patch with the ghoul and the makeshift mummy, the boys who had stolen his candy.

"And what about that Old Joe geezer?" The skeleton went on, "What's so scary about Mr. Grandpa Army Man?"

The idiot doesn't get it. Old Joe isn't supposed to be scary. He's the gatekeeper, the master of ceremonies, Charlie thought, ducking behind the largest pumpkin he could find. When he was crouched down, the pumpkin was almost as big as he was.

"Ooo, scary, the headless horseman. Same old fake horse that used to sit in front of the feed store. Remember that thing?"

Charlie sat down with his back against the pumpkin and closed his eyes. Old Joe said that when he was in the army, they were told that it was harder for people to see your hiding place if you avoided direct eye contact with them—a practice that Charlie and Billy put to the test in their frequent games of hide-and-seek.

"With this fog, it's so dark out here I can't see a thing," the ghoul grumbled as they passed Charlie's pumpkin.

"Oh yeah?" the mummy said. "Put your hand in front of your face."

Charlie heard a loud slap.

"Hey!" the ghoul cried. "You hit my hand."

"I was giving you a high five."

"But you told me to put my hand in front of my face—"

"Come on," the skeleton broke in. "This sucks. Let's go check out the stupid barn again."

Charlie waited until their voices faded, and pulled off his

rubber werewolf mask. Compared to the inside of the mask, the night air felt cool on his face. His head was hurting again and felt heavy, so he closed his eyes and listened to Old Joe fumbling with the "scary sounds" record that was playing over the loud-speakers. He was tired, as tired as he ever remembered being, and soon, to the scratchy chorus of howling wolves, rattling chains, and distant screams, Charlie fell into a deep, deep sleep.

— *chapter 5* —

Into the Pumpkin Patch

$\mathcal{H}$E WAS BACK there—out on the vast, empty plain. There were birds now too, clouds of them, swirling and screeching just above his head. As always, Charlie could see Billy there in the distance, walking alone in the shadows toward the setting sun. He called to him, shouting to be heard over the screeching birds, but Billy did not answer. He never did. Even so, there was something besides the birds that was different. Charlie could hear the sound of a heavy bell ringing somewhere close by, and this time in his dream, Charlie started to walk. This time, Charlie followed Billy.

The bell was still ringing when Charlie woke. He could still see the place, hear the birds, almost feel the strange sand and jagged rocks under his feet. But he knew he wasn't there. It was cold, much colder than it had been earlier, and the blanket of fog that hung over the pumpkin patch was wet with the coming rain. Charlie sat up; there were a few costumed witches and

ghosts left milling about on their way to the exit, and he wondered how long he had been asleep.

I missed it, Charlie realized, feeling the lump on his forehead. The blood had dried and the throbbing had become a dull
headache. *I slept through Halloween.* But then he paused, his
thoughts interrupted by the trail of a long black cape sweeping
over him in the fog. The cold seemed to follow the shadow, and
Charlie shuddered when it passed.

It was hard to tell with the mist, but it appeared as though
the hooded cape was part of a vampire costume worn by a tall,
slender figure.

"Billy?" Charlie was dizzy and had to lean against the
pumpkin to stand. *It can't be, can it?*

Charlie looked toward the barn. *Billy,* he thought. Billy was
here. Charlie's mind started to race.

Billy was back; Old Joe must have known and sent him
through the woods to scare the last of the crowd as they made
their way home, *just like he used to.* Charlie looked around the
pumpkin patch and saw the cloaked figure slowly making its
way toward the trees at the top of the hill.

"Hey, Billy," Charlie called. "Billy, is that you?"

But the cloaked figure continued on its way.

"Billy, over here!" Charlie shouted, stumbling out of the
pumpkin patch to follow the figure. "Billy, where are you going?
Wait for me, Billy, wait!"

It grew darker as he entered the woods, and with the heavy
mist, it was even more difficult for Charlie to see.

"Billy!" Charlie called out, catching a glimpse of a shadow moving ahead of him in the fog. "Billy, is that you?"

There was still no answer. Charlie followed anyway, running after the figure through the brush and trees as best he could. It seemed like they ran this way for hours. Charlie wondered where Billy was going and why he wouldn't wait for him, or at least answer his calls.

They continued deeper and deeper into the woods, and Charlie noticed that the forest floor had become wet and marshy. He slowed as his feet sank into the cold mire and soon realized that he was in a part of the woods that he no longer recognized. He stopped, glancing at the gnarled branches overhead to try to get his bearings. When he looked down again, the shadow was gone.

"Billy! Billy, where did you go?" Charlie called out to the thunder and croaking moans of the swamp, but still no one answered.

Counting out a hundred paces at a time, Charlie moved forward, looking for signs of the shadowy figure. The muck turned to a cold, watery slough, which slowly rose almost up to his waist the farther he went. *I can't be by the river.* Charlie shuddered, retracing their steps in his mind. *We came into the woods from the hill, and the river is in the opposite direction. Maybe this is the back of the old army base?* The thunder was getting closer now, and Charlie could no longer tell if his shivering was from the cold or the fear that he was lost.

"Billy!" Charlie cried out in a panic. A wolf howled from somewhere over the mountains. "Where are you?"

The thunder brought rain, which blinded Charlie, but he felt a sandbar underfoot, so he waded in that direction until he was able to pull himself up onto a low bank at the edge of the bog.

"Hello?" Charlie called. "Anybody out there?"

He was alone in a small ring of trees. On the other side, there was a low, rusted wrought-iron gate, but the rain and thick gray mist prevented him from seeing much farther.

"Hello?" he whispered again, and then, almost in response to Charlie's hushed tone, the swamp went briefly silent. Charlie turned back around to the bog. "Billy?"

Charlie froze. With a splash, the swamp was suddenly alive again. Something large was running directly at him from the thick underbrush along the bank. Charlie let out a loud yelping sound that was a shock even to him. He backpedaled as fast as he could, but slipped in the mud.

"Help!" he cried before recognizing the big, wet dog running up the bank. "Ringo!"

The dog jumped on Charlie, pinning him to the muddy ground—but Charlie was too happy to care.

"Am I glad to see you! Where've you been? I figured you would have made it back to the barn hours ago."

Ringo whimpered, and his eyes shot from side to side with every sound that rose from the bog behind them.

"What's wrong, boy? You look like you've seen a ghost. You can get us home now, though, can't you? Or are you lost too?"

Ringo's ears shot up and he turned in a circle.

"What is it? Did you see Billy?"

A cold gust ripped through the trees. Ringo barked.

"Oh no, you don't." Charlie reached to grab him, but he was too late. Ringo ran toward the rusted gate, which left Charlie with little choice but to follow.

chapter 6

Here Be Monsters

*A*PPROACHING THE GATE, Charlie noticed that there were faces twisted into the wrought iron. They looked like ghouls and hobgoblins. Beyond them, he could just make out the start of a cemetery that seemed to be more trees and vegetation than actual graves. He thought about leaving, but what about Billy? Where did he go? Besides, he wasn't even sure of how he'd gotten here, let alone how to get back.

Charlie heard the creak of the rusted gate before he even realized he had opened it.

"Ringo?"

He entered the graveyard. The rainy mist was so thick that he could barely see. He took another step, and another, and then, just like that, Ringo was back at his feet.

"What are you doing?" Charlie scolded. "Stay close."

He looked around again, but after just a few paces, he had already lost sight of the cemetery gate. The one he had just entered.

"Billy!" Charlie cried. "Where are you?"

With Ringo by his side, Charlie crept forward, moving deeper into the fog, fighting past the brambles, fallen headstones, and broken statuary. When they emerged from the mist, they found themselves in a sloped area where the headstones continued up toward the base of the mountains above them.

"I've never seen this back here, you?" Charlie whispered. Ringo replied with a sharp turn of his head.

"What is it?" Charlie's eyes followed Ringo's gaze. Something was moving ahead of them in the dark.

He ducked down behind a crumbled statue of an angel and peered out over its broken wing. Through the rain, Charlie could see the cloaked shadow that he had been following. The shadow was stooped and struggled to remove a heavy stone door from the front of an overgrown mausoleum.

"Billy!" Charlie shouted. He stood and took a few steps, stopping short when the shadow entered the mausoleum and disappeared into the darkness.

"Billy! Is that you? It's me!" Charlie yelled, sloshing through the mud toward the crypt. "Please, Billy! You can't just leave me here! I'm scared!" But his words faded.

"I don't understand," Charlie said to Ringo. His voice now quivering, he stared at the open doorway. "Where is he going?"

Charlie tilted his head back to the falling rain just as a loud crack of lightning lit up the sky. He knew that it could be dangerous to be out, cold and wet, for this long, so he forced his feet forward. With Ringo at his heels, Charlie stepped through the stone door frame and felt his way along the uneven steps that led down into the mausoleum.

"Billy, you here?" Charlie called when they reached the bottom. His voice sounded hollow as it echoed through the small room. The fire of a lone torch crackled and danced in the far corner, casting animated shadows on the stacked-stone walls. "I guess we're out of the rain at least, right, Ringo? We can wait it out here and find our way back after the storm if we have to."

A loud thunderclap spilled down the stairs, almost, it seemed, in agreement.

Charlie crept forward but paused when he heard the sound of grinding stone. He turned back to the stairs of the crypt.

"You hear that?"

Ringo cocked his head and howled; the crypt's heavy rock door was closing behind them.

"No, no, no!" Charlie cried, running up the steps and throwing his hands onto the cold stone. He tried to push the door, but his effort had little effect. Ringo looked up at Charlie, his howl turning to a whining whimper as the echo of the sealed stone faded to an uncomfortable silence.

"Believe me," Charlie said to the big dog, "I don't like this either."

Charlie dropped back down into the tomb and noticed that there were intricate carvings of ghouls, goblins, and other monsters cut deep into the walls. The creatures looked to be engaged in battle, and one featured a fierce monster on a large horse. The monster was enormous, wearing armor and holding a heavy battle-ax in one hand. Charlie left the gruesome image and went farther, stopping at a huge sarcophagus that was laid out in the center of the room. Beyond that, there was a tunnel with a sign carved into the stone above the entrance that read in large block letters, HERE BE MONSTERS.

"'Here be monsters'?" Charlie read aloud. "What's that supposed to mean?"

Ringo barked at the open passage.

"Don't worry. We'll be all right," Charlie said, trying to reassure him through his chattering teeth. "I-I-I think."

Ringo barked again at the darkness.

"No, Ringo!" Charlie shouted, but as usual Ringo ignored him and took off down the tunnel.

Charlie turned to the small stairs that led to the entrance of the crypt. The door at the top was still closed.

"Here be monsters," he said again and took a step into the tunnel. "One," he counted out loud, and then, "two . . ."

With each step, Charlie could just make out the flickering of a torch farther down the narrow passage.

"Billy, is that you?" he called, but again the only answer was the fading echo of his own words.

His hands trembling, Charlie felt his way along the wet, mossy walls, until he saw the glow of the torch again.

"Come on, Billy, I'm scared . . . ," he started to say. Then he heard Ringo bark. The sound was high-pitched and sharp.

"Ringo!" Charlie panicked and ran toward the light, following the tunnel around a long bend, the end of which revealed the shadowy figure in the hooded cape standing at a second stone door.

Charlie stopped. He was out of breath. "Billy? Is that you?"

It was still hard to see, but the figure seemed to be studying the carved inscriptions that spiraled around the door frame's heavy rock edges. Ringo sat beside the door whimpering, and much like the strange figure, the dog failed to acknowledge Charlie's presence.

Even so, Charlie was glad to have caught up with them, and with a sigh of relief, he stepped from the shadows and reached out for Billy's hand.

"Hey, Billy, it's me . . . " Charlie froze. The hand he held was cold, very cold. Charlie had expected this to a certain degree—after all, his own hands were numb—but this was a different kind of cold entirely. It was a kind of cold difficult to associate with living things. Charlie slowly looked up at the figure, the icy hand now holding his firmly.

"*Hey, Billy?*" the figure snapped back, tightening his grip.

Charlie could not move.

"*W*hy have you been following me?" the shadowy figure in the hooded cape asked in a peculiar accent. The odd intonation of his words seemed to struggle to keep his *W*'s from slipping into more natural-sounding *V*'s.

Charlie could not speak.

"Well?"

Charlie stared, mesmerized by the hooded figure. He thought he saw the hint of a pearly white fang flash as the ghastly profile turned to face him.

"You seem to have *lost* your ability to speak."

The hooded face was thin, long, and angular. Pale skin, the

texture of a fish's belly, sagged in folds under his eyes, giving his features the drooped appearance that they were melting. It did not look like any Halloween costume that Charlie had ever seen. This, he thought, did not look like a man.

Charlie felt the cold seep into his hand and slowly crawl up his arm.

"I beg your pardon, but I am not in the habit of repeating myself."

"I-I-I'm s-s-sorry," Charlie stuttered. "I think I s-s-saw you earlier, in-in-in the pumpkin patch."

"Ah, the pumpkin patch." The creature smiled, revealing two long, pointed fangs that seemed to drip from the roof of his mouth.

"I-I-I mean, I was following my cousin Billy . . . or I thought I was. I-I-I guess I thought you were him."

"But alas, I am not."

Charlie struggled to pull his hand free of the creature's grasp. Ringo barked.

"Please, my young friend. I mean neither you nor your mongrel harm. After all, you are the ones who *followed* me."

The creature released his hand, and Charlie stumbled back and fell against the wet stone wall. Charlie thought about running, but now, in this tunnel, in the back of the graveyard, he also found that he was strangely drawn to the situation.

"Wh-wh-where are we?" Charlie stammered, his curiosity getting the better of him.

"You are either brave or foolish to wander into a place of which you know nothing. Especially a place, well, a place such as this," the creature replied with a hiss. He turned back to the stone door and ran his long, bony fingers along the carved runes. "Where are you, you ask?" he continued. "Why, my young friend, you stand in a tunnel dug by monster hand. You stand on the very threshold of *Vampyreishtat*, or if you must, in the common vernacular, *Monsterland*."

"M-M-M-Monsterland?"

"I must admit, it surprises me how quickly the outside world forgets." The creature raised a long finger again and tapped his temple with a fingernail that was almost as long. "Monsterland . . . the places in between, the places stuck in the shadows, in the cracks, in the dark . . ." The creature's voice trailed off, as he seemed to be distracted by the thought for a moment. "*Vampyreishtat*, itself," he abruptly continued, "lost in the places where no one *wants* to go . . ." The creature pushed on the great stone door. It moved slightly, the heavy rock grinding against itself. "Care for a peek?"

Wind gushed from the darkness. The air was hot and cold at the same time, filled with the putrid, sweet smell of honeysuckle and rancid meat. Ringo growled. Charlie peered into the tunnel and then looked back at the creature.

"I-I don't understand. Wh-wh-who are you?" Charlie heard the question before he decided to ask it.

At that, the creature removed his black hood, revealing the rest of his face.

"Who am I? Or what am I?" He laughed, clicking his long fangs. "I will grant you one guess."

Charlie gasped at the grotesque features; his ears were pointed, each one scarred and tattered, and he did not have a single hair on his face or head. And those fangs, the way he gnashed his teeth sent a shudder down Charlie's spine. Fearsome as the creature was, Charlie noticed that there was also something oddly calming about him—a strange warmth and sad longing behind his yellow bloodshot eyes. *A vampire?* Charlie thought, but this did not look like any that he had ever seen in the movies or Old Joe's monster magazines. No, he couldn't be.

Charlie felt his head spinning. The vampire turned and appeared to sniff the air through his open nostrils.

"Ah, I smell chocolate . . ."

"I don't under—" Charlie was struggling to catch his breath. "I don't understand . . ."

Ringo barked and Charlie took a step back, his legs starting to buckle beneath him. The vampire reached out to catch him, but Charlie stumbled. Then he collapsed on the cold stone floor.

chapter 7

Mrs. Edith Winthrope

W HEN CHARLIE OPENED his eyes, he found himself in the center of a large bed draped in dark red curtains. With his bad dreams and sleepwalks back home, it wasn't unusual for Charlie's memory to be a bit hazy in the morning, but this was definitely not his room. And the old-fashioned hospital pajamas he wore were definitely not his either. He sat up and pushed open the curtains to reveal his new surroundings.

The room's walls were littered with antlers of every sort and oil paintings of portraits whose subjects looked to be long dead. Ringo sat as still as a statue staring into an immense fireplace that held the last of the night's fading embers. His dark brown fur seemed almost a part of the bearskin rug that lay beneath him.

"Ringo," Charlie whispered. He felt groggy, and even the simplest movement reminded him that his head, while now neatly bandaged, still hurt.

"Ringo, come here, boy."

Ringo turned to Charlie, the reflection of the dull embers lingering in his eyes. The dog crossed the room, pausing to look back at the fire, then lifted his head to uneasily lick the boy's hand.

"I don't understand," Charlie said. "Where are we?"

Ringo whimpered.

"Have ye woken in there, young sir?" The words came with a loud cracking knock on the room's heavy wooden door.

Charlie jumped and Ringo barked before sheepishly circling back behind the bed.

"Uh, yes," Charlie said, struggling to find his full voice. "I'm awake."

He heard a set of ringed keys jangle, followed by the clang of a metal lock. Then the door flew open, and a short, plump woman with graying red hair tied up into a bun burst into the room. She wore a blinding-white apron over a long black frock that swept the floor behind her. Her dress was buttoned up to a fur-lined collar, and she spoke in a thick Irish brogue.

"Aye, good to hear. Slept well, I hope? That bed is particularly comfortable, and I tried to keep the fire going best I could. It gets dreadfully cold in the old castle this time of year—that is without debate."

In just a few steps, she was at the fireplace stoking the coals with a log in hand.

"I am Mrs. Edith Winthrope. At your service at the bequest of my employer, so I hope we made your stay as pleasant as possible."

"I'm Charlie. But I'm sorry, I-I-I don't understand. Where am I? I was in the woods . . . I got lost . . . and then I met a . . ."

Charlie thought he felt the blood freeze in his veins. His hand quickly shot to his neck, checking for any open wounds. There were none.

"Ah, yes, Charlie. The Prime Minister found you in his wanderings last night and brought ya here to protect yer well-being. Looks like you've taken a knock to the head, but strange a young man such as yerself would be off wandering in the night . . . in that part of the woods and on All Hallows' Eve . . . of all nights . . . my goodness."

"The Prime Minister?" Charlie said. He was beginning to think that he was still sleeping.

"Yes, the Prime Minister. Your host," Mrs. Winthrope replied, moving quickly around the room, opening the curtains and straightening the framed portraits that hung on the walls. "You must be hungry," she said. "We'll get ya something to eat and wait for the Prime Minister to rise. He's better to explain all that to ya."

Charlie saw the sun peeking through an overcast sky and wondered how long he had been asleep.

"Excuse me, but do you think there is a phone I could use? You know, to call home. They might be worried," Charlie said, knowing Old Joe would be expecting his help down at the pumpkin patch.

"A telephone? My goodness, of course not," Mrs. Winthrope scoffed as though Charlie had asked to borrow their rocket ship. "Yer clothes looked like you'd been through a swamp, so I've taken the liberty of having them laundered for ya. You can get freshened up and come down when yer ready, and don't worry, Charlie, yer in good hands here. The Prime Minister is an exceptional host when he cares to be."

And with that, Mrs. Winthrope disappeared, pulling the heavy oak door shut behind her.

"No phone? What do you think of that?" Charlie turned back to Ringo, only to see him crawling farther under the bed.

Charlie found his clean clothes folded on an oak chest that sat at the foot of the bed, just as Mrs. Winthrope had promised. Next to his clothes, meticulously arranged, were the contents of his pockets: his photograph with Billy, the werewolf mask, the plastic fangs, and the Hershey's bar that Ms. Hatchet had given him.

"That's strange," Charlie said, turning the chocolate over in his hands. Charlie could plainly see that the bar had been opened and a small piece was missing, though the foil and paper wrapper were so neatly folded over that the bar might appear at first glance to be fully intact. "I don't remember eating any. You didn't have some, did ya, Ringo?" Charlie asked, wishing the dog could respond. "No, I guess not."

He set the chocolate down and picked up the photograph. It was damp from the rain, its edges curled slightly, but he could still see Billy smiling back at him.

Slowly waking up now, Charlie began to replay the events of the night before in his head. The older boys stole his candy . . .

he hit his head . . . there was a pumpkin . . . he ran . . . was lost . . . the graveyard . . .

"Monsterland, Ringo. That's what the vampire said, *Monsterland.*"

Charlie felt colder as he said it. The sensation crawled from the floor up his legs. His lips trembled and his teeth slowly shook to a chatter. Charlie knew it wasn't just the chill in the air; he understood Ringo's odd behavior and was very afraid.

— *chapter 8* —

The Vampire's Castle

RINGO FOLLOWED CLOSE behind as Charlie opened the heavy door and crept out of the room. They were in a long, dimly lit hallway lined with more portraits and some odd assortments of taxidermy. Charlie squinted, trying to make out the paintings, but it was too dark to distinguish much more than shadowed shapes and silhouettes.

"Wh-wh-what do you think, Ringo?" Charlie rattled off through his chattering teeth. It was colder away from the fire and Charlie thought he could see his breath. Ringo only whimpered.

There was a light at the end of the hall, so Charlie counted his steps in that direction, suddenly missing not only his parents and Old Joe, but also Mrs. Winthrope, despite the fact that they had only just met. After his third step, Charlie thought he heard someone or something behind him, but turned to find nothing but a damp draft. At his feet, Charlie heard something else scratching its way along the baseboards, but again, when he strained his eyes to see through the darkness, the hallway was empty. Ringo jumped at the scurrying sounds and nosed around for some sort of explanation.

"Don't look at me," Charlie said, scratching the dog's ears. "I'm beginning to wonder if this isn't some kind of a joke. You know, like on TV, hidden camera or something."

Charlie and Ringo continued, passing ornate candelabras dripping what looked to be a hundred years of wax down the walls. It was even harder to see in the pockets between the sconces, so Charlie crawled up the bust of a stone gargoyle and removed a stub of candle from the sculpture's extended claw. He had to protect the flame from the strong gusts that raced down the winding corridor as they walked. A booming roll of thunder crashed outside, quickening their pace to the top of a tall stone staircase that wound down into an immense foyer. Charlie saw through the stained glass of the arched windows that rain had joined the thunder. Trembling, he stopped when they reached the grand staircase.

"I don't know about this," Charlie whispered. "Maybe we should just get out of here—"

A loud crack of lightning interrupted him, splattering the steps in a bright flash and illuminating another series of portraits, which were hung neatly along the turn of the stair's spiral. At the second flash of lightning, Charlie noticed something familiar about the subject—or subjects. Standing on his toes, Charlie held the candle before the first painting. Though the face was drastically different from what he remembered, he immediately recognized the man in the portrait as the vampire from the tunnel. It was the sadness in his eyes.

Charlie held the flickering candle up to the next portrait. It was the vampire again, but this time he appeared younger and not as pale. His hair was jet black in the painting and plastered back behind his pointed ears, which were not tattered and scarred as Charlie remembered them from the night before. The next portrait was also of the vampire, and Charlie realized that each painting seemed to be from a drastically different period in history. In some, he wore elaborate military uniforms. In others, suits of the finest fabrics layered with vests and shirts with high collars. As Charlie moved down the stairs, the vampire became younger while the clothes he wore continued to reflect the fashion of a much older time.

Another lightning flash revealed suits of armor, masks, swords, battle-axes, and other curious oddities neatly hung between the endless rows of portraits. One object looked somewhat like a stuffed dragon's head, but Charlie quickly dismissed the thought, assuming it was something from Australia that he must have missed in *National Geographic*.

Finally, they reached the bottom of the stairs and the very last painting. Right away, Charlie could see that this portrait was different. It seemed more alive and did not possess the somber tone of the others. With his broad grin, the vampire looked pretty human in it, and wasn't more than a few years older than Charlie was now. He sat in an elaborate chair and next to him, with her hand on his shoulder, stood a beautiful girl. She was about the same age as the vampire and her eyes seemed to almost sparkle, as did her smile. Charlie's gaze turned back up the stairs to the portraits that seemed to span hundreds of years. In each one, the vampire appeared increasingly weary, as though each artist's rendering had managed to capture one last moment, just before that year's toll had been taken.

Ringo barked at the next crack of lightning, startling Charlie. He stumbled back, tripping over the dog, who let out a yelp. A hound of some sort answered from somewhere deep in the castle. Then the sound grew to a whole pack of dogs howling back and to the storm.

"What have we gotten ourselves into?" Charlie whispered to Ringo, deciding that it might be best if they just kept moving.

They wandered through grand ballrooms, neatly arranged libraries, and dusty sitting rooms. Winding corridors gave way to more stairs, and just as Charlie was about to give up all hope of ever finding the front door or Mrs. Winthrope, he noticed Ringo sniffing at the air.

"What is it?"

Charlie inhaled deeply, trying to smell what had caught the dog's interest. A glorious aroma drifted to them from the far end of the dark hall. Ringo licked his drooling lips.

"Kinda reminds me of Christmas," Charlie said. He was hungry and could practically taste the rib roast and potatoes that hung in the air. "Come on," he said, now willing to let Ringo's senses lead the way. "Can't be too bad, right?"

—— *chapter 9* ——

Mrs. Winthrope's Kitchen

*M*AKING THEIR WAY down the hall, Charlie and Ringo found themselves in Mrs. Winthrope's large, orderly kitchen. There was an oversize wood-burning stove and a cooktop on which several brass pots and cast-iron pans sat simmering. There was also a little boy standing on a chair at the end of a sturdy wooden table. He had a long knife in his hand, a toothpick tucked into the corner of his mouth, and he was mumbling some sort of a nursery rhyme to himself.

> *"One for sorrow,*
> *Two for joy,*
> *Three for a girl,*
> *Four for a boy,*
> *Five for silver,*
> *Six for gold,*
> *Seven for a secret never told..."*

The little boy's hair was thick and unkempt, which lent a general scruffiness to his appearance. He wore an ill-fitting dark suit that seemed to be homespun and of awkward construction, with his arms and legs dangling loosely from the cuffs. The little boy was peeling potatoes with the knife, and judging from the size of the pile behind him, it would be some time before he was finished with the chore.

> *"Eight for a wish,*
> *Nine for a kiss,*
> *Ten a surprise you should not miss,*
> *Eleven for health,*
> *Twelve for wealth,*
> *Thirteen beware it's the—"*

"Hello," Charlie interrupted, at which point the boy looked up and immediately stopped his recital. Ringo whimpered softly at Charlie's side.

The boy cut a piece of potato and offered it to a small magpie that had jumped onto his shoulder. The bird took the bit of potato in a single bite.

"Yer looking at me magpie, aren't you?" the little boy asked after several uncomfortable moments of silence. "Well, I saved 'em. It's a juvenile. He hit the stain glass you saw out there on the staircase in a storm. He was stunned, so I brought him in, now nursin' 'em back to health. When he's ready, I'm gonna release him back to the wilds. You ever been there? To the wilds?"

"I don't think so. I only just got here."

"You just got here?" the boy said, scratching behind his ear with the tip of the knife. "Whattaya supposed to be, the new kitchen boy?"

"Why, no, I don't think I'm the kitchen boy."

"I see, already trying to get out of some work. And as you said, just got here. So, if yer not the kitchen boy, who are you?"

"Well, I'm Charlie . . . and this is my dog—"

"Charlie?" The boy cut him off. "Well, I never heard of you. I suppose you'd be waiting for Mrs. Winthrope, then?" The little boy tilted his head as though he heard something. "I believe this is her now."

Charlie couldn't hear anything other than the crackling of the open fire and the bubbling pots on the stove, but he noticed that Ringo had his head tilted in the same manner as the little boy. A second later, Mrs. Winthrope pushed through the double doors, just as the boy had predicted.

"Aye, ya made it, Charlie," she said, "and I see you've met Oscar."

The little boy with the magpie on his shoulder gave a slight wave. Charlie couldn't help but notice that the bird was staring at him.

"I thought about it after I left ya upstairs. I should have sent Oscar to fetch you or given ya some direction here to the kitchen," Mrs. Winthrope continued. "This place can be tricky to get around if ya don't know all the ins and outs. It's just been so long since we've had a proper guest, I suppose we're all a bit out of practice."

Ringo licked Mrs. Winthrope's hand and moved toward the open fire, sitting beneath the long wooden handles that led to loaves of baking bread.

"Well, I suppose that all this may be rather confusing," Mrs. Winthrope said. "It is a bit hard to take at first. I'm afraid with the storm the Prime Minister didn't know what else to do with ya but to bring ya here." She picked up a heavy cast-iron skillet and set it on the stovetop. "He does crave human interaction, the Prime Minister, trying to understand ya better, I suppose. It's as though he's forgotten what it was even like."

Charlie fidgeted uncomfortably under the magpie's gaze. He did not like the way the bird was blinking at him.

"Aw, listen to me. You must be hungry. Here, let me prepare something to tide you over until dinner."

"That's okay, Mrs. Winthrope," Charlie said, trying to ignore the bird. "Thank you for everything, but I should get going."

"It wasn't a question, Charlie." Mrs. Winthrope picked up a large metal ladle and dipped it into one of the steaming caul-drons. "It's porridge like I used to make back in the old country."

Mrs. Winthrope put the porridge in front of Charlie and dropped in a chunk of butter, which quickly melted on top.

"There you go. That'll warm ya."

Charlie looked down at the steaming bowl. The aroma poured into his nostrils and pulled at his growling stomach.

"No, really, Mrs. Winthrope. My parents might be getting worried. I should be getting home."

"Home? Well, the trail washed out last night with the rain,

so we'll have to check the Prime Minister's schedule for that. You can ask him at dinner later. Now, go ahead, dig in . . ."

Charlie did not move.

"Ah, yes. Ya see, Oscar? His mother raised him wisely. I forget that we're all strangers to ya 'til last night." Mrs. Winthrope scooped a wooden spoonful from Charlie's bowl and took a bite. "See? Now, if we were the kind of cretins or ne'er-do-wells who would taint a bowl of a child's porridge, would I do that? Come on, eat up . . ."

"I guess that makes sense," Charlie said, thinking it was about the only thing that was making any sense.

Unable to resist any longer, Charlie picked up his spoon, sank it into the wooden bowl, and brought it up to his lips.

"Besides, if the Prime Minister wanted ya dead, I am afraid that we wouldn't be having this conversation, now, would we?" Mrs. Winthrope sprinkled some brown sugar on top as Charlie dug in for another spoonful. "Mmmm, delicious . . ."

Charlie couldn't agree more, as far as the porridge was concerned.

"Now, if you don't mind me asking, what were ya doing out there, in that section of the woods? Alone in the dark and rain with the way it is these days?"

"What do you mean, *these days*?" Charlie asked through a mouthful of porridge.

"What does she mean, he asks." Oscar laughed.

"What do I mean? Why, with the Headless Horsemen back at war with the Headhunters, of course," Mrs. Winthrope replied. "And there's word that Tok's marauders are back to conducting raids into the Mumiya-held Agrarian Plains, is what I mean; you were lucky to have stumbled upon the Prime Minister when ya did."

"Lucky, lucky," Oscar added, chopping a potato in half.

Charlie looked up from the porridge. "I'm sorry . . . but who did you say was at war?"

"Who isn't? 'Tis a dreadful state we're in." Mrs. Winthrope turned to the fire and sighed. "When your government started all this, it worked for a while, I suppose. It was a refuge, Charlie, a place where we could just be. But now, with the security cutbacks . . . and my goodness, the lost souls they're bringing in these days . . ."

Charlie lowered his spoon and wiped the stray porridge from his face. Could what the vampire had said last night be true? *Vampirestat . . . Vampirestaid . . .*

"Vampyreishtat," Mrs. Winthrope corrected, though Charlie had not said a word.

"Monsterland?" Charlie asked.

"Well, some call it that. Yes, Monsterland."

"What? How . . . I don't understand—"

"Oh, it is a pity what they fail to teach in yer history classes," Mrs. Winthrope interrupted, tying her faded red hair tighter into its bun. "How? Let's see. I suppose it's best to start at the beginning." Mrs. Winthrope seasoned a large roast as she spoke. "After the Second World War, the victors decided that while unified they would pool their resources and, in an effort to make the world *a safer place*, round us all up."

"Us?"

Mrs. Winthrope smiled at Oscar. She cut a rib bone from the roast and let out a low, guttural animal sound. Ringo's ears shot up and he crossed the kitchen to lick Mrs. Winthrope's hand again. She offered Ringo the bone and slid the panned roast into the large open-flame hearth.

"Most people are not what they seem, Charlie. On the surface at least . . ."

With the warmth of the fire, smells of the kitchen, and a belly full of food, Charlie suddenly felt dizzy. Maybe the bump on his head from last night was worse than he thought.

"Wait, I don't understand," Charlie replied. "Monsterland? Monsters?"

"Well, yer one to call us that," Oscar said, dumping another pail of potatoes on the table.

"*Monsters*, the strange and unusual, the gruesome, the different, and the feared," Mrs. Winthrope explained. "There was a time when we were able to coexist, humans and monsters as you say, but that, Charlie, was back when the world seemed bigger. There was more open space in those days. Room to roam, plenty of places to hide, to go undetected. If we were smart, we were left to live out our lives as we chose to live them, same as you."

Mrs. Winthrope paused, and Charlie saw the vampire's sadness in her eyes.

"It worked at that time, save for the occasional sighting, a creature on a foggy moor or under a full moon—literature is filled with anecdotes. But these sightings, back in those days, were for the most part dismissed. The figment, as they say, of someone's imagination."

"But monsters?" Charlie said. "You're talking about real monsters."

"Aye, Charlie, if you are going to insist on calling us that, real monsters. Some were—well, *are*—certainly a danger. A danger to the likes of me, even, but it didn't matter that only a few were a real threat. We were slowly hunted down and captured. Then sent to live here, and here we live. Self-sufficient, I might add. We have little in the way of technology with the trade embargos and all, but we manage. We grow our own food, make our own clothes. We've built towns and roads, our own central government even—"

"I'm sorry, but I still don't understand." Charlie looked around. "Where are we? I've lived just over, well, just over the mountains my whole life, and I've never heard of you or this place."

"Never heard of us . . ." Oscar snickered.

"Where is Monsterland, you ask? Why, Charlie, it's the places in between, stuck in the shadows, in the cracks, in the dark . . ." Mrs. Winthrope trailed off, apparently deep in thought for a moment. But she quickly snapped back, rattling off the rest. "Vampyreishtat, itself lost in the places where no one wants to go."

With that, Mrs. Winthrope cleared Charlie's bowl.

"Or that is at least the stock answer from the Prime Minister. He tends to have a flair for the dramatic."

"'Lost in the places where no one wants to go,'" Oscar repeated. "I always liked that part." The magpie let out a screech as if agreeing with him, making Charlie jump.

"In truth, Vampyreishtat, or *Monsterland,* if you must, is a valley," Mrs. Winthrope added. "A long, glacial valley created millions of years ago. The mountains on either side are too big and numerous to climb, so I suppose few ever came here. Then, in the days before air travel, mind ya, the valley was somehow left off the map."

Left off the map? Charlie thought about what he learned about the Oklahoma Territory in Ms. Hatchet's class the other day . . . Or was that today? Or was that yesterday?

"Your government discovered the mapmakers' mistake but decided to keep it that way. They had the foresight that someday they might need a place that did not exist, and soon enough they had it."

"How? How can they hide something so big?"

Charlie thought it would be hard to hide this enormous castle, let alone an entire land.

"Well, there are the mountains, odd weather systems, to say the least, and ya know, Charlie, your government has a way, if they do not want someone to know something, it tends to stay unknown. Besides, from time to time some stumble upon us. You are here, are ya not?"

"I'm sorry, Mrs. Winthrope, I still don't understand. Monsters here? They're all here?"

"All? Heavens no, but for the most part."

Charlie's face felt flush, and he thought that he might be

sitting too close to the fire or maybe the stove. Even with all of Old Joe's monster stories, he had never imagined this.

"And the government—our government in Washington— they know about you?" Charlie said. "The president?"

"Well, I don't know about the president, but yes, of course the government knows about us. They sent us here."

"Can you leave?" Charlie asked. He was now convinced that he must be dreaming.

"I suppose one could try, but why would we? Outside this valley, it's the old torches and pitchforks, isn't it?"

"Torches and pitchforks," Oscar repeated, shaking his head.

"Besides, the rules from yer government are very clear." Mrs. Winthrope turned to Charlie. "If we leave and are recaptured, we'll be, to put it simply . . . executed. As I said, that much is very clear."

"But the vampire, the Prime Minister, he was in the woods by my house. He was in the pumpkin patch, and that's on the other side of the mountains."

Oscar rolled his eyes. "The Prime Minister in the pumpkin patch . . ."

"Well, of course *he* was, Charlie," Mrs. Winthrope said in disbelief. "As Prime Minister, he is a bit of an exception, isn't he?"

Charlie did not know how to answer the question.

"The Prime Minister's role here demands that he—how should I say this—interact somewhat with the outside world. A liaison of sorts with your government."

Ringo sat gnawing the bone on the hearth by the fire, seemingly unaffected by this information. Charlie, on the other hand, was sure that they were the victims of some elaborate prank, or that the blow he took to the head was even more serious than he thought.

"I-I-I still don't understand—"

"Aw, I've gone on too much," Mrs. Winthrope said, cutting Charlie off. "You should go. Stretch yer legs before dinner. I know the Prime Minister is eager to speak with ya. It is best to stay in the castle, though, with nightfall almost upon us. Go to the tower. See if you can catch the last light of the day." Mrs. Winthrope returned to the hearth and busied herself with the dinner. "It's the spiral stairs just off the kitchen there. That's to the western tower. Best view for the sunset. Go on, the stairs don't bite." She motioned with a wave of her hand.

"I can show him the way, Mrs. Winthrope," Oscar said, leaving the magpie on a perch in the corner. "I was going to grab a few more potatoes anyway."

Charlie stood up slowly and called to Ringo, but the dog looked content with his bone by the fire, so Charlie left him with Mrs. Winthrope and followed Oscar up to the tower. The narrow staircase was lined with stones, and other than the spiderwebs, the walls were oddly bare compared to the rest of the castle. They climbed what felt like hundreds of steps, although Charlie lost count somewhere around the halfway point, so he couldn't be sure.

"This is where I leave you," Oscar said when they reached an upper landing. "What was it, *Charlie*?"

"Yeah, that's it."

"And you're from where, Charlie, what did you say, the other side of the mountains?"

"That's right," Charlie said, slightly out of breath from the climb. "And what about you, Oscar?"

"Me? I'm from all over the place. Traveled with a circus until Mrs. Winthrope found me."

"You were in the circus?" Charlie asked. He had never met anyone who had actually been in a circus, but it wasn't that hard to imagine Oscar and his magpie as some kind of junior acrobat or part of a high-wire act. "As what, a performer?"

"I guess I was more of an attraction, really. Like I said, until Mrs. Winthrope found me."

"And now you live here?" Charlie asked. "In this castle?"

"Me? No, not really. Well, kinda. I'm down in the moat."

"The moat?"

"Yep, the moat. I gotta get," Oscar said, scratching himself behind the ear again. "Potatoes calling."

Oscar turned into a narrow hallway that broke away from the landing.

"Nice to meet you, Charlie, and don't worry, keep climbing. You're almost there."

Charlie continued to the top of the stairs, where he found a large windowed room. The furnishings were spare. A drawing table, stacks of books, and several telescopes of various sizes and designs. A heavy oak ladder leaned up toward an open hatch. Charlie climbed the ladder and saw it wasn't too late. The sun was just setting.

THE VAMPIRE'S CASTLE SAT HIGH IN THE MOUNTAINS AT THE edge of a great precipice. Below it was just as Mrs. Winthrope had described: a massive valley with towering snowcapped mountains on either side stretching out as far as Charlie could see. A cobblestoned road wound down from the vampire's castle, across a covered bridge, and through a treacherous mountain pass. It snaked along a blue-green glacial river and on to a town that looked like a tiny spot on a map. The town, perhaps more of a village, really, was like the hub of a wheel with more roads splintering out in a multitude of directions. Looking down at it, Charlie quickly realized that this place couldn't be some kind of hoax or an elaborate prank; it was all so real, almost too real.

The wind outside on the parapet was fierce, and Charlie had to brace himself against the heavy gusts that threatened to pick him up and throw him over the edge. He felt his way along a waist-high wall toward a large fixed telescope, which was attached to a rotating track. Adjusting the lens, he could see farther down the valley and saw that it widened, the forest at the base of the mountains giving way to lakes and vast, wide-open plains. *Who knows what lies beyond that,* Charlie thought, pulling back from the telescope.

The wind picked up, followed by a freezing drizzle. Shivering, Charlie crammed his hands deep into the pockets of his sweatshirt. He felt the rough edges of the photograph between the sharpened points of his plastic glow-in-the-dark vampire teeth and could see the pumpkins in front of Old Joe's barn—he could see his cousin.

"I wonder what Billy would think of all this," he said aloud, listening to the hounds howling somewhere below. "Doubt he'd be scared."

Charlie looked out at Vampyreishtat, this Monsterland, and felt as alone as ever.

— *chapter* 10 —

Dinner with the Prime Minister

WHEN CHARLIE GOT back to the kitchen, he found Ringo playing with a large wolfish dog with gray-red fur. He watched as they chased each other through the main double doors and out into the hall. Music was playing somewhere in the castle, a violin alternating low moans and shrieks with a sad melody in between.

"Mrs. Winthrope?" Charlie called. "Oscar?"

But neither Mrs. Winthrope nor Oscar answered, so he followed the dogs to the foyer.

"Ringo . . ."

The dog came instantly, trotting around the corner, followed by Mrs. Winthrope, who was tucking her hair back up into its bun.

"Oh, Charlie," Mrs. Winthrope said, a bit surprised. "So how was it? Spectacular view, isn't it?"

"Uh, yes, ma'am. It was. Looked like I could see all of Monsterland . . . Uh, I mean Vampier . . ."

The music stopped.

"Vampyreishtat, but oh, no. No, no, no. You couldn't have seen the whole of it, my goodness," Mrs. Winthrope dismissed. "Please, Charlie, right this way. The Prime Minister would like you to join him before dinner."

The violin resumed its playing, although this time the melody, while still foreboding, rose with a flurry.

"Uh, yes, ma'am. Thank you, but my parents, they might be getting worried. I really should be getting home." Charlie thought that they would probably start looking for him soon, and he wasn't sure he really wanted to see this Prime Minister again anyway.

"Oh, it will be fine, Charlie. Just fine," Mrs. Winthrope reassured him. "Remember we were just aiding a fallen traveler, and I think you'll find that the Prime Minister can be quite charming . . . when he wishes to be."

With Ringo nipping at their heels, Charlie followed Mrs. Winthrope back through the foyer, up a small set of stairs, and into the library. The vast room was filled with leather-bound books on every wall from floor to ceiling; a narrow ladder on rails offered access to the volumes on the highest shelves. Their faded titles sparked gold in the light of a large, open fireplace.

Two high-backed chairs sat facing the hearth. Rings of smoke lingered in the air above the one on the left, which also appeared to be the source of the somber tune. The melody abruptly stopped at their approach.

"Aye, good evening, sir," Mrs. Winthrope said. "I have Charlie . . . oh my, I've realized I never got yer last name—"

"Cooper, ma'am. Charlie Cooper."

"Aw, yes. Well, Charlie Cooper," Mrs. Winthrope continued.

A long leg pushed back one of the high chairs, opening it away from the fire and to the room.

"Ah, *yessss*, our intrepid wanderer. Please show him in . . ."

The Prime Minister stood. The shadows from the fireplace had an elongating effect, making it appear as though he towered all the way to the ceiling. And he looked different than he had back in the tunnel. He seemed younger, like in the portraits from the middle stairs. His ears were no longer tattered, and his black hair, while streaked with gray, was full and slicked back from his forehead. But Charlie could still see, despite this younger appearance, the look of sadness that lingered in his eyes.

"Charlie, why, it is an honor to see you again," the Prime Minister said, extending his long, thin hand. "Welcome, please sit."

Charlie shook his hand, shocked once again by how cold it felt, as if he were just holding a snowball.

"And, Mrs. Winthrope. Would you be so kind as to bring Charlie some of your hot chocolate? His hand is simply chilled to the bone." The Prime Minister turned to Charlie. "You will not be disappointed."

Charlie could have skipped the hot chocolate, if just to keep Mrs. Winthrope and Ringo in the room, but he stayed and reluctantly followed the Prime Minister, sitting beside him in the other high-backed chair by the fire.

"Thank you for joining me before dinner. We are a bit

isolated here so high in the mountains, so always up for a bit of conversation. I trust your accommodations were satisfactory?"

"Uh, yes, sir," Charlie said. "Thank you."

Charlie noticed there were no portraits in this room. Instead, there were several framed photographs of older gray-haired men and women shaking hands with other older gray-haired men and women. Most of them wore dark suits, but some of them were wearing military uniforms.

They sat in silence for a while, listening to the crackling flames of the fire before the Prime Minister finally spoke.

"So, to the question of the hour, *why* is it, Charlie Cooper, why were you wandering in the rain, in a graveyard, all alone, and on All Hallows' Eve of all nights?"

"I guess I got lost," Charlie said softly.

"Easy to do in a wood that wild."

"Well, to be honest, I thought you were Billy at first . . ."

"Ah, *yesssss*. Your cousin, I believe you said."

"So when I saw you, I thought you were him, you know, from the pumpkin patch, and that you could help me, because I was lost." Charlie shrugged. "I guess I was wrong. It's just that he usually dresses up like . . . well, like you for Halloween."

"Billy does?" the Prime Minister asked as he plucked the strings of the violin with his long fingers.

"Yes. Or he did," Charlie said.

"He did?"

"Until last year." Charlie turned away and looked at the fire.

"And yet, you were following him, this year?"

Charlie was not sure what to say but thought that his parents and Old Joe, even Ms. Hatchet, would probably be asking him the same question.

"You must not tell anyone that you saw me there in the pumpkin patch, Charlie. It can be our secret, for now . . ."

"Yeah, okay, I mean yes, yes, sir," Charlie replied, knowing that no one would ever believe him anyway.

The Prime Minister plucked another string. "You know, I have seen you before, Charlie. Seen you there, on the other side, the other side of the mountains, as you call it."

"You have?" Charlie wasn't sure how he felt about a vampire watching him, even if he was a Prime Minister.

"*Yessss.* Sometimes I pass your *w*ay, through the *w*oods, and I have seen you alone late at night, sitting, sitting on your, how do you say it, *porch*," the Prime Minister said with a smile. "It appears *w*e share a similar nocturnal nature, does it not?"

"Yes, I guess so."

The Prime Minister plucked a few more notes and adjusted the strings.

"At times I have *w*ondered, *w*hy do you sit there, Charlie, alone on the porch so late at night?"

Charlie shifted uncomfortably and said, "I have trouble sleeping. Bad dreams. Nightmares, really."

Except for last night, Charlie thought. Last night was the first solid sleep that he'd had for as long as he could remember.

"Bad dreams?" the Prime Minister repeated. "I suppose *w*e all have them . . ."

"Well, they're not always bad. Sometimes they're all right."

The Prime Minister plucked another string.

"Please stop me if I appear too forward, but I am also troubled by sleep and wonder. What do you dream of, Charlie? What keeps you up at night? I must admit, I find the subject simply fascinating."

Charlie paused for a moment, thinking of the hot, arid plain from his dreams. The sun was bright, but he could see the boy in the distance. He could see Billy.

"Billy," Charlie said, feeling dizzy again. "I have this dream about my cousin Billy. He's lost somewhere, and I can't find him."

"Lost? Like you were?"

Charlie felt the blood drain from his face, and it was warm, too warm sitting next to fire.

"Yes . . . lost . . ." But Charlie's voice trailed off. He was confused.

Billy had been gone for over a year. They were working after school in the orchards with Old Joe the day he left. When they were done with their chores, instead of going back to the house to do their homework like Old Joe said, they climbed their usual tree, a weeping willow that reached out over the river.

In the summer, they hung their shirts and shoes in the branches and jumped from the tree to swim in the cool, swirling waters below. But it was October, and that day, the river was cold, too cold. Still, Billy didn't care. He said that summers should last forever and bet Charlie that he could swim to the other side despite the temperature. But Billy never came back up. And aside from his troubling dreams, Charlie had not seen Billy since.

Charlie felt his eyes welling up but willed himself not to cry. He hadn't cried, really cried, not since Billy first disappeared, and he was not about to start now in the presence of this strange creature. He coughed back the tears and continued, "Yes, sir, lost."

"There, there," the Prime Minister said, patting him gently on the shoulder. "No need to solve all that ails us this very moment, right? The night is young, and as I am sure you have gathered, Mrs. Winthrope knows her way around a kitchen."

The Prime Minister stood and took in the kitchen's aromas with a wave of his hand.

"Ah, hot chocolate. Come now. I am quite sure that a feast awaits..."

And feast they did. They moved to a formal dining room and sat at a long table lined with candelabras and more dripping wax. There was roast beef and potatoes, fish and ham, vegetables so large that Charlie could hardly believe what he was eating. And the Prime Minister, as Mrs. Winthrope had said, did turn out to be quite the conversationalist. They spoke of faraway places, great journeys, fantastic creatures, and many battles, which oddly enough made Charlie feel better. The Prime Minister told him more of the government's roundup of the world's monsters and agreed that when they had first arrived it was different, a more hopeful spirit to it all. Mrs. Winthrope concurred and just as Charlie thought he had eaten all he could, she moved on to dessert.

"Oh, Charlie," Mrs. Winthrope said, passing him a hefty strudel. "When we first arrived, we had more support from yer government, from the outside. But now, with the budget slashed, my, my, you wouldn't believe what it takes to keep the place going."

"But how?" Charlie said. "How did you all even get here?"

"Why, at night, Charlie, they used to bring us through the tunnel, the very same tunnel that brought you here," Mrs. Winthrope said, rather matter-of-factly.

"By my house?"

Charlie pictured the woods and the abandoned military base next to Old Joe's orchard. All these monsters, the world's monsters, had come here to this strange place through the woods by his house. Charlie shuddered at the thought, but then remembered what Mrs. Winthrope had said about the word *monster*—how it was not always a fair label. Charlie pondered this, concluding that perhaps his fears were inappropriate.

"Similar to the outside world, there is much that plagues us here besides our own true nature," the Prime Minister admitted. "Like any government, I suppose, balancing the needs of the many factions is a constant battle."

"We talked about that," Charlie said through a mouthful of strudel. "The Headless Horsemen being at war with the Headhunters."

"When are they not at war?" the Prime Minister said wearily. "While I must admit that the Headless Horsemen have a legitimate grievance, they are unfortunately the least of our concerns. The real issues that plague our valley are to the north in the Agrarian Plains, warring factions, neither side willing to yield or compromise..."

The Prime Minister turned to Charlie. "And how is a government, any government, expected to function *without* compromise? As I am sure you have learned in school, compromise is at the very essence of what a government is. It is by its very nature what it is supposed to do, is it not?"

"We did learn about that in school," Charlie replied, noting that the Prime Minister hadn't eaten anything during the entire meal. He just sipped at his cup of hot chocolate as he spoke about the troubles of Monsterland with a growing intensity.

"And as elected by the Council of the Congressional Caucus of Vampyreishtat, the Prime Minister is charged with—how should I put this?" Mrs. Winthrope said, standing up from her chair. "Sorting it all out."

"I suppose that is one way to put it, Mrs. Winthrope," the Prime Minister added.

"These are trying times to be sure," Mrs. Winthrope went on, collecting an armload of dirty dishes and loading them on a serving tray. "Trying times indeed."

"*Yessss*, it is hard to say what is next for your government's grand experiment with us, the apparent horrors of the world. Who knows what the future holds for Vampyreishtat and its many inhabitants?" the Prime Minister concluded. "This, from our shared insomnia, is what keeps me up at night, Charlie."

As Charlie ate the last of his strudel, Mrs. Winthrope left for the kitchen. Despite her absence, Charlie now felt oddly at ease with the Prime Minister. After their conversation, the fear he remembered overtaking him back at the tunnel and again before they met in the library had somewhat lifted.

The Prime Minister sat back in his chair, lit his pipe, and smoked silently until Charlie set down his fork.

"You know, he never said good-bye," Charlie said, looking at his plate. It could have been the food or the warmth of the fire, or maybe even the Prime Minister's own unexpected candidness. Whatever it was, Charlie suddenly felt compelled to tell the Vampire everything.

"Billy?" the Prime Minister replied, turning from his thoughts to the boy.

"They say he drowned. They dredged the river and everything, but they never found him. I don't believe them, though. Billy was one of the best swimmers in town, so I think he might have just run away. He's done that before. I tried going to look for him. I thought maybe he got lost, but my mom and dad stopped me."

"Do you still think that, Charlie?" the Prime Minister said. "That your cousin Billy has run away?"

Charlie looked up at the Prime Minister.

"I don't know anymore. But sometimes at night, in my dream, I can see him, and I think he needs me."

The Prime Minister took a long draw on his pipe. Charlie watched the smoke swirl into a cloud that hung just above their heads. The Prime Minister was quiet, seemingly lost in thought again. The ticking of a clock echoed from the foyer.

"Whatever Billy's fate, lost or otherwise, there is perhaps a way," the Prime Minister said after some time. "A way, Charlie, that you could see him again."

Charlie sat up. "Where? Here?"

"*Yessss*, here. I have only been there once, but there is a place in this valley, far beyond the horizon. A deep wood where the lost and the spirits gather. It is possible . . ." The Prime Minister leaned forward. "Perhaps, as you say, he is just lost, lost like you, and he ended up there. It happens. It is a long, hard journey, though. Not for the weak of heart. If you were to accept such a challenge, you will see things, horrible things, the likes of which you have never dreamed . . ."

Charlie thought about it. He knew that Billy wasn't back home. And they never did find him in the river. If he was what they said, maybe he was there. Or maybe, as the Prime Minister said, he was just lost. Lost here, over the mountains. Lost just like Ringo had been. Lost, just like him.

"But you think Billy might be there?" Charlie still couldn't believe his ears.

"He might be. I make no guarantees, though. The lost—they come and go in this place as they please." The Prime Minister set down his pipe. "However, a trip like this should not be taken lightly, Charlie; monstrosities aside, the terrain alone is treacherous, much of the route uncharted." The Prime Minister paused for a moment. "You will need a guide, and one who knows the mountains as well as the open range. There is only one I can think of who might be able to accompany you there safely. As we speak, he is preparing to go north to the Agrarian Plains on a diplomatic mission, an informal summit, really. Perhaps he could be persuaded to push a little farther. Might do him some good, actually."

After all he had heard about this strange valley, Charlie

tried to imagine what could possibly be ahead. He pictured himself walking down cobblestoned roads, through heavy woods teeming with bizarre creatures of every shape and size. There was no doubt about it—Charlie was scared. He thought of his parents, who surely would be concerned by now, and Old Joe, but at the end of the road, he saw Billy.

Shivering, he heard himself say, "I'll do it. I need to let my family know, but I'll go."

The Prime Minister looked at the boy quizzically. "So little tribulation. Are you not frightened?"

"No, sir, I am. To be one hundred percent honest, I'm already terrified. No offense," Charlie said, holding his shaking hands under the table. "But I know Billy would do the same for me, so I need to be brave. That's what he would want, is for me to be brave."

"It is that important to you, is it?"

"Yes, sir. Whatever happened, I need to talk to him. I think he's out there somewhere, and like in my dream, I wonder if he needs me."

"Well, your Billy is certainly lucky to have you for a cousin." The Prime Minister smiled, exposing his pearly fangs. "Then it is settled. Tomorrow, if you still want to go, I shall try to help you arrange the details." The Prime Minister stood. "Now, if you will excuse me. As we have discussed, I have pressing matters that require my attention."

Charlie stood as the Prime Minister crossed the room to the door.

"Sir, thank you."

"Ah, *yesssss*. It is my pleasure," the Prime Minister said, stopping in the shadow of the doorway. "Now, Charlie, it is important that you sleep tonight. This journey will push you to the limits of who you truly are . . . perhaps to the very limits of your soul. You will find yourself face-to-face with your greatest fears. Trust me, they are here."

The Prime Minister turned to leave but caught himself. "Oh, and thank you for the chocolate last night. It does help to stave off . . . certain unfortunate cravings. A necessity, I am afraid, in keeping up with this more palatable appearance. Well then, again I thank you for your company this evening."

With that, the Prime Minister bowed gracefully before exiting, leaving Charlie alone at the long dining table. As the clock in the hall struck midnight, Charlie heard the familiar jingle of Ringo's collar and was relieved to see his old friend entering the room.

"What do you think?" Charlie dropped to his knee to bury his head in the dog's thick coat. "You'll come with me, won't you, eh, boy? You're always ready for an adventure, right?"

Charlie helped Mrs. Winthrope and Oscar clear the rest of the dishes. Then Oscar showed him back to his room by way of the stairs in the kitchen. They passed through more endless corridors, and other great halls, somehow finding their way back to the top of the grand stone staircase. As they walked the landing, Charlie looked down the long row of paintings and was surprised to see the Prime Minister standing before the last portrait, the one with the smiling girl.

"It's how he tracks the years, I suppose, a tradition from a bygone era," Oscar observed as he continued down the corridor. "But I wouldn't concern yerself too much with the Prime Minister's affairs. It's rude and, from what I hear, unwise. Come on. Mrs. Winthrope said you have a busy morning ahead . . ."

So Charlie followed Oscar to his room, where the boy left him with a plate of cookies, a warm glass of milk, and Mrs. Winthrope's hopes of pleasant dreams. Oscar took Ringo back to the kitchen, to feed him again he said, promising to have the dog curled up next to the bed by morning.

Alone in the room, Charlie wandered around, eventually selecting a book from the shelves titled *The Nicest Monster* to keep him company. He dressed in the clean, pressed pajamas that Mrs. Winthrope had left for him and went to the window to look at the mountains and the moon that filtered through the breaking rain clouds. Once again, he could hear dogs howling from within the castle and out somewhere in the night.

As the moon disappeared behind the blanket of clouds, Charlie peered down to the stone drive that led over the moat at the front of the Prime Minister's castle. There in the shadows he saw a dog appear, stopping in his tracks playfully. Even from this distance Charlie knew it was Ringo.

Charlie watched as he went back into the shadows and then reappeared with the large wolfish dog from the kitchen. Charlie couldn't miss the larger dog's graying red hair a second time.

"Mrs. Winthrope? It couldn't be . . ."

The large dog ran down the bridge, followed by Ringo, and then, almost on cue, a wolf howled, followed by a large splash. Charlie stared at the moat that circled the Prime Minister's castle. There was a small boy swimming in the moonlight. The boy appeared to be covered in furry scales of some kind and did not seem to be affected by the frigid temperatures.

"Oscar?" Charlie whispered.

Vampires, werewolves, a fish boy*—it was all too strange. Charlie sighed, suddenly overwhelmed thinking of the journey that lay ahead. *I guess it's not too late to ask the Prime Minister to just take me back to the tunnel. Back home.*

Then Charlie pulled the photo from his pocket. If Billy were here, he thought, maybe he didn't have a way to get back home. Maybe he was just truly lost. Lost in a place that just so happened to be inhabited by, as Mrs. Winthrope was reluctant to say, *monsters.*

Charlie got into bed and stared at the photo. He knew it didn't matter how scared he was; he had to find out what happened to Billy. He could feel the tears swelling in his eyes again but still he would not cry. Instead, he drifted off to sleep and for the second night in a row, Charlie slept soundly.

---

* Charlie would later find out that Oscar was actually what is known in the common vernacular as a sea wolf, though it should also be noted that "The Fish Boy" was the name that was used to promote Oscar's talents when he was with the circus.

—— *chapter* II ——

The First Step

THE MORNING WAS busy, just as Mrs. Winthrope said it would be. Charlie found a breakfast of eggs, sausages, and piles of hotcakes waiting for him in the kitchen. He ate while Mrs. Winthrope packed food and dry stores in wooden crates. She then brought out a waxed canvas rucksack, a thick homespun sweater, a wool coat, and stiff work trousers.

"You'll blend in better this way," she said, stuffing his sneakers in his pack and handing him a pair of heavy leather boots. "You'll need these for the mountains."

She also added a wool cap, socks, mittens, long underwear, a bar of soap, a tin of tooth powder, and a wooden toothbrush with horsehair bristles.

"An adventure is no excuse for poor hygiene," Mrs. Winthrope advised, cinching the top of the rucksack.

As the wagon was loaded with the supplies, Charlie wrote a letter to his mother explaining he would be gone for some time looking for Billy but not to worry, though he felt he wasn't being entirely honest on that last line. He asked Mrs. Winthrope if she would see to its delivery.

"I'll make sure to drop yer letter in the post right away," Mrs. Winthrope promised. "Our system may be a bit antiquated, but it is reliable."

She assured Charlie that he would see the Prime Minister again soon, explaining that he had his own modes of transportation and that he would be joining them for dinner that very evening.

Before he knew it, Charlie had already waved good-bye to Oscar and was in the wagon bouncing down the road and into the valley below, Mrs. Winthrope giving him bits of history as they traveled and pointing out areas of interest along the way.

Despite the roughness of the road, Ringo managed to stay asleep on the heavy canvas tarp that covered their belongings. When Charlie pointed out Ringo's weariness, Mrs. Winthrope told him how Ringo had run with wolves last night, admitting she had been there in wolf form to ensure the dog's safety. And then, as they moved along with the dust and commotion of the wagon, Mrs. Edith Winthrope told Charlie the story of how she was turned.

"Before the war—the second one, mind ya—I was a librarian living just south of Cork, back in me beloved Ireland. But when the fighting broke out, my, how everything changed.

"With my background, I applied for the clerical staff of the Secret Intelligence Service, was immediately hired, and, after a bit of training, was sent toward the German front. The clerical work assigned to me was mundane, yet it was exciting, Charlie, to be there in the midst of it all, feeling as if ya were at least doing something to keep the horrors of war at bay."

The horses reached a steady pace as the road leveled a bit, allowing Charlie glimpses of the valley below.

"But one night, one fateful night, my life changed forever. We were working late and I stepped out of the office to take in the evening air. There was a park of sorts nearby and a warm breeze, so I suppose I'd wandered a bit . . . and then, well . . . that's when I met the German deserter known as Jurgen, Jurgen Schmidt. Only I wouldn't garner that information for years to come . . ." Mrs. Winthrope pulled back on the reins as they approached the next steep grade.

"Jurgen wasn't himself that night, and after the attack, I was never quite myself again either, but I learned to cope with my affliction. Control it almost, unlike poor Jurgen. I stayed on with the SIS, and as they soon learned, I had become more useful. At first, they didn't ask how I was able to obtain the information I did, but they were all too eager to accept it."

"You were a spy?" Charlie asked. "As a wolf?"

"Aye, as a wolf, Charlie. Although it wasn't long before I was discovered, until most of us were discovered, and in 1949, the authorities in West Berlin picked me up. I met yer host, the Prime Minister, shortly after, and have been in his employ here in this valley ever since."

Here in this valley, this strange place tucked away just over the mountains from Old Joe's orchards the whole time; it was all so fantastical that Charlie could hardly believe it. But between the conviction in Mrs. Winthrope's words and the long cobble-stoned road ahead, with its odd rock farmhouses and curious signs, it all seemed very real. And *monsters*, he thought, *monsters* had built all of it.

"When I got here I couldn't control my transformations as well as I can now, but when the moon was full, the Prime Minister still allowed me to roam. He would find me later, cold and shivering, wandering lost somewhere on the moors. Later on, he taught me how to gain better control over the animal inside, to harness it. Somehow, with all he's been through, the Prime Minister has still maintained some semblance of a benevolent soul, I would think."

"He's been awfully nice to me," Charlie said. He had to admit, after all of the movies he had seen, meeting a vampire had gone better than he ever would have expected.

"Aye, and there are perks," Mrs. Winthrope said with a wink. "I've never felt better, seem to age slower, actually, and you know, Charlie, it is a unique perspective to see the world through two different sets of eyes." Mrs. Winthrope smiled at Charlie and continued. "You see, you've nothing to fear with me. We all have choices to make. And I have chosen control. I've chosen to be a master of my impulses, not a slave to them."

Mrs. Winthrope put her arm on Charlie's shoulder.

"I won't harm ya and I think I can speak the same for the Prime Minister," she said, and then abruptly took the reins back into both hands and turned the team to avoid a particularly treacherous slide. "But I can't say the same for what else roams these lands. You still have tonight to decide, Charlie, but after tomorrow, once you've entered the wilds, it will be hard to turn back."

"Oh, I've already made my decision," Charlie said, determined to continue despite his fears. "Thank you, though."

"Have ya, now?" Mrs. Winthrope replied, raising an eyebrow. "Perhaps it's best to wait until you've met your guide."

Charlie looked out to the other side of the valley. Up on a particularly barren mountaintop stood another castle. But it was not like the Prime Minister's, and it was like nothing Charlie had ever seen. While still under construction, the castle seemed to be carved into the stone and clung to the rocky crags as if it were one with the mountain.

"Ah, that's where we're going, Charlie, the Charnel House, as he calls it. Now that we're down, it's time to go back up," Mrs. Winthrope said, returning her attention to the horses. "And up we go . . ."

—— chapter 12 ——

The Horseman

"CHARLIE, WAIT HERE," Mrs. Winthrope instructed. "Get down and stretch your legs, but don't wander off too far."

Charlie followed her orders, hopping down from the wagon with a thump. It had been a long day and he was stiff from the bumpy ride. He left Ringo asleep in the back and walked a little way down the stone drive until it wound around the side of the giant rock outcrop. There, carved from the stone in similar fashion to the castle, he found a carriage house, a stable, and two corrals. Although aesthetically they were nothing alike, there was something about the layout that reminded Charlie of Old Joe's barn back home. Then he wondered how his grandfather was getting along without him, and if anyone had thought to see to his chores in his absence, something he wished he had noted in his letter.

He followed a stacked stone fence to the first of the two horse pens. There, he saw a large, cloaked figure leading a giant black Clydesdale up toward the stable. The man brought the horse under the portico, whispering quietly in its ear, and as it lowered its head, he brushed back its long black mane. Charlie, not wanting to disturb them and also not sure of what else to do, stepped back into a stall and hid as best he could.

The cloaked figure was the biggest man Charlie had ever seen, much bigger than Old Joe or his dad. By the looks of the roof of the stable and the horse, the man appeared to be at least eight feet tall. His shoulders were broad and his heavy arms hung like tree trunks at his sides. The giant man threw an armload of hay into the horse's trough and then reached out to shut the gate. From his hiding place, Charlie saw that the man's huge hands dwarfed the latch, causing him trouble securing it. A scar, with crude stitching, circled his entire wrist and this simple motion seemed to tug at the sutures, pulling them to their very limit.

The giant started to leave but hesitated. He pulled back the hood of his cloak and turned his head, letting Charlie catch a glimpse of his gruesome features. The yellowing brown-green skin on his face was also pulled taut, so much so that it revealed each and every contour of the bone below. Hard lines of dead, white scar tissue divided his face in raised stitches of twisted skin, and his coal-black eyes were sunk back into the darkness of his visible eye sockets.

"You, you there in the shadows. Show yourself," the giant said in a gruff, rasping voice.

Charlie closed his eyes, hoping the giant wouldn't see him, but in two steps the giant man was already standing over the stall. He smelled of livestock and woodsmoke, of earth, death, and decay.

"Come now. I see you there."

Charlie edged forward from the shadows, realizing he had little choice but to comply.

"Who are you, then?"

"I-I-I'm Charlie," he said weakly. "Charlie Cooper."

"Charlie who? I've never heard that name. What are you doing in here?"

"I'm sorry. I was over by the wagon and saw the horses."

"The wagon? What wagon is that?"

"Mrs. Winthrope's. We just got here," Charlie said.

"Mrs. Winthrope? You have come with Mrs. Edith Winthrope?"

"Yes, sir."

The giant towered over Charlie. "So you must be the boy I have been hearing about . . ."

"I'm not sure," Charlie said.

"I would bet you are. Well, off with you. Back to the wagon. It's not safe to be wandering around here by yourself."

"Yes, sir," was all Charlie could think to say as he hurried toward the stable door. But then he stopped and looked back at the big black horse. "Excuse me, sir."

"Yes, what's that?"

"The horses, sir. Do you take care of the horses?"

The giant turned to Charlie, pulling the hood over his scarred face. "What kind of question is that?"

"It's just we have horses back home, but I've never seen horses like this . . . They're magnificent."

The gruffness in the giant's voice softened. "Ah, yes. They are . . ."

"Yes, sir, they are. I like horses."

"Charlie, where have you gotten to?" Mrs. Winthrope called.

Charlie pushed the door open, and the giant man stepped back from the harsh light of the setting sun.

"Thank you and nice to meet you, sir," Charlie said, closing the door behind him. The giant man just grunted.

"Who was that you were talking to?" Mrs. Winthrope asked when Charlie returned to the wagon.

"The horseman, he takes care of the horses. You should see them. They're huge. Almost as big as he is." Charlie paused to catch his breath. He looked out over the mountaintop, realizing that this castle was at a much higher elevation than the Prime Minister's.

"The horseman?" Mrs. Winthrope repeated, ushering him up the oversize front steps. "This way, Charlie. I'll show ya to your room and ya clean up for dinner. The Prime Minister will be here shortly after sundown."

She led Charlie and Ringo inside and up a wide staircase that was carved out of the side of the mountain and then down a hall to his room. At one end of the hall there was an open window, which blew cold with the mountain air. At the other end, there was a candle stand with stacked rows of unlit dusty votives.

"This way, Charlie," Mrs. Winthrope said, opening the door's heavy lock.

The room was large and brighter than the one at the Prime Minister's castle, though it also had shelves upon shelves of heavy leather-bound books.

"Here you go. See if you can't get a little rest before dinner. It's been a big day for you. Maybe go through your things, let me know if you need anything more for the journey."

"I will, Mrs. Winthrope. Thank you," Charlie said, scratching Ringo behind the ear.

He watched them leave and then dumped his pack out on the bed, wondering if the giant man from the stables would show Old Joe the horses he cared for someday. *Old Joe would get a real kick out of that,* he thought. *Well, out of all of this, really.* Looking over his supplies, he figured that Old Joe would be proud of him for continuing their search, but also that it would be a lot easier if he, or at least his mom or dad, were traveling with him. But Charlie knew they weren't. Going forward, he would have to rely on himself—well, that and this guide, and whatever could be expected from his old pal Ringo.

chapter 13

The Tip of the Iceberg

CHARLIE WAS DREAMING again. The sun was lower now out on the plain, and he could see Billy was farther away, almost on the horizon. The birds were there again too, but this time they were quiet and closer to Billy, off in the distance. Charlie moved fast, trying to follow his cousin, but had trouble keeping up through the deep sand. He called to him, but as usual, Billy did not answer. Then Billy, followed by the dark swirling birds, disappeared over a far-off dune. In an instant, he was gone.

Charlie sat up with a start, realizing he must have dozed off. The sun was starting to set and a bell was ringing somewhere in the castle. Worrying he might be late for his second dinner with the Prime Minister, Charlie straightened his new clothes and quickly retraced his steps from his room back to the entranceway. He reached the stairs and found it was much harder to go down the giant steps than up them. As he wound his way into the foyer, he heard the clang of what sounded like steel on stone. When he looked up to investigate, he lost his footing and fell down the remaining steps, arriving on the landing with a heavy thud.

"May-may-may I be of service?" asked a deep, reverberating voice.

The accent was Germanic and the tone hollow, as if the words had come from what could only be described as a tin can.

"Are you—are you injured?"

"No. I'm okay, thank you," Charlie replied, his eyes drifting up to see that he was talking to a figure made of large sheets of polished metal. Heavy bolts lined the sides of its torso, their seams dripping oil.

"Rohmetall, Steam Man Number Three, at-at your service." The figure gestured a mock bow, punctuated by a long hiss of vapor that shot with a whistle from the narrow pipe welded to the side of the contraption's head. He took a step forward, and Charlie could hear and see wisps of steam escaping from the metal couplings and articulated joints.

"Oh, hello. I'm Charlie—"

"Yes-yes, I have spoken with Mrs. Winthrope. Ch-Ch-Charlie Cooper," Rohmetall interrupted. "May I be of service, Ch-Ch-Charlie Cooper? You appear to be injured."

The palm of Charlie's hand was indeed scraped from his fall.

"Aw, it's nothing, really," he said, wiping the blood on his pants.

"That-that is not a good idea, especially out in the wilds. I will get you a ban-bandage," Rohmetall stuttered through his glitch. "Please come this way."

He took a clunky step and extended his hand. Each finger was also articulated, so it could move freely, although when together, they looked more like the vise that was clamped to the end of Old Joe's workbench back home. Charlie took hold and Rohmetall pulled him to his feet.

"Starting to-tomorrow it would be wise to pay better attention to your surroundings-dings."

Charlie looked at the smear of blood on his pants and was reminded of the Prime Minister's and Mrs. Winthrope's warnings.

"Do not fear. We will see to that stain as well."

Charlie followed Rohmetall down the hall. He was surprised by how quickly the steam man could move considering his crude construction.

"I was assembled here, in this very castle—very castle. There were two prototypes before me; I am the third-third-third attempt, and I would like to think the most successful. I have a steam-driven generator that is fueled by minimal amounts of c-c-coal or wood—coal or wood. The kettle door is on my left side, so please be careful as it can be hot."

They entered another foyer and Rohmetall stopped. "Please-please wait here."

Charlie watched him clank forward and disappear around a dark corner. Noting the faint smell of coal fire that was left in the air, he stood there waiting and couldn't help but hear the low mumble of voices that carried from a set of large double doors on the other side of the foyer. The doors were cracked slightly, allowing only a sliver of light to escape. Counting his steps to himself, Charlie snuck across the hall and paused when he reached the light.

"And *why* not? You *w*ill already be in the Agrarian Plains, easily two-thirds of the *w*ay . . ."

Charlie recognized the Prime Minister's distinctive accent immediately.

"Aye, yes," a familiar gruff voice replied. "But the final stretch is by far the most difficult and treacherous. Not many have crossed the sands, let alone the Vast Inland Sea, to even be sure of what lies beyond."

Charlie moved closer and stood against the wall beside the doors.

"All the reason more to make the journey," the Prime Minister said.

"I see what you're after. You've been trying to map that section of the wilds for years . . . or find someone weak-minded enough to do it for you . . ."

"You are mistaken. It is not just the maps. It's for the boy . . ."

"Yes. And that is the point. He is just a boy, a living boy, I might add. If you want to keep him that way, he has no place here. And what is it about this particular boy that has brought on this sudden benevolence? Has your own survivor's guilt reared its head as of late?"

"No. It is nothing like that at all," the Prime Minister

replied. "It just seems that he is troubled, angry—there is something that haunts him. A feeling I am sure you can appreciate. He needs *thisss*; he needs to understand."

"And you need your precious maps."

"I am afraid the boy has lost his way, and *we* can help him," the Prime Minister continued. "You of all people should know what it is like to be lost."

"Enough. It is too far, too dangerous. A human boy would never make it."

"Oh, I do not know about that. This boy, he has heart," the Prime Minister said. "I have never seen someone so gripped by fear, so very scared, yet he still *took* the first step forward. He willingly entered the tunnel, for someone else's benefit, not his own, I might add. Not too many can say *thisss*, and that itself says something."

"He came here, to this valley, willingly? I agree the boy is troubled, hopeless is what I'd say."

"Come now," the Prime Minister went on. "At least meet with him . . ."

"I met him this afternoon in the stables. He likes *horses*."

Charlie pulled back from the door. Could this giant, the horseman, be the lord of this castle? Was this towering, deformed creature supposed to help him find Billy?

"It is an honor that your Prime Minister has even asked this of you," the Prime Minister said. "It would be considered a duty served for your government."

"I am already in service with this ludicrous diplomatic venture to the Agrarian Plains, and now this? A fool's errand to some lost island with me playing nursemaid to a boy? Ha." The giant laughed.

"Well, as your Prime Minister, I am afraid I must insist . . ."

"You insist?" the giant said.

"Yes, I insist," the Prime Minister said, enunciating the final syllable with extra emphasis.

Then, it was silent. After a moment, Charlie leaned forward, trying to get a glimpse of the room, which appeared to be a large library filled with more books.

"Charlie, I believe that is you breathing heavily in the hall," the Prime Minister said, so suddenly that it startled Charlie. "Would you please come in, join us?"

"Uh, yes. Excuse me, sirs . . ." Charlie cleared his throat, pushed open the heavy double doors, and stepped into the room.

"May I present Mr. Charlie Cooper," the Prime Minister announced with a dramatic wave of his hand.

"Yes, yes, Charlie Cooper," the giant said dismissively.

The large, disfigured man turned to a desk and picked up a hefty tome. He seemed different from when they met in the stable. He stood straight and appeared quite dignified before the fireplace, no longer wearing his heavy, hooded cloak but instead a suit of fine hand-tailored fabric. His hair was jet black like a raven's wing, and he had it pulled back and tied in a tight braid that shone almost purple in the firelight. Charlie looked up at the giant and again saw the dark of his sunken eyes. But perhaps the shock of their first meeting had worn off, because now Charlie found him far less repulsive.

"Charlie, as a service to the Council of the Congressional

Caucus of Vampyreishtat, this gentleman has agreed to take you—" the Prime Minister started.

"Let us be clear," the giant interrupted. "I have done nothing of the sort."

"As your Prime Minister, *w*hy, yes, I think you have," the Prime Minister replied with a tight smile. "Now, there is much to discuss, plans to *w*ork out, so may I suggest that *w*e join Mrs. *W*inthrope for dinner," he said as he walked out of the room. "And young Charlie must get to bed early," he called back from the foyer. "Λ long journey lies ahead . . . much to discuss . . . yes, much to *discusssss* indeed."

Charlie supposed he should follow the Prime Minister to the dining room but lingered a moment as the hulking man read from one of his many books. Charlie wanted to tell the giant that he agreed with him. That he also wondered if he was capable of making this journey. And if they were being completely honest, he was scared.

"I suppose you are hungry, then?" the giant said without looking up from his book.

"A bit, sir. It was a long trip today."

"A long trip?" the giant roared. "Ha, you have no idea what awaits you out there in the dark, do you, boy? This is just the tip of the iceberg, as they say."

Charlie stared down at the leather of his new boots and saw that he had already scuffed one of the toes before the journey had even begun.

"Well, then," the giant said brusquely, snapping the book shut and crossing the room. "We will have a good meal, at least."

Charlie hesitated; he felt small and weak next to the giant.

"Come now, I will not invite you again."

Charlie did as he was told and followed. As they entered the foyer, he noticed that he was already having trouble keeping up with the giant's long strides, so he quickened his steps not wanting to lose the man, and this just on the way to dinner.

chapter 14

The Monster's Prayer

*I*T WAS ANOTHER fine meal. They sat under the stars at a long stone table, which stood at the edge of the courtyard overlooking the precipice. Rohmetall tended a fire nearby made from the trunks of large oak trees, and the fire burned steadily behind them, casting the night in an eerie glow.

It seemed that by the second course it had been decided. Once his official diplomatic business for the Council out on the Agrarian Plains had concluded, the giant would take Charlie as far as the edge of the woods where the spirits were known to gather. It was apparent from his demeanor that the hulking man was still reluctant to accept this assignment, but he sat as a proper host regardless, and once the dinner plates had been cleared, he offered his pipe tobacco to the Prime Minister. They smoked as they discussed the proposed plan, often veering off course into debates over politics, philosophy, or science. Despite the occasional gruff response, Charlie was impressed by how calm the giant was as he argued his case or point of view. He thought that the entire evening was fascinating and found himself, much like the previous night at the Prime Minister's, strangely at ease in this intimidating man's presence.

As they waited for dessert, Mrs. Winthrope debriefed the table on the current state of each of the regions that they would pass. They would travel light, riding upon two of the giant's Clydesdales with a third pulling a supply cart that would be driven by Rohmetall for as long as it was needed, or capable of passing over the rough terrain that they were sure to encounter once they had moved out of the previously mapped territories.

For the first leg of the trip, they would be considered on "official business" to the Agrarian Plains. Once there, the giant was charged with the delivery of documents from the Council of the Congressional Caucus of Vampyreishtat and would speak with the Mumiya in an effort to curtail an all-out war between the various disputing factions. Then from the Agrarian Plains, they would cross the desert and the Vast Inland Sea to the island where the woods were said to be located. The Prime Minister would join them along the way as his schedule would allow but warned he should not be counted on, as his visits would be brief and, because of security reasons, largely unannounced. Still he promised he would be watching and kept abreast with news of their journey via the giant's official dispatches and other sources, which would go unnamed, also because of security reasons. He reiterated his expectation that they would survey and map any previously uncharted territories and that he looked forward to seeing the result upon their return, which he projected would be before the heavy snows covered the high mountain passes. As the discussion wound down, Charlie made a mental note to write another letter home, thinking his family would appreciate the update and latest schedule.

After dinner, the party moved to a large room, a laboratory under the giant's courtyard. The room was filled with contraptions and heavy machines, not to mention hundreds of books, some on shelves and some in random towering stacks. Charlie recognized what he was sure were the various parts and remains of Steam Man Numbers One and Two, sitting steamless on workbenches, their eyes empty and hollow, much like their creator's.

"You should read this cover to cover," the giant said, handing Charlie an extremely large book.

Surprised by its weight, Charlie almost dropped it.

"Be careful there," Mrs. Winthrope said. "That book is very old."

Charlie looked at the spine and read out loud, "*'The Crypto-zoologist's Cyclopædia of World Creatures.'*"

He blew the dust off the cover and opened the book's moldy pages to a sketch of the Mongolian death worm. Though the image was in black and white, Charlie could see that its fanged teeth were dripping with bloody drool.

"Oh, a perfect suggestion, a little light reading just before bedtime," the Prime Minister said, shifting through a stack of astrological maps and charts. "I must say, I am particularly fond of the author."

Charlie turned to the back page and found a portrait of the Prime Minister in his more youthful days.

"Oh, we could go on through the night, but young Charlie here needs his rest," Mrs. Winthrope said, ushering him toward the door.

"Ah, yes. We should all retire, I would think," the Prime Minister added. "You will be leaving before the dawn, Charlie. The sooner you sleep, the sooner you will find yourself on your way."

"Yes, sir, and thank you, to all of you," Charlie said, not sure what to expect of the coming day.

Rohmetall led Charlie out of the laboratory and back across the courtyard. The night was clear and the stars abundant. Charlie stopped and looked up at the sky. He wondered, as he took it all in, if Billy or his parents and Old Joe weren't looking up also and, just like him, wondering if he might be doing the same.

"May I be of service, Ch-Ch-Charlie Cooper?" Rohmetall asked, stopping next to the boy.

"No, just looking."

The steam man leaned back and tilted his head. His eyes rotated as their three separate lenses layered on top of one another clicked into place.

"Yes, *via lactea*. Latin. Direct translation is 'milky road.' Known in the present day as the Milky Way-Way." Rohmetall's eyes shifted again. A whistle of steam emerged from his head and disappeared in the wind. "'No one regards what is before his feet; we all gaze at the stars.' Quintus Ennius, 239 to 169 BC-BC."

The steam man turned and took a heavy metal step toward the castle.

"Ch-Ch-Charlie Cooper, this way, please."

Charlie followed Rohmetall through the corridors to the steps and the foyer. A bell rang in a distant part of the house and the metal man stopped.

"That would be another guest who may require my service. Excuse me, Ch-Ch-Charlie Cooper, but do you know your way from here?"

"Yes, I can manage. Thank you, Mr. Rohmetall."

"Then, please-please excuse me." The metal man turned and clanked a few steps down the hall. With a display of his remarkable flexibility, he stopped and looked back over his shoulder without turning his lower half.

"'I have loved the stars too fondly to be fearful of the night.' Sarah 'Sadie' Williams, 1837 to 1868." Rohmetall continued on his way, calling, "This is where we first met, Charlie Cooper. This is where we first met."

Charlie watched the odd metal man go. Then, tucking the thick encyclopedia under his arm, he climbed the stairs, again noting their unusual size. *They must be for the giant man,* Charlie thought. He found his way to the landing, but stopped when he heard the thud of a closing door down the hall. The cold wind still blew in from the open window, although now the candles in the votive stand at the end of the corridor were lit, their flames flickering against the wall. Charlie looked down at the doorknob to his room. With the day's excitement, he was tired, and knew he should just go in, but now in this strange place, his curiosity once again got the better of him.

At the end of the hall, to the side of the candle stand, Charlie found a wooden door, which was decorated with intricate carvings of mountains and a stream that led up to a great arctic ice field. He removed one of the candles to look closer at the scene and could see that there was a small figure standing on a mountaintop. The figure was staring out into the tundra and seemed lost among the many glaciers that were carved into the wood. Charlie leaned forward, but an icy draft blew and extinguished the candle. In the darkness, he could see a flicker of light from the other side, so he peered in through a star that had been hollowed out along the door's border.

The room was dark except for a second set of votive candles. The giant, wearing his heavy cloak, knelt before the stand with a length of knotted rope wrapped through his immense fingers. Charlie watched as the giant lifted his head toward the candlelight and could see that his body seemed to almost collapse as he spoke.

"Oh, Frankenstein, my creator, generous and self-devoted being, I ask thee to pardon me; I, who irretrievable destroyed thee by destroying all thou

lovedst. Alas, you are cold now, and cannot answer
me. But I wait and listen patiently for your guidance."

The giant dropped his head; the knotted rope tumbled down from his hand.

Frankenstein. Charlie stepped back, taking a deep breath. *Frankenstein?* He turned and hurried down the hall, quietly opening the door to his room. The fire was already lit, so he pulled off his boots and quickly slipped under the bedcovers.

In bed, Charlie continued to turn the idea over in his mind. *Frankenstein. The giant said Frankenstein. Creator? Was he? Could he be?* Charlie thought about the Frankenstein movies he had watched back home. Old Joe loved monster movies, especially those about Frankenstein, and Charlie would have bet money that they had seen almost all of them at some point or another, but the real Frankenstein's monster? Charlie pulled the covers up to his chin and looked over at the book that had just been given to him.

"*'The Cryptozoologist's Cyclopædia of World Creatures,'*" he read aloud, prying open its heavy pages. "*F*'s—'Fafnir, Familiars, Fenghuang, Foxfire, Frankenstein . . .'"

Charlie turned the page, only to find a chapter on Frost Giants.

He turned back to the last page of the chapter on Foxfire, realizing a section was missing. Charlie pulled the encyclopedia open as far as he could and found jagged edges that ran the length of the book's spine. Someone had torn out the chapter on Frankenstein.

Flipping through the ghastly pages of his required reading, Charlie could not believe what he had agreed to; the horseman, this giant whom he was supposed to travel with to find Billy, was actually the monster, the one created by Dr. Victor Frankenstein, *the Frankenstein monster*? It was really sinking in now, and as he looked down at the encyclopedia and the many horrors that awaited him in Monsterland, he realized that once again sleep might not find him at all this evening.

VOLUME II

— *chapter 15* —

The Departure

CHARLIE GOT OUT of bed at the sound of horses below in the courtyard. Dawn was just arriving, and from the window he could see Ringo and Mrs. Winthrope, in the form of the large gray-red wolf, politely herding the black Clydesdales into a loose circle. Charlie slowly got ready, though his stomach was in knots and he thought that he might be sick. He looked at his picture with Billy. While the journey ahead gave him some hope, he had to admit that he was afraid of where he was going; he was afraid of the unknown that lay ahead.

And the encyclopedia that had kept him up all night didn't seem to help—from banshees to ogres, trolls to vampire cats. The trolls seemed to be the worst of the lot. Trolls were vicious, the book said. With their long, razor-sharp fingernails and the way they gnawed on their victims' bones until they were dust. They traveled in numbers and could turn themselves to stone, like a turtle retreating into its shell, at a moment's notice. Charlie took a deep breath, trying his best to remain calm.

After all, this was a book, and certainly could be exaggerated as most good books are. He had already met a few creatures, two of which, vampires and werewolves, had been horribly described. Yet both had proved to be most affable and impeccable hosts. He also reminded himself of the giant's quiet confidence and the Prime Minister's air of certainty that one could not help but find contagious. He would trust them—he had to, no matter what they were, thinking that if anyone could, his new guides would be able to help Billy, wherever he might be.

Charlie thought about his mother and wrote her another letter. It was short and to the point.

Dear Mom,

So far so good. I am good too. We haven't found Billy yet, but don't worry, we will. We have a plan now, and they say I should be home before the snow covers the pass. Please say hello to Dad and Old Joe. Oh, and forgot to tell you, Ringo is with me, so don't worry about him either.

Love,
Charlie

PS—Please also tell Old Joe that he wouldn't believe the horses here and some other crazy things too.

That was enough; Charlie knew if he took too much time with the letter, or tried to explain more, going through the absurdity of his situation again might actually change his mind. So he folded the letter, tucked the photograph in his pocket, pulled on his boots, and stuffed the encyclopedia into his pack with the rest of his belongings. It was time to go.

The courtyard was buzzing with activity when Charlie arrived. Mrs. Winthrope, no longer a wolf, and Rohmetall were at the cart tightening a heavy tarp that covered their supplies. The Clydesdales shifted and shook as the giant stood in the dark, straightening the saddles and adjusting his gear. The larger of the saddled horses, Faust, was heavy with arms of every sort. There were swords and hammers, an ax, a crossbow, and lengths of thick chain. The giant wore his hooded cloak and boots of polished leather. Through the open cloak, Charlie saw that he also wore a short sword, a knife, and a coarse vest of armored leather.

"Here, boy," the giant called. "Put this on under your coat."

He threw Charlie a smaller version of the vest. The unexpected weight of the garment knocked him back.

"Ahh, Charlie, the grandest of journeys starts with a single step."

The horses trembled uneasily as the Prime Minister appeared from the shadows behind them.

"Keep these with you at all times," the Prime Minister instructed, holding out a roll of parchments. "These are your papers of transit, my guarantee of safe conduct. Present them if you must."

"Yes, sir," Charlie said, taking the papers and securing them in the pocket of his coat with his photograph of Billy, the fangs, and the rest of his chocolate bar.

"Let us hope you find no reason to use this, but best to be prepared." The Prime Minister held out a long object wrapped in thick red cloth.

Charlie took the bundle and felt the weight of it in his hand. The fabric fell away, revealing a bone-handled sword similar to the ones that the gladiators had used. Charlie pulled the weapon from its scabbard of hand-tooled leather. The blade looked old, but its edges were razor sharp. There were odd engravings carved deep into the aged metal.

"It's a gladius, isn't it?"

"Well done, Charlie. Well done."

"I did a book report on gladiators when I was in the fourth grade."

"Well then, you may be interested to know that the hilt of this particular gladius is dragon's tooth. Strongest bone on earth," the Prime Minister said.

"Thank you, sir. Thank you for everything. And, sir"—Charlie pulled the Hershey's bar from his pocket—"I'd like you to have this."

He handed the chocolate to the Prime Minister.

"Why, Charlie," the Prime Minister gasped. A spark had appeared in his tired eyes. "Most generous of you. Now it is I who must thank you."

"Oh, it's nothing. I remember you saying you liked chocolate and that it was good for you and all, so it's the least I could do."

The Prime Minister bowed graciously as Mrs. Winthrope joined them holding a covered basket.

"There's food for you in there and a lump of coal for Rohmetall. He knows where the rest of it is in the cart, so don't ya worry about that. Come now."

Mrs. Winthrope and the Prime Minister walked Charlie to his horse.

"This here is Goliath. A fine horse," Mrs. Winthrope said as she secured Charlie's rucksack to the back of his saddle. Goliath was smaller than Faust, the giant's horse, but still towered over Charlie.

"Come now. Up ya go."

Mrs. Winthrope clasped her hands for Charlie's foot and hoisted him up onto Goliath's back.

"You cut a fine figure in the saddle, Charlie," the Prime Minister said with an eye to the rising sun.

"Now, you do what yer told, and you'll be all right," Mrs. Winthrope said, but Charlie detected a hint of apprehension.

"Will you mail this one for me too?" Charlie pulled the letter to his mother from his coat.

"Of course I will," Mrs. Winthrope promised. "Such a good boy—yer family will welcome an update."

Goliath shifted his hooves and turned slightly to Faust. The giant sat tall in the saddle, his armaments at his sides and on the horse's flanks.

"So, you are sure about this?" the giant said.

"Yes, sir," Charlie replied. "I'm sure. And you, sir?"

"As if I had a choice in the matter. Well then, let's be on our way."

Faust stepped forward and Goliath followed.

"You be careful with my horse, you hear me, boy?" the giant warned as he rode. "Valuable stock, so mind yourself. I don't want any mishaps."

"Yes, sir," Charlie said, looking back across the courtyard. Rohmetall sat at the top of the cart, which rocked forward after them across the cobblestone. Ringo stood next to Mrs. Winthrope, licking her hand, but the Prime Minister was already gone.

"Go on, now," Mrs. Winthrope said, petting Ringo goodbye. The dog ran forward and leapt into the back of the cart. "Take care, Charlie. We'll see ya on your return!"

"And to you, Prime Minister!" the giant called out as they traveled away from his castle. "You will remember that it was I who said this was a bad idea, who feared for the boy's safety."

"I'll be sure to tell him," Mrs. Winthrope shouted after them.

"Oh, he hears me," the giant yelled. "He hears me."

Mrs. Winthrope answered, although her words were stolen by the wind. Charlie watched her wave from the courtyard for as long as he could but lost sight of her as they rounded a bend in the road.

Charlie rode Goliath up next to the cart where Ringo stood on the heavy bundles happily wagging his tail.

At least Ringo's up for it, Charlie thought, and pushed Goliath forward, trying his best to stay in stride with the giant.

chapter 16

The Ride to the Tavern

*I*T WAS ONLY midday, but Charlie's eyes were already heavy as they rode. The sun shone warm and bright, and the skies that stretched out over the mountains were the deepest blue.

"Odd weather. Not often we see the sky in this valley," the giant said, turning back in his saddle. It was hard to see his face beneath his hooded cloak. "If yer tired, you can ride in the cart."

"I'm fine. Thank you, though."

"Didn't sleep much, did ya? I find the night to be long myself, especially before a trip."

Charlie thought about his problems sleeping, realizing that last night was the first night since he had been in Monsterland that he had been bothered by his insomnia. The first two nights he had fallen asleep right away, and his dreams did not seem as troublesome here. More than likely, he concluded, because of the very real nightmares that already inhabited this place.

"I read the book, though, like you said," Charlie responded.

"Good, the more you can learn about what frightens you,

the less you have to fear. And it's never a bad idea to know what you're up against."

Charlie urged Goliath forward to keep up with the giant. "Uh, and, sir..."

"Yes, what is it?"

"I'm sorry, sir," Charlie said. "But I'm not sure I know your name."

Charlie thought he might have missed it in all that had happened and wondered, with what he had seen last night, if the man should simply be called Frankenstein, even though he was actually the doctor's creation. Old Joe would know, of course, but Old Joe wasn't here to tell him.

"I looked it up in the book. But the pages on Franken . . . well, Frankenstein were torn out."

"Were they, now? I wonder how that might have happened," the giant grumbled.

"Well, you know, with the pages torn out and all, I guess it left me wondering..."

"My name?" the giant growled impatiently. "You want to know my name?"

"Yes, what should I call you?" Charlie asked, hoping he wasn't insulting him with his question.

"What to call me?" the giant said, turning his head to Charlie. "An interesting question, as I have been called many things through the years: 'fiend,' 'daemon,' 'wretch,' 'it,' 'a vile insect,' even . . . but a proper name? I suppose I am most commonly known as the *Monster*."

"The Monster? I should call you Monster?"

"That will do," he replied, digging his heels into Faust's flank and trotting ahead. "Come now, enough of this. We have a long ride ahead."

"Monster?" Charlie called after him. "What kind of a name is Monster?"

They rode on over open country and deep green pastures, passing alongside a stream and crossing it twice. The travel was pleasant and the weather was good.

In the late afternoon, they went past a slow wagon moving in the same direction driven by two hooded creatures.

"Goblins," Rohmetall announced with an asthmatic whistle. "*Goblin*. English. Anglo-French *gobelin*, or *gobelinus* in Latin. From *kobalos*, Greek meaning *rogue*. A creature of legend, often described as 'grotesque' and 'evil.' Known for their greed. Also known as excellent metalsmiths and for their woodwork. Danger level . . . calculating . . . calculating . . . danger level . . . high . . . tic . . . tic . . . high."

The goblins scowled as they rode by and steered their wagon clear of the Monster. When the wagon was well out of sight, the Monster turned back in his saddle.

"We will stop earlier tonight than usual, need to pick up additional provisions. Up here at the tree line, there's a village. We will stay at the tavern. Let's move, though, we do not want to be roaming these streets at night."

As they entered the village, the gravel road turned to cobble-stone. It was quiet save for the few oddly shaped creatures that hurried about their business here and there. Charlie pulled his werewolf mask from his pack and slipped it over his head.

"What is that?" the Monster asked, looking down at him.

"It's my mask. You know, from Halloween? I thought it might help me blend in," Charlie said, but through the rubber slits he could see that the Monster did not share his enthusiasm.

"I suppose that could work from a distance, but at close range it will only draw attention," the Monster said, pulling Faust to a stop at a wooden two-story building. "Take it off."

Feeling childish, Charlie removed the mask and returned it to his pack.

"The dog can stay with the horses. Might serve as a decent sentry, even. This place will pick up come sunset. Believe me."

As they dismounted, the Monster instructed Rohmetall to secure the horses and cart and to stay with them at the stables for the night. Charlie joined him as they crossed the road to the tavern.

"You will be safe in here for the most part," the Monster said, approaching the tavern. "There are a number of humans who work in this village—more than what's typical for the valley—but still mind yourself. They're all profiteers, really."

The Monster entered the tavern, dropping his head to avoid hitting the door frame. It was dark and smoky in the low room with just a few shadowy figures, who sat silently in the corner. A tall, thin man appeared from a door behind the bar. His skin was pearly white and his eyes were bloodshot.

"We require rooms for the night and a meal," the Monster said, tossing a thick gold coin in the innkeeper's direction. The coin bounced with a ring on the bar before the innkeeper caught it in an outstretched hand.

"We can oblige your request, but first allow me to inquire as to your manner of being," the innkeeper said, looking the Monster up and down.

"My manner of being?" the Monster replied, removing his hood.

The innkeeper stepped back.

"Ah, I see, sir. Your cloak . . . I did not recognize you. I beg your pardon. As you may imagine, some requests come from guests who require, *ahem*, additional responsibilities—potential damages, which must be considered and perhaps even compensated in advance. However, this is, of course, not your concern."

"No, it is not my concern. But seeing that we are fed is."

"I understand," the innkeeper said, bowing his head. "Right this way."

They were seated at a table in the corner with their backs to the wall, facing the open middle of the room. The crowd was thin, although the two goblins they had seen on the road had now joined the shadowy figures in the corner.

The innkeeper brought out two wooden bowls and a large pot of steaming stew.

"And some fresh bread for ya," the innkeeper announced, leaving them two rock-hard loaves.

The Monster took a spoonful of the stew and then pushed his bowl forward.

"This swill is intolerable. We would be better off over an open fire, but that will be soon enough."

Charlie forced the stew down. The Monster was right. It

wasn't the tastiest, making him wonder what exactly they ate in this land, and what strange ingredients might be lurking in the bowl before him.

"I will see that the innkeeper hears about this," the Monster said, getting up from the table and pushing open the door to the back of the tavern. A loud commotion of pots and pans clanged from the kitchen.

"You may consider this bog water *stew,* but I certainly do not!" the Monster bellowed.

Charlie stared down at his bowl. There was a small claw bobbing at the surface of the murky liquid. He picked out the claw, hoping it was from a crab or crawfish, and set it on his plate with a grimace. When he looked back up, there was a goblin standing at the table. He was short and stocky with thick greenish-gray arms, pointed ears, and a long, tangled beard.

"Those were fine mounts we saw you on out there on the road today," the goblin said, exposing his pointed yellow teeth.

"The horses?" Charlie said.

"Aye, the horses," the goblin said, joined by the other goblin, whose beard was equally long. "A heavy purse needed for horses such as those. Yer a rich, young fellow, then, aren't ya?"

"Why, no, not at all. They aren't my horses."

"And you expect us to believe that horses as magnificent as that would belong to the ogre you seem to have in your employ. A likely story . . ."

The other goblin leaned forward. "Could you spare a few coins . . . for me and my friends here? We've just arrived in this place and find ourselves without sufficient funds."

"No, there's been some misunderstanding," Charlie said. "He's not an ogre and he doesn't work for me. I don't have any money."

"So the big fellow holds your coins for you, is that it?"

"Holds what coins? I don't have any coins—"

"A likely story," the other goblin added.

"Likely indeed," the first goblin said.

The Monster reentered the room from behind the bar carrying a large tray with what looked like turkey legs sticking out on top.

"You two, what do you think you are doing there?" the Monster said gruffly.

The goblins retreated to their table.

"Beg your pardon. Just talking to the boy. No damage done."

"You have no business talking to the boy, or to me for that matter. Be on with you."

The Monster set the tray of what he was able to scavenge from the kitchen on the table. He grabbed a large drumstick and ripped into the flesh with his rotten teeth. Breathing heavily, he sneered at the goblins in the corner.

"What was that about? What did I tell you about minding yourself?"

"They were asking about the horses," Charlie said.

"The horses? My horses? Why is that their concern?" The Monster pushed the tray toward Charlie. "Eat. I look forward to ridding ourselves of this vile burg in the morning, you can be sure of that. Vile place . . . vile."

Charlie ate what he could and soon found himself following

the Monster and the innkeeper up a narrow wooden staircase. It groaned under their weight.

"Not to worry, made of the choicest timber, by the finest of the goblin craftsmen," the innkeeper said, leading them to their rooms on the upper landing.

The rooms opened to the hall and faced the road where they had left Rohmetall with the horses. They were connected and the Monster moved quickly, inspecting the locks on the doors and windows.

"This will do," the Monster said, tossing the innkeeper another coin. The innkeeper caught it, bowed his head, and left, closing the door behind him.

"I will check on the stables," the Monster said, dropping Charlie's rucksack on the bed. "You will hear all manner of sound as the night wears on, but rest assured. You are safe here."

The Monster looked out the window and then pulled the dingy, threadbare curtains closed.

"Shout out if you need me, and remember, study your book."

The Monster went into his room, bolting the door between them. Then Charlie heard him lock the doors to the hallway outside, followed by his heavy steps as he crossed the landing and went down the stairs.

Charlie double-checked the locks, propped his photo with Billy up against an oil lamp on the nightstand, and got into bed. He took out the book and read two chapters, one on the physiological nature of the Persian manticore and a second that debated the various ways to disarm a hostile gnome. The wind picked up and slammed a shutter roughly on the side of the window frame while he read. As the night wore on, it howled and blew harder. Charlie could hear the cries of wolves and something screaming off somewhere in the hills that surrounded the village. From the street below, he heard low voices that grumbled and growls that echoed off the narrow buildings.

Charlie set down the book and pulled his blanket up higher, almost above his head. *At least Ringo and the horses are safe,* he thought, looking at the photograph again. When he blew out the lamp, he wondered if the same could be said for Billy.

——— *chapter* 17 ———

Just a Few Coins

*B*ILLY. CHARLIE COULD see him clearly this time. He was close. Right there, standing in front of him out on the desolate plain. And he was shouting. Billy was shouting something, but there was nothing coming out of his mouth; his lips were moving, but it was silent. He shouted again, and then, as quickly as he had appeared, the shouting stopped and Billy was gone.

Charlie opened his eyes; it was still dark, but he knew that he was in his bed at the tavern by the howling winds that raged outside the window. There was something else, though—a faint clinking sound, metal shifting on metal, and it was coming from the door to his room. As Charlie sat up, he saw the doorknob slowly turning.

"Just a few coins."

The door creaked open, and Charlie saw the outline of a goblin.

"There, there, young sir," the goblin whispered, crossing the room, his counterpart following closely behind. "A few coins is all we're after, just a few coins . . ."

The goblin stood over the bed. He had a long, curved knife in his hand. The other goblin had a similar knife in his teeth and was riffling through Charlie's coat in the corner.

"So where might they be? Your coins, that is?"

Charlie saw the bone handle of the sword that the Prime Minister had given him sticking out of the top of his rucksack. It was glowing in the moonlight, right there, but he couldn't move. He was too scared. He tried to call out, but his words were tangled and lost.

"Just a few coins," the goblin repeated, following Charlie's eyes to the blade. "Well, well, what is this? A bit of an old relic for a young sir such as yerself."

The goblin bent down to retrieve Charlie's sword but stopped short as the door to the adjacent room broke open. Knocking the door off its hinges, the Monster was on top of the goblin in the corner in a flash. He roughly grabbed the creature and threw him against the wall, then turned toward Charlie. It was all happening so fast; still, Charlie could have sworn he heard him roar.

The goblin next to the bed scrambled to his feet and pointed his knife at Charlie's throat.

"N-n-n-not another move," the goblin stuttered, obviously shaken by the sight of the Monster.

The Monster paused halfway across the room.

"There, that's it. Like I said, we're new here, just weary

travelers in search of a few spare coins," the goblin explained, stepping closer to Charlie. "We'll take what we're after and be on our way..."

"New here?" the Monster said. "A few words, then. Some introductory advice, if I may. You will take nothing, and it would be wise, medically speaking, to just leave the boy be..."

"Ah, well, you're not really in a position to be giving out *advice*, are you?"

The Monster slowly pulled back his coat, revealing the sheathed long knife that hung at his belt.

"That's enough of that," the goblin said. "Put your hands—"

But before the creature could finish, the Monster drew and threw his knife, hilt-first, hitting the goblin squarely in the forehead with its heavy handle. The goblin dropped his weapon, took another step, and then fell forward, unconscious.

The Monster turned back to the other goblin with a menacing glare. Fearing for his life, the second goblin ran out into the hall, jumped over the railing down to the landing, and tumbled down the remaining stairs.

"Get your things. It is almost morning. We will move out," the Monster instructed. "And next time, Charlie, call for help. I cannot protect you if I do not know that you are in trouble."

"I tried," Charlie said. "But nothing came out..."

"Try harder."

The Monster left in pursuit of the second goblin, and Charlie hurriedly stuffed his belongings into his pack. From the floor below, he heard another roar, followed by a shirking yelp that made Charlie wonder where the Prime Minister and Mrs.

Winthrope were and what they would have thought of all this. He looked down at his trembling hands as he secured the sword to the side of his pack, and thought about his parents. What would they think of this, or Old Joe for that matter? But then, when he stepped over the unconscious goblin to leave, he thought that Old Joe would have at the very least found it interesting.

The downstairs of the tavern was dark, and Charlie was startled when the innkeeper stepped from behind the bar.

"I heard the commotion," the innkeeper said. "I did not know—I promise . . ."

He was holding a kerosene lantern and followed Charlie out to the street, where they found Rohmetall driving the cart and pulling the other horses. Ringo rode in the back barking at the small crowd that had gathered, torches in hand, to see the excitement.

"You should have called for help, Ch-Ch-Charlie Cooper," Rohmetall called.

"I know," Charlie said, reaching for the pommel. He tried to pull himself up into the saddle but slipped. He tried again and was surprised by the grace of his second attempt before realizing the Monster was lifting him.

"The sun will be up soon." The Monster dropped Charlie onto the horse. "This danger has passed."

"You should have called for help, Ch-Ch-Charlie Cooper," Rohmetall repeated.

"Yes, you should have," the Monster said, swinging up into his saddle. "And if you're in trouble, be quick about it."

They rode toward the edge of the village with the mob of

curious onlookers following on foot. A shriveled woman with wild hair twisted in dirty knots did not seem concerned with the pace and walked briskly between the cart and Charlie's horse.

"So this is the boy?" the old woman asked. She was looking up at Charlie from under the brim of a wide felt hat.

"What boy?" The Monster pushed his horse forward through the growing crowd.

"Aye, my lord," she cackled. "The word is out . . . You travel with a newcomer. A boy. A living human boy . . ."

"As I said," the Monster continued, looking down at her. "What boy?"

"Ah, yes. *What boy* . . ." The old woman walked closer to the cart. Ringo whimpered as she reached a long, bony hand out and stroked the dog's heavy coat. "I hear there's strange goings-on the farther one ventures."

"We have heard the same," the Monster replied.

"You're headed into the wilds now, boy," she crowed, pointing a knobby finger at Charlie. "You best take care of yourself."

"He will," the Monster promised, taking his horse to a gallop. "I guarantee."

The old woman stopped and removed a handful of dried leaves from the pocket of her apron. Charlie wasn't sure how, but she lit the clump and then waved it about the cart and horses as they passed.

"Well, safe travels to ye," she said, watching them ride across a small bridge where the cobblestone turned back to gravel. "Safe travels."

— *chapter* 18 —

The Function of a Name

THE CARAVAN RODE on out of the village, moving higher into the tree line. They traveled throughout the day without incident, allowing Charlie to take in the magnificence of the trees, which towered above them. There were giant pines and redwoods, heavy hemlock, and silver birch. Some of the trees' trunks were as wide in diameter as ten men. Charlie thought about Billy, wondering if he too had traveled this way and seen these very trees. They stopped midday to water the horses, and Charlie followed the Monster as he walked up a small incline and knelt with the knotted rope in his hand before a pile of rocks that served as some sort of a roadside shrine. Charlie stood to the side, dwarfed by the trunks of the giant trees around them.

"Why are you always lurking about, coming up behind me?" the Monster said after some time had passed. He was still on his knees, and asked the question without looking back at the boy.

Charlie picked at the oversize bark on the trunk beside him.

"Speak up," the Monster commanded.

Charlie took a deep breath. "It's just . . . I don't know where to be sometimes."

The Monster sighed and turned to Charlie. It was quiet except for the wind in the high trees and the gurgle of a small stream.

"Do you know where we are going, boy? Do you even know why you want to go there?"

"Of course I do. I need to see my cousin Billy. I need to talk to him. I want to tell him that I miss him and I want him to come back," Charlie said. "I need to find him and tell him I'm sorry . . ."

"Sorry?"

"That I couldn't do more, that . . ." Charlie could feel his throat tightening up and stopped.

"And you cannot say these things to him here? Beneath these trees?"

Charlie looked at the ground.

"I see. I too have known these feelings," the Monster said. The stern look on his face had softened a bit but quickly returned as he finished his thought. "Well then, no need to look so glum about it. We are going, aren't we?"

"Yes."

"So get your chin up—no more of this sulking, you hear me?"

"Chin up, yes, sir," Charlie said, wiping his nose on his coat sleeve. "You know, my grandfather back home, he says that too, chin up . . ."

"Does he?" the Monster said, turning back to the shrine.

"Yes, sir, he sure does." Charlie felt better. He sat down at the base of the tree and waited. Then followed the Monster back to the cart and horses when he was done.

THEY RODE THROUGH THE AFTERNOON, AND AT DUSK THEY dropped down into a low gully lined with heavy rock and divided by a clear mountain stream. The Monster pulled his horse around, surveying the site.

"Rohmetall, see to the horses. Charlie, you will gather wood for the fire and fetch water. These are your duties, Charlie. We all have to pull our own weight."

Charlie gladly slipped down from his horse. If he thought he was stiff from the wagon ride the other day, that was nothing compared to how his legs felt now. They were loose like rubber, and he had trouble walking as he set out to complete his chores.

The Monster spurred Faust out of camp with Ringo running behind him. Charlie found a bucket in the cart and carried water to Rohmetall for the horses and then went off to gather the firewood.

He piled the wood in the center of the clearing and looked up at the setting sun. The forest around them came alive with howls and cries, and Charlie hoped that the Monster and Ringo would return soon.

When they did appear, the Monster had a large stag tied over the haunches of his horse.

"What is this?" the Monster asked. "It is almost dark. And the fire is not lit?"

"Yes, Ch-Ch-Charlie Cooper. Why is not the fire lit-lit?" Rohmetall sputtered. He was carrying a heavy crate of cooking supplies toward them.

"Well, you are not much help, are you?" the Monster said to his metallic creation.

"Yes, Ch-Ch-Charlie Cooper. Why is not the fire lit?" Rohmetall repeated.

"Uh, I wasn't sure what to do. I did what you said but . . ."

"Come on, boy, what is the point of the wood if there is no fire?" The Monster was now down off the horse. "And do you think this is sufficient fuel to make it through the night?"

"I'm not sure . . ."

"Well, I assure you it is not."

"Yes, sir," Charlie said, and worked his way toward the edge of their camp for more wood.

"And you," the Monster said to Rohmetall. "You could make yourself useful, help the boy."

"Help Ch-Ch-Charlie Cooper. Charlie Cooper needs my help."

Rohmetall joined Charlie and began breaking small tree trunks into usable fuel.

"Helping, helping . . ."

Charlie stepped behind a rock outcrop and took in the sight of the rising moon. The forest was raucous now with unseen movement, and the sound of creatures moving in the dark around him urged Charlie quickly back to camp with his last armload of wood.

He returned to a roaring fire, with Rohmetall tending the blaze. The Monster stood away from the flames, cutting hunks of the stag with his long knife, Ringo paying close attention beside him.

"I was once afraid of fire, but now worry that some nights we will not be able to have one for fear of what it may attract," the Monster said.

Charlie dropped the load of wood.

"You can organize that, there. Kindling, middle-sized, on up, you understand?"

"Yes, sir."

With Ringo eagerly watching, the Monster brought the bloody chunks of venison toward the fire and stuck them on the ends of sharpened sticks.

"I realize now that it was my mistake last night at the tavern, Charlie, not yours," the Monster admitted. "Call out next time, but I should have been more diligent. Been holed up in the castle too long, I suppose. Losing my edge for the wild. I should have left the dog with you too, and for that I am sorry."

"That's okay," Charlie said, glancing up from the kindling that he was separating. "I was pretty scared. I'm sure glad you were there."

The Monster grunted softly and turned back to the meat.

"I'll try to be more brave," Charlie said, picking up a small log and throwing it on the fire. He then looked back at the Monster. "And, uh, sir . . ."

"Yes. What is it?"

"Well, I was wondering, with me supposed to call out and all, other than Monster, have you ever had a name? A real name, you know, like I do?" Charlie asked.

Rohmetall's head spun around toward the Monster.

"You know, like Charlie or Rohmetall?"

"Rohmetall. Noun of Germanic origin. Translation to English: 'raw or crude metal.' 'Raw or crude,'" the steam man stated.

"Enough. I thought we had settled this," the Monster grumbled.

"I know you said *Monster*. But that's like calling me *boy* instead of Charlie, isn't it?"

"Yes. I suppose it is, if you happen to be the boy of all boys . . ."

Charlie was having second thoughts about bringing up the subject again, but he was curious, so he continued anyway.

"Come on, you must have a name."

The Monster cleaned his long knife in the grass.

"I do. It's Monster."

"But that means so many things. How about something that I can call you? And only you?"

"I am aware of the function of a *name*," the Monster said, shifting his weight, his shoulder dropping slightly out of socket. He seemed to be lost in thought for a moment. Then he continued, "Mary Shelley once called me Adam, but I believe it was meant as ridicule."

"Who's Mary Shelley?" Charlie asked, wondering if she might have been his mother.

"M-M-Mary Wollstonecraft Shelley (née Godwin), 1797 to 1851," Rohmetall announced. "Author. *Frankenstein; or, The Modern Prometheus* . . ."

"Shut up with all that claptrap," the Monster snapped.

Charlie looked up at the Monster. "So it's true?"

"Is what true?"

"Frankenstein . . . the story," Charlie said, thinking that Old Joe would be thrilled.

"True?" the Monster said. "Perhaps *inspired* is more accurate. Shelley was a writer of her time, and there were stories—rumors, really—in the hills where she vacationed, so she wrote about them—"

"Like ghost stories," Charlie interrupted.

"Not ghosts, quite the opposite," the Monster said. "Stories of a living creature assembled by a madman's profane fingers; dissecting rooms, slaughter and charnel houses were said to have furnished its gruesome materials. So this Mary Shelley took the tale and then embellished it, as most writers do. But true? I suppose to some degree. I am here, am I not?"

The Monster turned to Charlie.

"A name, you ask? Who is to know all the names that provided the sum of my many parts? Too many to recall and too long ago . . ."

"We could make one up," Charlie said. "You have to have some name that you like."

"It is odd for a person to pick his own name. Besides, who is to use it once you are gone? The Prime Minister?" the Monster asked, hooking a disjointed thumb to the steam man. "Herr Rohmetall there?"

Charlie thought about it for a minute.

"What about Frank? I could call you Frank . . ."

"Frank?"

Charlie smiled. "Yeah, get it? Frank N. Stein."

The Monster did not look amused, but for a split second, Charlie thought he saw something in his dark, empty eyes—a flicker appeared for the briefest of moments.

"Frank. No, not Frank . . . Franklin, perhaps," the Monster said, stoking the coals with the tip of his long knife. "I doubt it will stick, but I have always been fond of that name."

"I like Franklin," the boy said. "Reminds me of Benjamin Franklin. You know, the kite and lightning? He was an inventor and a statesman, just like you."

"If it pleases you, then, and if it will put an end to this tedious conversation, you may call me Franklin."

The Monster seemed generally amused with himself.

"As for a last name," the Monster continued, looking back to Rohmetall, "how does Prometheus sound?"

"Franklin Prometheus," Charlie announced.

"I said that in jest."

"Prometheus," Rohmetall recited, "a Titan. Credited in ancient Greek mythology for his aid toward mankind. Some say man-man-mankind was his creation. Also credited for . . . the gift of f-f-fire."

Rohmetall rotated his head to Charlie.

"In reference to the title of the 1818 Mary Shelley novel *Frankenstein; or The Modern Prometheus*, Shelley considered Prometheus a devil responsible for bringing fire to earth-earth, which led to the cooking of animal flesh or meat, which is said to have led to the downfall of man."

As if to emphasize the point, the skewered venison dripped hissing on the coals.

"Enough," Franklin growled.

"No-no-notable quote from the novel, the Monster to Herr Frankenstein, 'My food is not that of man; I do not destroy the lamb and the kid to glut my appetite; acorns and berries afford me sufficient nourishment.'"

"Acorns and berries?" Franklin huffed, turning the meat from the flame. "What did I tell you about that story? Like to see ol' Mary survive on acorns and berries in this place."

"Franklin," Charlie said again. "Franklin Prometheus!"

"And now that this pressing issue has been resolved, can we please see to dinner?" Franklin Prometheus said. Ringo barked with approval.

They began their meal, and Franklin was right: The food tasted much better over the open fire. They ate the venison and dug into a sack of turnips from the cart. After dinner, Rohmetall brought out bedding, and Charlie laid his blankets next to the fire.

"The book," Franklin said, handing him a lit lantern.

So Charlie settled in beside the blaze and went over his studies by the lantern light. He searched the tome for more on

Prometheus but found little else, save for the section about the monstrous eagle that ripped out the Titan's liver daily, only to have it grow back again—his punishment for giving man fire.

Charlie lay by the fire, listening to the crackling flames and the humming howls from the trees, thinking how grateful he was for Prometheus's gift and sacrifice.

— *chapter* 19 —

The Monster's Rage

CHARLIE WOKE UP from a troubled sleep. It was the dream again, the desolate place with its vast emptiness, the jagged rocks and blowing sand. But this time there were no birds; this time there was no Billy. He sat up and looked around the camp, finding Rohmetall slouched down on a boulder near the horses. The lantern was out and the fire had settled down to glowing hot embers.

"Ch-Ch-Charlie Cooper is awake," Rohmetall said, suddenly at attention.

Charlie pushed Ringo off his bedding and climbed out into the cold night air. "Yes, just need to visit the trees."

"Charlie Cooper visits-visits the trees."

Leaving Rohmetall, Charlie wandered to the edge of the firelight and peered up at the moon, which drifted lazily behind a veil of black clouds. The night's cries were thick in the air around him, until a horrible roar that pounded like thunder abruptly interrupted the growing murmur. The roar was followed by a wailing moan that sent shivers down Charlie's spine. He turned to run back to the campfire but stopped himself. Every part of him wanted to leave, but once again, his curiosity got the better of him. Charlie ventured forward, counting his steps until he was perched on a rock overlooking a lower tree-lined bowl. It was almost like an amphitheater and there in the moonlight, center stage, he saw Franklin.

The Monster clung to a large tree. Shaking it to its very roots, he was ripping the trunk from the ground. With unharnessed rage, he flung the tree across the clearing, and then turned his attention to a boulder, which he lifted and hurled, smashing it against the other rocks. There were more trees and more boulders, and this continued until he dropped to his knees, raised his head to the moon, and let out a howl that again sent shivers up Charlie's spine. Then Franklin fell back and clawed at his chest, his cry growing to the terrible roar that Charlie first heard in the tavern.

Charlie had seen enough. He ran stumbling through the woods back to camp, where Rohmetall was calming the horses. They stamped in place, shaken by the Monster's furious display. Ringo was whimpering at the metal man's feet.

"Charlie Cooper has returned from his visit to the trees-trees."

Rohmetall appeared calm, almost oblivious to the Monster's cries that echoed in the forest around them.

"Yes, it's me," Charlie said, climbing into his bedding. He flinched when another ghastly roar boomed from the trees.

"Do not concern yourself, Ch-Ch-Charlie Cooper. According to Mrs. Winthrope, this is how the Monster cleanses his rage," Rohmetall said blankly. "His anger at the world and the horrors of his past that tor-torment him."

Charlie was silent. He lay back while the outburst continued, thinking about what it would be like to go through life without ever having a name. Without ever needing a name because there was no one to use it. What it must have been like to be that isolated, that lonely. Charlie knew he felt lonely sometimes, but there was always someone around, someone who knew his name, at least.

He turned the thought over in his mind, letting the next roar bring some comfort in this frightening place. What would dare attack them with such a beast in their presence? He fell asleep again listening to the anguished cries of his protector. He hoped that the Monster, now named Franklin Prometheus, could find some peace someday, but was also glad that he had found an outlet, as Charlie did not wish for it to be him.

— *chapter* 20 —

The Lester Mortlocks
of the World

*T*HEY RODE FOR the next three days, climbing higher and higher into the mountains. The road became narrow, winding up rocky passes and down into heavily forested valleys. The travel was good, but late on that afternoon of the third day Charlie felt an eerie presence, as if they were being watched. Franklin must have sensed it too, as he studied the trees that lined the trail with more diligence than he had for the past two days. Ringo was also uneasy. On narrow stone passes or under the dark canopy of the great trees, the dog barked at movement that no one else could see.

With the trees behind them, they soon approached a traveler on foot in an open meadow. The traveler wore a hood that hid his face from full view.

"Nice day for a wander, I'd say," he said in a voice that was hoarse and cracked.

Franklin continued without reply, so the traveler gave Charlie a wave as he passed.

"It is a nice day," Charlie said, returning the gesture.

The traveler looked up, revealing his face, which broke into a craggy smile. Charlie could clearly see an *X* branded onto the side of his pockmarked cheek.

"Yes, it is. Safe travels to you. Safe travels to you all," the stranger replied, watching as they rode away.

"To you-you-you too, sir," Rohmetall added, drawing a glare from Franklin, which made Charlie laugh.

"What's so funny?" Franklin barked.

"Nothing," Charlie said, clearing the chuckle in his throat. "Nothing at all—"

"Well, mind the horse there, you hear me?"

"Yes, sir, I will."

Charlie felt good, he thought. Better than he had in days, weeks, maybe a year. He wasn't sure if it was Franklin and Rohmetall's ongoing back-and-forth, or the pleasant weather, or if it was just the feeling that he was doing something important. Their little group was well on their way, and he was finally going to find Billy.

They left the man standing in the meadow and continued up over the rise of a small hill that was covered in wildflowers. But on the way down the other side, the solid path turned to loose gravel, making the horses slip as they trotted along. Rohmetall pulled on the cart's brake, but instead of stopping, it skidded off the road, hitting a boulder that was hidden in a patch of mountain daisies. Franklin quickly turned his Clydesdale, caught the harness of the cart horse, and forced the entire rig to a stop.

"Charlie. Dismount and hold the reins."

Charlie did as he was told. Rohmetall set the brake and climbed down from the cart.

"May I be of service, F-F-Franklin Prometheus?"

"No, you've done quite enough," Franklin growled. He crouched down on one knee and ran his hand along the edge of the wheel, inspecting the damage. "Lost the rim, but it can be fixed."

"May I be of ser-ser-service?" Rohmetall inquired a second time.

"Yes," Franklin sighed. "Take the horses and go find water."

Rohmetall turned to unhitch the cart horse.

"Charlie. You stay here," Franklin ordered, looking over his shoulder at the boy.

Once more, Charlie did as he was told and sat on the hill in the wildflowers, watching Rohmetall lead the horses to a stream at the edge of the meadow. In no time at all, Franklin had the cart propped up on a stack of rocks as high as the loose gravel would allow; with the wheel in hand, he hammered the clamps in place.

"Come here, boy," Franklin said.

Following Ringo, Charlie ran down and stood next to the Monster.

"The wheel, put it in place," Franklin instructed. From one knee, he rested the cart on his shoulder. "When I stand . . . ready . . ."

Franklin stood, lifting the cart and all the provisions.

"Now, Charlie."

Charlie struggled with the wheel; he tried to pick it up but could only bring it a few inches from the road.

"The wheel, Charlie," Franklin repeated.

"I'm trying!" Charlie gasped, doing his best to lift the heavy wheel again, but it barely moved.

Suddenly, a shadow cast over them. With the weight of the cart bearing down on him, Franklin twisted to look behind him. "Who's there?" he called. Ringo barked.

"Here, allow me to give you a hand," a raspy voice replied. It was the traveler from the road. He knelt beside Charlie, lifted the wheel, and slid it onto the axle with ease. "Ah, there, tighten her up, and with a little goose grease, good as new."

Franklin set the cart down and stood towering over the man. He shook out his lumbering arms and brushed his hands on his heavy trousers.

"I am sure we could have managed," Franklin said.

At the sight of Franklin's gruesome features, the traveler began to turn away but caught himself and looked straight at the figure above him.

"Ah, yes. I see now that you could have. A strong man, a strong man, to be sure." The traveler moved uneasily, a hint of apprehension in his eyes. "Well, yes. There's a stream ahead, the water's not bad. I could give you a hand with the cart."

Franklin looked back up the hill behind them.

"Oh, but my help? What would a strong man like you need with my help?" the traveler added, walking quickly ahead down the slope.

"Charlie, in the cart," Franklin ordered abruptly, stepping away from the wheel.

Charlie looked back over the hill at the tall flowers. They swayed in the late-afternoon breeze in shimmering waves across the meadow.

"Only a bit farther . . . the stream, that is," the traveler called back to them.

"Where's he going?" Charlie said.

"The cart, boy, now," Franklin repeated, glaring uphill.

Charlie ran to the cart as Franklin reached under the tarp and pulled out a heavy club. Behind them, at the crest of the hill, Charlie saw the first of the ogres appear.

It was about Franklin's size but rounder in the middle. Its meaty head was bald and caught glints of the sun as it slowly lumbered forward. Two more of similar build followed close behind, spread out in a clumsy formation.

From his place beside the cart, Charlie looked ahead toward the stream. He could see the traveler was running away from them, down toward some boulders below.

"Sorry about this! Just business!" the traveler yelled back. "Now, you ignorant beasts, now!"

At this, Rohmetall abandoned the horses and went after the traveler, just as more ogres appeared from the trees behind him. Charlie reached for his sword with a shaking hand, but Franklin stopped him.

"We will be fine, if you promise to do what I say," Franklin said, swooping down to pick up the boy.

"I promise."

"What have you learned from your studies?"

"They're ogres, right?" Charlie was breathing heavily. "The book said that they are slow and dim-witted . . ."

"Aye, ogres, slow and dim-witted," Franklin said, setting Charlie down in the cart. "Remember, the more you can learn about what frightens you, the less you have to fear. Now, let's see that justice finds these ogres and this malicious *Samaritan*."

The ogres grew closer, bumbling toward them with unexpected speed. Franklin stepped away from the cart, preparing himself for their attack. He lifted the heavy club over his head and roared as he brought it back down to earth with incredible force. Charlie felt the cart shake.

Franklin greeted the first ogre with a forceful blow to its sagging belly. The ogre bent over and rolled down the hill, howling past Charlie. Ringo ran after it baring his teeth. The second ogre took a hit squarely to its head, collapsing on the spot, while the third tripped over its own feet and somersaulted sideways toward the tree line.

Franklin turned back to the cart, a faint smile on his face. "See, Charlie, slow and dim-witted." He picked Charlie up and threw him onto his shoulders. "Hold on tight."

Charlie did, and they ran down the hill toward the stream so fast that tears welled in his eyes.

"Rohmetall," Franklin called, setting Charlie down by the boulders at the bottom and gripping the club in both hands.

Rohmetall cocked his head. He was holding the traveler by the scruff of his neck. "Ogre. *Ogres.* Of French origin. Danger level for . . ."

"Enough of that; secure the boy now!"

"Securing. Securing," Rohmetall responded, dragging the pleading traveler behind him as he moved to protect Charlie. Then he shouted, "Ogres! Ogres!" when more ogres appeared from behind the rocks.

Charlie spun around clumsily, trying to pull the sword from its scabbard to face them.

"No, Charlie, not now!" Franklin growled, bringing his club down on the first ogre he could reach. "Remember your promise and do as I say!"

The other ogres turned their attention to Franklin, stumbling over to surround the Monster. Franklin just stood there calmly, shifting the giant club in his hands. Charlie stepped back behind Rohmetall, but found he was more scared for the Monster than for himself.

"Stupid, pathetic creatures. You will pay for the unfortunate company you keep," Franklin bellowed, slamming the club down on the ground again. Letting loose a mighty roar, he set upon the ogres with such fury that Charlie jumped back with a start. One after another, the Monster knocked them to the ground. But two ogres managed to get past him; one wrestled the club from Franklin's hand while the other locked the Monster's torso in its powerful arms. The second ogre lifted Franklin off his feet and spun him toward the stream. Charlie could see the sutures along Franklin's neck ripping under the strain and gasped, wishing he could help him. But the Monster fought to get his feet back to the ground, where he was able to throw the ogre over his shoulder.

Three of the ogres lay unconscious, unable to rejoin the fight. The three that remained circled Franklin again before attacking in unison. Franklin fought them back, but without the club, he had trouble keeping them at bay.

"Get him!" the traveler shouted. "Get him—"

The traveler stopped short, his eyes suddenly wide. Charlie followed his gaze, wondering what could have possibly spooked him in the midst of such chaos. He turned and saw it immediately. Behind them, up in the tree line, there was something moving on all fours, and it was moving fast.

"H-h-hold on, wh-wh-what is that?" the traveler stammered.

The figure looked like a wolf, the biggest Charlie had ever seen, bigger than Mrs. Winthrope's form and much bigger than Ringo. The wolf paused at the top of the hill, let out a long howl, and then sat back on its haunches, which appeared slightly more human than lupine.

"No, no, no." The traveler struggled against Rohmetall's grip. "Let me go, please . . ."

In response to the howl, a pack of wolves appeared from the woods behind the creature and ran down the hill toward the scattered ogres. The large wolfish animal rose higher, extending its front limbs to the ground. They were armlike but covered with thick straw-colored hair.

"You don't understand! We have to get out of here!" the traveler cried.

The beast howled following the wolves down the hill. It was faster than the others, its gait closer to that of an ape than a wolf, and it leapt onto the closest ogre, knocking it to the ground, and then turned to the next. One ogre tried to race back up the hill, but Ringo and the pack of wolves ran it down; the others were soon subdued by the sight of Franklin's brutal fists and this new beast's snarling teeth.

The wolflike beast stood again on its crooked hind legs and stepped forward, showing its claws.

"Stop! Stop!" the traveler cried.

Two of the ogres broke away, but the howling wolflike creature followed them into the heavy timber.

"P-p-p-please stop," the traveler repeated.

Franklin dropped the ogre he was pummeling with a grunt and turned to the traveler.

"I-I-I-I'm sorry. With the hood before, I didn't recognize you for what you were," the traveler pleaded.

"And if I were not what I am, you would deem this caper acceptable?" Franklin snarled.

"Ah, no." The traveler cracked a weak smile. "But if you were not what you are, I do believe I would have found this caper to be more of a . . . heh . . . heh . . . a success—"

"I see that mark on your face, malefactor," Franklin said, pushing him aside.

"Mark?" The traveler tried to cover the branded X with his hand. "What mark?"

"Not uncommon here. We are all running from something,

but your actions make its point. Charlie, fetch the rope from the wagon."

"Rope?" the traveler cried. "What on earth would you need that for?"

Charlie brought the rope back, and together they bound the traveler and ogres by the wrists, attaching them to one another in a long line. The ogres moaned and groaned, their lumps and bruises already showing. The traveler continued to whine.

"Come now," Franklin said, pulling on the end of the rope. "You have quite a journey ahead."

"Journey?" the traveler whimpered.

With Charlie at his side, Franklin led the sorry group up the hill and back to the road. After some persuasion, Franklin extracted the bandit's name, noting it in his pocket ledger.

"So, *Lester Mortlock*, with this step your new life begins. Start walking," Franklin ordered.

Lester pulled at the rope, looking up in disbelief.

"You can't just send us off like this. Our hands bound? Not here. Not in this place!"

"If you stay on the road, you should meet a party who recognizes you for what you are; hopefully they will bring you to a proper justice. Now, on with you," Franklin said, clearly restraining himself.

The ogres staggered forward, dragging Lester with them.

"Ya can't just leave me like this. Show mercy . . ."

"I have shown mercy. If it were not for the boy's presence,

you would have received a much different fate," the Monster growled.

Charlie and Franklin stood on the hill and watched as Lester Mortlock and the ogres crossed the meadow and disappeared into the high trees.

"A weak mind preying on the weaker-minded," Franklin spat. "Come now, we must see to the horses."

—— *chapter* 21 ——

A Boy Named Dwight York

WHEN THEY RETURNED to the stream, they found a tall, lanky boy in a floppy, wide-brimmed hat sitting under a tree with Rohmetall. The boy couldn't have been more than a few years older than Charlie, almost Billy's age, and he held a long blade of grass in his teeth. Ringo licked the lanky boy's hand and nipped at his ankles. As they approached, Charlie noticed that the boy did not seem shocked or repulsed by Franklin's ghoulish features. He simply stood and extended his hand, which Franklin accepted.

"Dwight York," the older boy said with an accent that reminded Charlie of the British spy films that Old Joe liked to watch.

"Franklin. Franklin Prometheus."

Charlie smiled at his use of the name, though Franklin seemed to avoid meeting his gaze.

"A fine name. A fine name indeed, and although I recognize

your face, it's not a name I've heard in these parts," Dwight York replied, turning to Charlie. "And you?"

"Charlie Cooper."

"A pleasure to meet you."

"There is something familiar about you as well, Dwight York," Franklin said, examining the sutures along his wrist that had opened in the fight. Charlie looked at the boy's shaggy hair and noted that it was the same straw color as the wolf creature.

"And you too, sir," Dwight York said to Franklin.

"Well, I have been here a long time."

"Perhaps that is it . . ."

"Please join us for a meal this evening," Franklin offered. "A show of our gratitude."

"From the look of things, I am not sure I was needed."

"I insist."

"Well then, if you insist, it would be an honor," Dwight York accepted. "There's a pleasant spot ahead."

After they retrieved the horses upstream, Charlie went with Rohmetall to bring back the cart. When they returned, they found Dwight York and Franklin surveying the campsite, which they had started to lay out against the side of the mountain.

"With the stone to our back, it should be easy enough to defend," Franklin said, looking up at the great trees.

"Agreed," Dwight York said, securing his satchel. "Now, if you'll excuse me, I'll be back with something for the pot."

Charlie watched as he disappeared behind the rocks and then went about his camp chores with Rohmetall. Franklin took out a large roll of maps, spread them across the back of the cart, and busied himself writing dispatches of their progress to the Prime Minister. After he gathered the firewood, Charlie joined the Monster at the cart. He looked at the map of the previously charted territories, easily spotting the Prime Minister's castle, and realized that their journey was really just beginning.

"Ah, you can see it on this old map, can't you? We've a ways to go still," Franklin said. The wooden box that contained the bulk of his surveying equipment was open and holding the charts down in front of them. "Now, if you notice here, we've already entered what they call the wilds."

Charlie could see that the border of the area was clearly outlined.

"So, while not quite off the map yet, we should be prepared to start making some corrections along the way. I expect that you will help me with these cartographer's duties."

"Yes, sir. I can help."

Franklin grunted softly at Charlie's response, then turned to point at the contents of the wooden box. "That right there is a sextant, here is a compass, and this is what they call a theodolite, and that is the Gunter's chain, you got it?"

"I think so," Charlie said, looking back at the path that Dwight York had taken out of the campsite.

"What is it?" Franklin said, following his gaze. "Out with it. It's obvious there's something on your mind."

"Aren't you suspicious of him?"

"Suspicious?"

"Yes, of another stranger?"

"Who? Dwight York?" Franklin said, shutting the wooden box and securing it beneath the tarp. "He extended us a great kindness. It should be returned, should it not?"

"But it could be a trick. The man on the hill, he started out helping with the wheel. Lester . . ."

"Mortlock. Yes, and this was my mistake. It was foolish for me to think you could lift it on your own, and this led to our ambush. It seems I have grown a bit rusty."

Charlie thought about their encounter with the ogres, and standing next to Franklin, he felt small and weak.

"Besides, I know this boy Dwight York, somehow. I am not sure from where, but I have seen him before," Franklin said, shifting his weight and pushing his loose arm back into its socket. "I'm certain he's the one who has been up in the trees following us these last few days, not those dimwits. With the current lack of security, I'd bet this Lester Mortlock and his companions just lie in wait, preying on poor fools who pass through this meadow. And for what, a few coins?" Franklin scoffed. "More than likely loosened the gravel that damaged our wheel themselves. I am afraid that the Prime Minister and the Council have underestimated the situation. It is worse out here in the wilds than we thought."

"What do you mean, you know Dwight York but you don't remember him?"

"So many faces, Charlie. When you have been alive as long as I have, maybe you will understand. Now, I must return to the Prime Minister's correspondence. See to the fire. Ask Rohmetall for help if you need it."

As Charlie gathered the kindling, he thought about their conversation and wondered how old Franklin was. If the rumors of the Monster were the inspiration for Mary Shelley's book, then Franklin would have been alive when it was written. Charlie did the math in his head: Rohmetall said the book came out in 1818. So that would make Franklin, well, almost two hundred years old. Or older, depending on how long he had roamed the hills before Shelley started her tale. It was a lot to take in.

JUST BEFORE SUNSET, DWIGHT YORK RETURNED WITH SOME fat pheasants and a grouse.

"It might be wise to keep our wits about us tonight," he said, laying out his catch. "Strange goings-on in these woods, my brothers, strange goings-on indeed."

They prepared the game birds for the fire, and as darkness fell, the aroma filled the camp. Ringo and the wolves that accompanied the lanky straw-haired boy were restless through dinner. They stood with their eyes fixed on Dwight at the edge of the firelight and were only calmed by his attention.

After they ate, Charlie and Rohmetall cleaned the dishes at the stream before joining Franklin and Dwight York by the fire. The wind picked up as they settled in, whipping through the treetops overhead.

"It's coming off the mountain," Dwight York said. "It'll be a cold one tonight."

Franklin sat on a thick saddle blanket by the fire, examining his loose stitches. He dug into his worn leather bag and pulled out a small box that looked to Charlie like his mother's sewing kit.

"So, Dwight York, what brings you to these woods?" the Monster asked.

"I tend to roam these hills. It's far away from the majority of the populace. So besides the wolves, I usually have the run of it to myself."

Franklin opened the box and removed a long, thick needle and coarse string. With his fat fingers, he had trouble threading the eye but, after several tries, managed to get the string through.

"Stumbled upon that Lester Mortlock fellow and his cohorts a few days back, so when I saw your party traveling in their direction thought I would turn round," Dwight York added. "It gets to me, their general disrespect of this place. It's just not supposed to work that way."

"It irks me as well," Franklin said, pushing the needle through the thick skin of his neck.

"Can I give you a hand with that?" Dwight York offered.

"While I thank you, no. I have become accustomed to this inconvenience," Franklin replied, feeling his way along the seam. Though his hands seemed to be a hindrance, he slowly made progress stitching the gaping wound closed.

"And you? What brings your curious caravan this way?" Dwight York asked.

"Business out on the Agrarian Plains," Franklin answered.

"Ah, you ride toward trouble. I hear that Tok and his marauders' raids have taken a toll on the Mumiya's holdings this year."

"Yes," Franklin said. "We have heard the same."

"I was told it is over a land dispute. Some old family business between Tok and this Queen Tuya. They are brother and sister, you know." Dwight York poked at the fire with a stick. "Well, not your concern just yet."

"But soon enough." Franklin turned his attention away from his stitching. "You seem to be well informed for such a young fellow."

"I do what I can to stay abreast of the situation." Dwight York threw the stick in the fire. "Read the *Times Monthly*, of course."

Franklin paused, studying his face. "What is it about you, boy? I can't put my finger on it."

Dwight York looked over at the wolves and Ringo. Then took a moment before answering.

"I am afraid I have not been entirely honest," he admitted. "About recognizing you earlier . . ."

"Is that so?" Franklin said.

Dwight York removed his hat.

"Yes, sir. I am afraid it is. We have met. Two summers ago, I believe. You were recruiting."

Franklin's furrowed brow relaxed. "Aye, now I see, it was at Ranger School."

"Yes, sir, Ranger School orientation, actually. You spoke to the new inductees."

"That's right, along with the Prime Minister. That is it. Well, you've certainly grown."

"As boys do," Dwight York said, sitting up a little straighter.

"Ranger School?" Charlie interrupted.

"Yes, Ranger School. No proper university in my future. And to think, all I ever wanted was to be a professor like my parents. Literature, the classics . . . these were my interests."

"It's coming back to me now," Franklin said. "Your class showed real promise."

"Wait, hold on, I don't understand," Charlie persisted. "What's a Ranger?"

"Why, Rangers are the peacekeepers here," Dwight York said. "Empowered by the Council to ride the high-line, ensuring that the charming inhabitants of Vampyreishtat stay where they are supposed to stay and do what they're supposed to do, as well as other policing duties." He raised his hand in a quasi salute. "Entrusted with patrolling this land and all of its many inhabitants!"

"And there's a school?" Charlie asked, trying to imagine Ms. Hatchet teaching social studies to a classroom of werewolves back home.

"Ah, yes, takes training to contain the world's horrors," Dwight York answered.

Franklin leaned forward, closer to the fire. "And why, may I ask, aren't you at Ranger School now?"

Dwight York sat back a bit, intimidated by the Monster's sudden proximity. "Well, if you must know, I have taken a . . . uh . . . a leave of absence."

"A leave of absence, eh?"

"It just wasn't my cup of tea, really, a bit too on the military end of things for me. Hup, two, three, four, and all that."

"Your *cup of tea*?"

"I think I might be better suited for the Witches' School, actually."

"The Witches' School," Franklin muttered.

"Your Rangers haven't given up, though. Saw one of them just the other day, actually. Tried to recruit me back into the program," Dwight York said. "But enough about me, right?"

"Oh no, on the contrary," Franklin said. "I think this conversation has just begun."

Franklin told Charlie to break out his bedroll, which he did diligently. But instead of sleeping, Charlie lay in the firelight, reading up on werewolves in the encyclopedia and listening to Franklin and Dwight York talk well into the night. Ringo slept with the wolves at the fire's edge, and when Charlie did sleep, he slept soundly, knowing that tonight, in this company, they would certainly be safe from whatever else might be watching them from the shadows.

— *chapter 22* —

Travels with Dwight York

IN THE MORNING, Dwight York tracked Lester Mortlock and the ogres for a while, curious if they had tried to escape their bonds to double back for another ambush.

"Perhaps those big oafs learned their lesson," Dwight York said when he returned to the camp. "They stayed to the road, as far as I can tell."

Franklin was going over his maps while Rohmetall and Charlie finished tying down the loads in the cart.

"Might I join you for a spell?" Dwight York inquired. "I was going that way and know the terrain."

"Please do," Franklin said, rolling up the maps and eyeing the former recruit. "The current *lack* of Rangers in this region may warrant another set of hands."

Dwight York walked next to Charlie's horse as they rode. He ate clumps of grass, claiming it was good for his digestion, and would disappear with Ringo into the woods from time to time, sometimes leaving them and the trail for hours. He usually returned with information about what lay ahead or options for clean water—though other times he would silently rejoin them, almost as if he had never left. As they traveled along, Charlie explained to him that he was looking for his cousin Billy, who was lost, and Dwight York told Charlie more about why he left the Ranger School.

He said that since his transformation, he preferred to be alone, present company excluded. This made the Rangers, or any group for that matter, "a tough sell" for him. He did not feel comfortable in the confines of an official pack and chose instead to wander on his own, finding his lupine cousins often better company than his fellow lycanthropes or other humanoids. He told Charlie that he, not the moon, was in control of his curse, so while still a burden, he was able to transform only when he wished to.

He told Charlie about his journey, how the government showed up at his school and brought him to the valley; first caged in the hull of a ship, then a train, and finally to the tunnel, blindfolded in the back of a truck.

"Were you scared when you first got here?" Charlie asked, picturing the tunnel next to Old Joe's orchard. "I was. Still am, really..."

"Of course I was frightened. Who knew what they had in store for us? But once here, I quickly adapted, and the solace of this place agrees with me. There's a peace to be found here for those who are willing to accept it."

He spoke of creatures who did not adapt so easily, and of others, citing Lester Mortlock by name.

"I find that there are some here who are difficult to understand. Hard to tell what type of creature, even. Could be a random human without affliction who just stumbled upon this place the same way you did, but for reasons known only to them, they chose to stay. I suppose it's just their nature, the Lester Mortlocks of the world, their inclination to exploit, to wreak havoc, and I'm afraid the opportunities for those sorts of endeavors abound in these valleys." They rode through the day, stopping here and there for Franklin to oversee their mapping duties. Late that afternoon, they passed a pack of ghouls greedily devouring the remains of a fallen elk. The ghouls were gaunt creatures. Their bluish skin dangled loosely from their long, thin arms as they pulled at the carcass with their claws and tore at the flesh with their long, pointed teeth.

"This lot's easy enough to understand. Pure hunger is their motivation," Dwight York said, nodding at the desperate creatures, and to which Rohmetall added a thorough definition.

The next day, as they entered the heart of the mountains, the road worsened and the terrain became more treacherous. The Clydesdales labored up and down narrow passes that wound through deep ravines, and Franklin had to lean back against the cart to control it down the steep slopes. The incline made their mapping duties more difficult, but Dwight York promised that they would be through this rough patch soon enough.

"Ah, yes, the pass is just ahead, see down below, the source of the great river. I'll have a look."

He left with Ringo and was gone for most of that afternoon. When he returned, Dwight York abruptly announced his departure.

"There's one of your Rangers in the area I wish to avoid, if you don't mind," he said, pulling down the brim of his wide hat. "Nice enough fellow, just a bit of a bore, to be honest—rah-rah, that sort of thing. I must admit I am not quite ready to go back just yet, and who is to say what he wants with me this time?"

Dwight shook Franklin's hand, said good-bye to Rohmetall, and patted Ringo on the head.

"We will speak again, then," Franklin said. "Continue our conversation about your studies and your duty . . ."

"I look forward to it," Dwight York replied with a sly grin. "Now, the trail follows the river for a few days. From there, it's up a bit more and then the long descent to the plains."

Charlie noticed that Dwight was emptying the contents of his pockets and moving them to his satchel as he spoke.

"You take care, Charlie. I hope you find what you are looking for," he said. "And remember, we all live with some sort of a curse, some sort of burden, don't we? I've always thought that it is how we handle the trouble that reflects one's true nature."

Charlie nodded, sad to see him go.

"I will find you again if you pass this way," Dwight York continued as he wandered off between the rocks. "Till then . . ."

"Good-bye," Charlie said, pushing his horse forward, but

Goliath refused. With his nostrils flared, the horse leapt back, startled by the straw-colored werewolf that was now perched on the rocks just above them. The creature was wearing Dwight York's satchel across his back.

"It's all right," Charlie whispered to Goliath. "He's our friend."

Charlie waved. The werewolf lowered his head respectfully before turning to scramble up the steep incline. Charlie calmed the big horse and watched until Dwight York was over the ridge and out of sight. Then he spurred Goliath forward to catch up with the cart.

— *chapter 23* —

Up in the Mountains

$\mathcal{T}$HAT NIGHT THEY camped under a rock shelf until a cold rain came in, interrupting their sleep just before dawn. They broke camp early and trudged on through the mud, following the trail as it moved away from the river and up to a high mountain glen. They rode under the shelter of the trees for the day and soon found themselves in a rocky area with boulders littered about the trunks. The rain continued steadily, making it difficult to see.

"We will push a bit farther," Franklin shouted back, rain pouring from his hood. "See if we can find a dry spot in these rocks."

Franklin and Charlie rode ahead, leaving Ringo barking and Rohmetall driving the cart on through the mud. They pushed forward, skirting a series of large boulders. As they continued, Charlie thought that the tight weave of rocks might as well have been Old Joe's Halloween maze. They rode on until, in a flash of lightning, Faust leapt sideways, almost throwing

Franklin to the mud. The Monster steadied himself, calmed the horse, and turned him back around to Charlie.

"We need to be mindful here—" the Monster began. Then stopped, raised his crossbow, and yelled, "Charlie, behind you!"

"What? Where?" Charlie cried just as a set of long claws ripped into his shoulder.

Goliath bucked wildly, throwing Charlie from his saddle. He hit the ground hard, and something heavy landed on top of him. Then he heard an arrow whistle past his ear and thud into the mass. Exhaling its last putrid breath, the creature collapsed, pinning Charlie to the ground under its weight and covering his face in its wet, matted hair.

"Trolls," Franklin said. He had dismounted and was pulling the dead creature off Charlie when the second attacked.

Charlie fumbled as he tried to draw his sword, but there was no need. Franklin had already knocked the beast to the ground. The troll scrambled back with Franklin in pursuit and howled out as the Monster brought his heavy sword down upon it, but the blade sparked and glanced sideways as the metal struck solid stone instead.

"Cursed creature has turned on me." Franklin picked up the heavy, troll-shaped rock. He held it over his head and then smashed it to pieces against a large boulder.

"Let us see you turn yourself back from that, *troll*," the Monster growled, then returned to Charlie and pulled the boy from the mud.

"It got you there, on the shoulder," Franklin said, examining Charlie's wound. "I told the Prime Minister this was a mistake, and here's your proof. Can you ride?"

"I think so," Charlie answered, although he found it difficult to move his arm.

Franklin carefully lifted Charlie back in his saddle and handed him a bundled piece of cloth.

"You hold this to your shoulder. We have to keep moving. We are lucky to have stumbled upon such a small grouping, but they will be back. We will see to your injury when we have put some ground between us and this place."

Rohmetall came over the rise behind them and pulled the cart to a stop, Ringo barking at his side.

"May-may I be of service?" Rohmetall asked, rusty water dripping from his rivets.

"Hold the dog," Franklin ordered. "We have to keep moving."

The metal man looked at the fallen troll on the ground as Franklin pulled the arrow from its carcass.

"Trolls," Rohmetall said. "Troll. *Trodfolk*. *Bjergfolk*. See Scandinavian folklore. Related to the Anglo-French *troil*, *trolle*. Found in isolated mountains. Danger level—"

"Enough!" Franklin growled. "We obviously all know what a troll is . . ."

They rode higher up into the glen, and the farther they traveled, the more difficult it became for Charlie. Every sway of the saddle worsened the pain in his shoulder, and he could feel his warm blood dripping between his skin and his cold, wet shirt.

Charlie felt disoriented and thought he saw something ahead of them in the trees. It was hard to make out at first, but then he could see him clearly. It was Billy.

"Billy?" Charlie called out, trying to keep his cousin in his sights. But the dizziness overwhelmed him and he slumped forward in the saddle, mumbling, "I'm sorry, Billy, I'm sorry . . ."

Franklin stopped the horses and eased the boy down while Rohmetall hung a tarp. They built a small fire against the rocks, and Franklin gathered his medical supplies.

"I will see to this. Take the dog. Have a look around," Franklin told Rohmetall. "See if the trolls have had time to regroup."

Rohmetall clanked off against the rocks, and Franklin bent his head to step under the tarp.

"I'm fine," Charlie heard himself say. "We can keep riding."

"Not likely," Franklin said, taking out his sewing kit and lighting a lantern. "I am sorry, boy. As you can easily see, my abilities are crude, but we have to stop the bleeding."

He cleaned Charlie's wound with some water and threaded a needle. Without the constant movement of the saddle, Charlie felt better already. He struggled to sit up straighter.

"Stay still now," Franklin said, wiping the blood away from the claw marks.

Charlie looked at the Monster's roughly sutured wrists. They were discolored and yellow with oozing infection between the stitching.

"Does it hurt?" Charlie asked.

"Does what hurt?"

"Your wounds. The stitching?"

"Not as much as this will hurt you, I'm afraid. But yes, I feel it."

Franklin looked distraught as he held the needle to the lantern light.

"Oh, these cursed digits." The needle looked tiny and trembled in Franklin's huge hand. "You ready?" Charlie nodded.

Franklin pinched the skin around the wound together as he started the coarse thread through the first loop. Charlie felt the point of the hot needle pierce his skin. He tried to distract himself, listening to the rain as it beat down on the tarp.

"There, one . . . ," Franklin said, but then he quickly turned his head out toward the storm. "Who is there?" the Monster bellowed.

The rain came down in sheets, making it difficult for them to hear any response.

"I will not call again," Franklin grunted.

A figure appeared from the shadows. "I wish you no harm. Just saw the firelight."

"Then show yourself." Franklin left his needle and thread to step out from under the tarp. "Now!"

Charlie leaned against the saddle blanket. From where he sat, he could barely see the back of Franklin's legs. The rain hissed as it fell on the fire.

"*Show yourself,*" the voice answered. "I am at as much a disadvantage as you."

"I have no time for games!" Franklin roared, moving toward the figure in the rain. When the figure reached under his cloak for his sword, Franklin did the same. Charlie craned his neck to see better and felt the one stitch pull open as he moved.

"I am warning you," Franklin growled.

The man took another step, then stopped. "Ha, I don't believe it!" he exclaimed with a laugh.

"You think this is funny?" Franklin barked.

"Why, it's me, Ignacio, you old lunk!" the man said, throwing back his hood. "Ignacio Santos!"

Franklin's shoulders relaxed.

"I should have known your voice, but for this driving rain," Igancio Santos went on. "My apologies. It has been a while."

"Aye, it has. But no time for reunions," Franklin said, turning back to Charlie. "And what are you up to, sneaking about in the night?"

Ignacio followed him. "I see you haven't changed a bit. And what do you mean, sneaking about? Why, I'm out on patrol . . ."

They stepped under the tarp, and rain streamed down from their cloaks.

"Patrol? Well, your patrol was little help to us," Franklin scoffed.

"What's this?" Ignacio said, his eyes adjusting to the lantern light. "A boy? A real boy?" He poked Charlie with his finger as a test.

"He is real enough to bleed," Franklin replied, holding the lantern higher.

"Ignacio Santos, Ranger." The man knelt down to examine Charlie's wound. "Looks like you've encountered some trolls along the way."

"And I am afraid these profane fingers of mine have trouble with such delicate tasks," Franklin said.

"Still, I see you've managed to keep yourself together all these years." Ignacio turned back to the rain. "There's a cache nearby with supplies and dry wood. I was just on my way. We'll be more comfortable there and can see about closing that shoulder properly."

"I can ride," Charlie said, trying to sound stronger than he felt.

"There, now," Ignacio said. "That's the Ranger spirit!"

—— *chapter 24* ——

The Ranger's Cache

CHARLIE'S SHOULDER THROBBED, but at least he was warm and dry, wrapped in a blanket near the fireplace of a small stone cabin. Franklin and Ignacio Santos sat at a stout wooden table with Ringo curled up at their feet. The maps were spread out under lantern light, and they ate as they spoke. Charlie recalled little of their ride to the Rangers' post, but he remembered being in Franklin's arms, his large hood protecting him from the rain as they rode, and then being carried in and set on the cabin table. It was Ignacio who'd stitched the gash in Charlie's shoulder, with Franklin, he was later told, looking on attentively.

"Let me know if you're in need of repair as well," Ignacio had said to his old friend. "It'll be like back in your rangering days."

This was the last thing Charlie remembered them saying.

"AH, THERE HE IS, BACK FROM THE DEAD," IGNACIO ANNOUNCED when he saw that Charlie was awake. The Ranger picked up a flask of water and a wooden bowl from the table and brought it over to the fire. Ringo followed, resting his head in Charlie's lap.

"How's that shoulder? Didn't look too bad. But you'll feel it for a few days to come." Ignacio handed Charlie the wooden bowl. It was filled with a thick stew and rice. "I'm afraid with the recruitment shortage there's been no one at this post for some time, so can't vouch for the freshness of these stores, but did the best we could."

The stew was warm and Charlie was so hungry that he would have eaten the rancid stew from the tavern again. Franklin stood behind Ignacio, his head almost hitting the ceiling.

"Your coloring's returned," Franklin said with an approving grunt. "I will see how Rohmetall is doing." Franklin turned to the door and stepped out in the rain.

"Off to check on his precious horses, more likely." Ignacio pulled a stool up to the fire. "You'll find he's not the most trusting soul. Do-it-himself sort of fellow, helluva Ranger, though, helluva Ranger. But that—that was a long time ago . . ."

"So you're actually a Ranger?" Charlie asked with a mouthful of stew. "You went to the Ranger School?"

"Yes, Ignacio Santos, Mountain Division, at your service. Entrusted by the Council with patrolling this land and all of its many inhabitants . . ."

Charlie looked around the small cabin. It was indeed outfitted for a patrol. There were maps on the wall that indicated hot spots in red, while the other wall held a variety of weapons, and another was lined with crates of food and barrels of dried goods. There was something about it that reminded Charlie of Old Joe's workbench back home. "HQ," as he called it, was tucked back under the low-slung annex of the barn and also had maps and ropes and other supplies strewn about, although it wasn't as well organized. On a rainy day, HQ was probably Charlie's favorite place in the world, especially when Old Joe had a project going and was telling stories from his army days.

"And Franklin, Franklin was a Ranger?"

"Franklin?"

"Yes, his name is Franklin now."

"The Monster of all Monsters has taken a name? Curious, but it has a certain ring to it. Yes, Franklin, as you say, was a Ranger. And not one to back away from a fight."

Charlie did not have any trouble imagining this with what he had seen of the Monster so far.

"He was here in the beginning, trained me, actually, but that was years ago. It was rough on the big fellow back in those days, so many creatures arriving at once, unsure of themselves and their new surroundings—it was a bit of a free-for-all, really. And Franklin and the Rangers managed to establish some semblance of order, all that being relative, of course. Made some enemies along the way, I'd imagine. But did some good too."

"So he's no longer a Ranger?"

"Not for years, unfortunately, but he served his time." Ignacio picked up a log and stoked the fire with it. "We could sure use him, though. With the budget cuts these days, there just aren't enough of us to patrol a place this big anymore. And it's hard to fill the soldiering ranks here with all the different wars going on out there in the world. But we do what we can."

The Ranger took the empty wooden bowl from Charlie.

"And what of you? What brings you to these parts, traveling in such esteemed company?"

Charlie thought for a moment and then pulled the photo of Billy from his pocket. He handed it to Ignacio and told him all about his cousin, how he wondered where he went and how he had to see him again.

"I need to find him, to talk to him," Charlie said. "So we're going to the woods past the desert."

Ignacio raised an eyebrow. "Are you, now? Well, that is quite a journey. I wonder how our old Ranger friend got talked into that—"

"The Prime Minister, he asked him to go. After his meetings, you know, for the Council," Charlie replied, hoping Franklin wouldn't be mad that he had shared this information.

"Asked? Ha, should have known that the Prime Minister would somehow be involved," the Ranger said, looking down at the picture. "Well, searching for a lost friend is a noble errand for such a young soul." Ignacio smiled and handed the photograph back to Charlie. "Noble indeed, and these days that alone should be celebrated."

chapter 25

Heaps of Trouble

$\mathcal{F}$RANKLIN AND THE Ranger decided that it would be best for Charlie to rest for a few days before their journey continued. They had examined the wound and agreed that it was healing nicely, although Charlie told them it itched horribly.

"That means it's getting better, so let it itch," Ignacio told him.

Franklin and Ignacio spent most of their time huddled over their maps and charts, while Charlie stayed on his blanket by the fire, buried in his book or writing letters back home of their progress. When they weren't discussing logistics, Franklin, Rohmetall, and the Ranger took turns staying at the cabin with Charlie, patrolling the area and hunting for small game nearby. By the second day, Charlie already felt stronger. So after their patrol that morning, they allowed him to move around outside the cabin, just as long as he stayed within shouting range, which, for Franklin and an old Ranger like Ignacio, was farther than one might expect.

"Not too far, now," Franklin warned. "You will need to get your things together later. I'm afraid we must leave tomorrow if we have any hope of reaching the plains in time for our summit."

He gave Charlie his brass telescope and let him wander over to the river to sit on the rocks in the sun with Ringo and his book. From there, Charlie could see that the river dropped into a series of waterfalls, and after a while he thought he would stretch his legs, so he followed them to the rim of a great canyon. The canyon continued on the other side, but below the ledge, the river widened and opened to a spit of gravel beach. Back against the trees at the edge of the gravel, there was an odd collection of corrugated rust-streaked metal buildings. A narrow pier stretched out from the main building, and at the end of the pier, there was a small, broken shack.

Through the telescope, Charlie followed a long, heavy chain that was attached to the building and stretched down the length of the dock. The chain moved, periodically forcing Charlie to refocus the lens. When the image cleared again, he saw a little girl stepping out from the shadows; the chain was fastened to a thick iron cuff on her ankle.

The little girl's hair was unruly, curly red, and tucked as best it could be under a soiled bonnet. She was dressed in layers of tattered clothes and was working hard, pulling a large net to the river's edge, where she gathered it around her, then waded into the swift water. Charlie lowered the telescope and moved closer to the rim of the canyon. The height was dizzying. He looked through the lens again but had trouble locating the girl.

He took a step to refocus, and another before he realized he was too close to the edge; his foot was slipping. Charlie dropped the telescope and stumbled sideways, trying to catch himself. He saw Ringo. The dog looked puzzled. Then Charlie felt nothing but air.

The icy water stole Charlie's breath when he landed. He fought the current with all his strength, but Charlie knew that the river had him. He thought of Billy, and looking up, he saw a strange, shimmering light that seemed to take on an almost human shape. Was it Billy? He reached for the light, pushing off the bottom and swimming up, his arm extended as far as the riptide would allow. But as he approached the surface, both Billy and the light were gone. His lungs burning, Charlie knew he was out of air. Sinking now, he reached again for the surface, then saw a net spread out above him like a veil. His shoulder throbbing, Charlie wrapped his arm in its web, and the net pulled him up, bursting to the surface, and he was dragged toward the shore.

He tried to stand in the shallow water but stumbled at first before collapsing on the sand, and then lay there, breathing heavily and staring into the eye of one of the many discarded fish heads that littered the beach.

"You need to leave here."

Charlie could see the little girl in the raggedy clothes and soiled bonnet standing over him.

"Leave, or there will be trouble," the girl continued. She was small with delicate features browned by the sun. Her ice-blue eyes, almost translucent, seemed to stare right through him. Charlie sat up, still breathing heavily.

"Thank you."

"For what?" the girl asked. "I had hoped to land a fish."

"Well, thank you anyway," Charlie said, looking back at the crumbling building behind him. It was quiet except for the river and the loose, bent sheets of metal that methodically banged the sides in the wind. He followed the girl's chain with his eyes back to the dock and the rusting steel shack. "You live here? Over there on the dock?"

"What business of that is yours?" the girl said, pulling in the net.

"I guess it isn't." Charlie's breathing had calmed. "But the chain..."

"Again, not your concern."

"I guess it's not. Well, my name is Charlie—"

"My name is Abigail, Abigail Rose. Now you must leave," the girl interrupted. "And please don't come back here or there will be heaps of trouble for me."

Charlie stood. His wet clothes clung to his goose-pimpled skin.

"Okay. I'll go." Charlie shivered.

He left the little girl on the beach and found his way to the rocky crags that led back to the Ranger's cabin. At the top of the canyon, he found the telescope and his book, but Ringo was gone. As he gathered his things, he decided that he would take one more look, just to check on the girl, he told himself. When the telescope came into focus, Charlie could see that there was an old man in a long black tunic on the beach now, and that he was walking toward Abigail and her empty net. The man was shouting and waving a heavy stick, then Charlie lost them in the shadows of the dock.

What did she say? Charlie thought, looking back toward the cabin. *Heaps of trouble?* He couldn't help but think that her troubles might be his fault—he had to do something. He knew he should take the time to run for Franklin or the Ranger, but the old man had a stick. It might be too late—he had to be brave. Billy would want him to be brave, Old Joe too, and maybe, he thought, even Franklin. He hoped that Ringo might alert them at the cabin, and then, against his better judgment, he ran back down the trail to the beach and to the girl.

There was no sign of the old man or the girl when Charlie dropped down to the sandy gravel. He ran, forgetting to count his steps along the water's edge, and ducked behind a rowboat beneath the dock. He then followed the pier to the base of the building, where he climbed up to the long chain that held Abigail prisoner. It now led into the shack, snaking under the dingy tarp that served as a door.

The other end of the chain was welded to a metal plate, which was attached to the building with heavy rusted bolts. Examining the plate, Charlie could see wet, rotten wood under the tin siding. Using the blade of his sword, he was able to pry the plate loose, and he had to jump back to keep it from crushing his toes when it fell.

With the chain free from the building, Charlie ran down

the length of the dock, sword in his hand. The shack was small, the size of a playhouse, and as he approached, he heard sobbing.

"Abigail . . . ," Charlie whispered, throwing back the canvas.

The little girl sat wrapped in a tattered blanket next to an apple crate in the corner. There was a tin bowl, a dented cup, and a small lantern on the crate, but otherwise the dirty room was empty.

"Charlie?" Abigail looked up, bewildered by his sudden appearance.

"Yeah, it's me." Charlie knelt down next to her.

"I told you, you mustn't come back. You have to leave."

"We both do, come on . . ."

Abigail tugged at the chain.

"I've taken care of that, but we have to go," Charlie said.

"The chain?" Abigail stood up.

"Yes, now, come on."

"Where will we go? He'll find us," she said.

"I have friends. You'll have nothing to worry about when we find them—trust me."

Charlie opened the tarp as Abigail gathered her cup and bowl and wrapped them in her blanket. She turned back to the light, and Charlie saw that her eye was red and swelling.

"That old man hit you?" Charlie said.

Abigail turned away from the light. "I didn't catch no fish."

"We have to go," he said firmly, feeling his anger rise at the sight of the small girl's growing bruises.

Charlie reached out to take Abigail's hand, but she pulled it away quickly. Her fingers, much like the Prime Minister's, felt like icicles.

"I'm coming," Abigail said.

Charlie picked up an armload of chain. "I don't know what to do with this. I guess we'll just have to drag it."

They moved quickly down the dock, dragging Abigail's heavy chain behind them as quietly as they could. There was still no sign of the man with the stick, so they dropped the length of chain and metal plate to the beach and jumped down after it. The chain was easier to manage in the sand, but as they stepped out from under the shadow of the dock, Charlie saw the old man staggering toward them, waving his stick.

"Heaps of trouble," Abigail repeated.

Charlie looked back toward the dock.

"The rowboat."

Charlie and Abigail turned, dragging the chain behind them, and found the boat under the dock. They piled the chain in the bow, and together they lifted the plate and dropped it in with a clang. Abigail pulled herself aboard and Charlie pushed the rowboat until it was floating, feeling the stitches in his shoulder strain.

He was standing in knee-deep water when the old man brought the stick down. It caught him by surprise, glancing off his good shoulder, but Charlie did not freeze from his fears this time. He reached for his sword, drew the blade, and blocked the next blow, then slashed out at the man. The old man stepped back, swinging the stick again. Charlie countered and cut the stick in half.

The old man threw down the two pieces in disgust. He looked sad and defeated standing at the shore under the dock.

"I keep her chained but not so she don't run off," the old man called as he tried to gather his breath. "I keep her chained to stop the creatures from running off with her—I swear!"

"Stay back!" Charlie said, holding the blade out in front of him and backing toward the boat.

"Lookee here, I'm the one that found her off wanderin' in the woods there. What was I supposed to do, leave her? I've taken care of that girl. Gave her a place to live, tried to feed her, although I admit she don't seem to eat much . . ."

The old man took another step toward Charlie.

"I said stay back!"

"Ya can't just take her!" the old man pleaded. "Who's gonna catch the fish?"

"I'm not taking her," Charlie shouted. "This is a rescue!"

The boat caught the current, so Charlie had to swim to reach it. He dropped the sword over the side and pulled himself in. Abigail was huddled near the bow and the old man was still screaming on the shore. Drifting out into the stronger current, Charlie saw that the canyon narrowed ahead. He looked in the direction of the camp and saw Ringo run down from the rocks, followed by Franklin and the Ranger.

The boat swayed in the rougher water, and a length of chain that was left draped over the side caught the current. Abigail fumbled with it, and Charlie could see that the pile behind her was shrinking. The chains disappeared over the side, one link at a time, moving faster as its weight pulled it down below the swirling surface of the water. Charlie reached for the last of the links as they whipped overboard, but the chain slipped through his fingers. Abigail looked over her shoulder at him with a blank expression on her face. Then the chain went tight, jerking her forward, and the little girl was gone.

Charlie looked over the bow and caught a glimpse of Abigail's red hair and rags waving around her like broken wings as she sank. Without hesitation, he dove in after her and swam to the bottom. He found the length of chain and tried to lift it but couldn't. Then he saw something, although it was much larger than Abigail. It must be Billy, he thought. Like before, in the river and in the woods, after the trolls. He reached out for him but instead felt a rough tug on the chain, and he was pulled up, bursting to the surface. Charlie gasped, filling his lungs with air.

"Let go of the chain," Charlie heard a deep voice bellow.

Between the waves that broke over his head, Charlie could see Franklin in the water. He was hanging from the side of the rowboat with one hand, the length of chain in his other. Abigail was drenched but huddled safely in the bow. Charlie dropped the chain and swam over to Franklin.

Franklin glared at the boy. He slung him with his free hand into the boat and Charlie landed on the pile of chain next to Abigail and lay there gasping for breath. Franklin finished securing the heavy links and pulled himself aboard next, his weight almost flipping the boat, then he sat with his back to Charlie as he put the oars into their locks. In the distance,

Charlie could see the Ranger and Rohmetall waiting for them on the shore. The old man was already gone.

"The current is too strong. We will meet them downriver at the crossing," Franklin said, turning the boat around. "We called to you, Charlie. You are fortunate that we came looking for you and found the dog when we did."

Franklin guided the boat through one series of rapids, then another, and as the waters calmed, he looked up at the high canyon walls.

"Darkness will find us soon. We will have to stay in this canyon tonight," he said, rowing the boat to a narrow rock beach. "Charlie, quickly, a fire."

Shivering, Charlie jumped to the shore and gathered a pile of driftwood. Franklin pulled the boat in and then carried Abigail up to the dunes between the canyon walls. He set her down in the sand and took off his drenched cloak. From his pockets he removed a small bundle wrapped in waxed canvas that held a flint and tinder.

"At least this is dry," he said, placing the tinder in the driftwood. Then, using the blade of his knife and the flint, Franklin lit a fire.

Charlie emptied his pockets as well, but all he had was his photo with Billy and the plastic fangs.

"My pack is back at the Ranger cabin," Charlie said, laying the photograph on a rock near the fire to dry. "I'm sorry . . ."

"We will make do. More wood," Franklin grunted at Charlie as the flames grew.

Charlie left the warmth of the fire to search for more drift-wood. He looked up and saw the sun disappearing over the deep walls of the canyon but knew that they were safe. He closed his eyes and, once again, thought about how he had a Monster to thank.

chapter 26

The Burden of Abigail's Chains

WHEN CHARLIE RETURNED to their makeshift camp, Franklin was coiling Abigail's long chain in his hands. Charlie stacked the driftwood and joined Franklin as he knelt down next to the girl.

"With your permission," Franklin said softly.

Abigail nodded and with his left hand steadying the iron on her ankle, Franklin wrapped his right hand in a length of chain and pulled. The heavy chain twisted, and then, with a metallic snap, it broke, leaving three links hanging down past her tiny foot.

"I will have to see about that iron cuff in the morning when there is light."

"Thank you," the girl said. "I don't have much memory before that dock. It feels strange to be on different sands, that's for sure."

"There's spring water from the walls of the canyon just

there," Charlie offered. "Wish we had some food for you, but it's all back with the Ranger."

"I am not thirsty, or hungry, just tired," Abigail said. "As tired as I've ever been."

So Franklin made her a pallet of his cloak and her tattered blanket, and the girl lay down to sleep in the sand with Charlie and the Monster at her side.

Franklin added a piece of driftwood to the fire and sat staring out at the river with his legs folded below his elbows. They did not speak for some time, until Franklin broke the silence.

"We should turn around after what happened today, for your safety. Same with the trolls, I could not forgive myself if something more were to happen to you," Franklin said, and then muttered to himself, "I warned the Prime Minister, with his futile attempts at diplomacy, his charts and maps . . ." Franklin shifted, adjusting his shoulder, which seemed to have fallen from its socket. "You must listen to me, Charlie, if we are to survive in this place. What did I say before?"

"You said to stay close to the cabin," Charlie said, unable to look at Franklin.

"And what did you do?"

"I didn't."

Franklin glanced over at the boy. "It was foolish to go on your own to help this girl. But it was also brave, Charlie. Selfless. And for that I am proud of you."

Franklin threw another piece of driftwood on the fire.

"But from here on out, if you wish to continue, you will listen. Is that understood?"

"Yes, sir," Charlie said softly.

"What's that?"

"Yes, sir. I understand," Charlie said, then went on to explain that the little girl's name was Abigail Rose and that she had been chained to the dock, forced to fish for the old man. He told Franklin of the squalor of her shack and the old man going after her with the stick.

Franklin shuddered. "It saddens me to hear of such treatment. I too have been chained like a beast, and while I cannot speak for this Abigail Rose, like a beast I acted." The Monster rubbed his scarred wrists, lost in thought. "Back then, in those chains, I was angry and afraid. Sometimes confused. I did not know why I was feared. But now that I have broken my shackles, I see things more clearly. I am not so different. We all go through life angry and scared at times. As sad as that is, it is also a sort of comfort, knowing that we all face the same demons at one time or another."

Franklin looked over at the little girl and sighed.

"Let us hope that this Abigail Rose will find some kind of peace with her newfound freedom and not the shackled burdens we discuss."

The fire sparked before them, shooting up embers that seemed to float overhead.

"Abigail said she couldn't remember much before that dock, but the old man said he found her wandering in the woods. How come she can't remember that?" Charlie asked.

"It is difficult to say. It could be this place. When you have been here long enough, it is hard to remember anywhere else," Franklin said. "My own memories are clouded. At times I wonder if they are even mine and not some odd remnant of my parts' expired lives instead."

Charlie watched as Franklin looked up longingly at the stars.

"You know, I wonder, Charlie, as I gaze upon the glory of these heavens, if I were to have a soul, is it mine or did it once belong to someone else? Perhaps this Abigail Rose shares a similar plight . . . a similar confusion. Or her memories could just be experiences better forgotten. Hard to say."

Franklin glanced over at Charlie, and again the boy saw a faded glow beneath his coal-black eyes.

"There must be something in there," Charlie said with a smile. "I believe that. Monster or not, you agreed to help me find Billy. And just today you pulled us from the river. You didn't have to do that. Would have made your trip a lot easier . . ."

Franklin almost returned the smile. "At least we will rest tonight knowing that we saved a fellow tortured soul," he said, patting the boy on the back. "Get some sleep, Charlie. As the Prime Minister is fond of pointing out, you will need it."

Charlie did not dream that night and woke in the morning to find Franklin and Abigail standing next to the rowboat at the river's edge. The Monster held the long chain and the cuff that he had managed to remove from her ankle in his hands. He said something to the girl and then hurled it out to the middle of the river. Abigail watched the chain land with a splash, then disappear into the depths.

"Thank you," Abigail said once the chain was out of sight.

"It is my honor," Franklin said politely, dropping his head. "Now to rejoin the horses. I'm afraid we've still a long way to go."

— *chapter 27* —

The Baroness Draguta Flori

*A*BIGAIL SAT WITH Charlie in the bow, and as the canyon opened, the current slowed, making the morning's travel seem leisurely. They passed a passel of hobgoblins who threw rocks at them from the banks of the river, but they ran to the shelter of the trees when Franklin shot an arrow in their direction. At midday, they encountered another set of heavy rapids, which Franklin navigated successfully and then hugged the shore as the river widened at the bottom. Staying near the rocky bank, they rounded a bend to find a hand-pulled ferry secured to a stone jetty. Ignacio was paying the ferryman as Rohmetall drove the cart and horses to land.

"Ah, you made it. A pleasant enough day for a row, I suppose," the Ranger said. "There's lodging here if we can convince the owner. Might not be a bad idea. The temperature is dropping and this fine fellow says it looks like snow tonight."

Franklin lifted Abigail Rose and handed her to Ignacio, who set her gently on the dock.

"Ignacio Santos, Ranger. And who might you be?"

Ignacio took Abigail's hand to shake and Charlie noted his slight hesitation at the coldness of her skin.

"She is Abigail Rose," Franklin said, pulling the boat to shore. "And I would imagine she could do with a good meal by a fire."

"That way," the ferryman offered, pointing a long, bony finger up toward the trees.

Charlie tried to see his face, but the ferryman pulled his hood down farther.

"The lodge is up behind the rocks, back in the pines."

"We thank you," Ignacio said. "Is the baroness in?"

"Hard to say," the ferryman answered, turning back to his business. "She comes and goes as she pleases."

Rohmetall pulled the cart and horses around, and they were soon mounted, with Abigail riding in the back next to Ringo. The dog was reluctant to join the girl at first. With his ears pinned back, he whined and almost cowered in her presence, but he soon came around, and Abigail seemed to enjoy his company.

Charlie and Franklin rode ahead, finding that the trail narrowed as it entered the deep pine forest. And, as the ferryman had said, back, high in the trees, sat a large lodge made of stacked rock. Over time, the pines had grown over the structure, cracking the stone and forcing their way in, almost becoming one with the building.

Franklin pulled his horse around and dismounted. "Wait here," he instructed, handing Charlie his reins.

Franklin took the worn stone steps to a thick wooden door and pushed it open. Charlie dropped down from Goliath's back. He was tired and stiff, and the stitches in his shoulder were tight and throbbing.

"Hello, Ch-Ch-Charlie. I will take the horses to the stable-stable," Rohmetall declared, grabbing ahold of the reins and leading the horses next to the cart.

"Fantastic, isn't it? The way the trees have joined the stone," Ignacio said as he rode past.

"It is," Charlie answered, watching them go.

Ignacio continued on to the stables, and Charlie, figuring the horses were taken care of, climbed up the stone steps and entered the lodge. The first room was large and open with long tree trunks cut into rough-hewn tables with heavy benches. And the forest had certainly found its way in; branches curled through cracks in the corners of the ceiling and wound back on themselves across the length of the building.

"No one is about," Franklin said. He stood hunched at a stone counter over a large dusty book. "Doesn't seem like any-one's been here for some time. But it is stocked. Well provisioned. I signed us in on this ledger."

Franklin dropped a gold coin on the counter.

"See about a fire, Charlie. I'll go and fetch Miss Abigail."

Charlie crossed the room to the large fireplace. There were neat stacks of wood and kindling, so he took some dry moss and twigs and lit them with a long match that he found on the mantel.

He sat back as the flame caught, but a cold draft blew

down the chimney, threatening the struggling flicker. Charlie thought he could almost see the gust for a moment, a small, vaporous cloud, but then it was gone.

The door opened and Ignacio entered to find Charlie staring at the ceiling.

"What is it?"

"Nothing. Just thought I saw something," Charlie said, turning back to the fire.

Franklin and Rohmetall brought in their gear, followed by Abigail. The small girl walked into the room and immediately looked up at a corner.

"It must be the Baroness, Draguta Flori," Ignacio said. "She'll show herself soon enough."

"A Baroness." Abigail continued to stare at the ceiling. "I'd like to meet a Baroness."

"Or what remains of her," Ignacio added with one eyebrow raised.

"Like a ghost . . . ?" Charlie asked.

"*Ghost*. Middle English—*Gost*, from Old English *Gast*. *See* Old High Germanic *Geist*." Rohmetall set down his load and announced, "A spirit or soul of the deceased that may appear to, or their presence felt by, the living. Sanskrit root *Heda* denoting 'fury or anger.' Also see 'the undead,' 'poltergeist,' 'wiedergänger'—"

"'Specter,' 'kelpie,' 'banshee'—this list goes on," Franklin said, cutting off the metal man and turning to Abigail. "Come, girl. Stand next to the fire."

Ignacio stepped up onto a bench and looked toward the

ceiling. "Ah, yes, Draguta Flori. Have you never heard of the pouty princess?"

"I haven't," Charlie said.

"Me either," Abigail added.

"Oh, a curious tale indeed. Why, she was a Baroness whose father controlled lands that stretched as far as the eye could see. He owned great houses and manors and castles—what castles! But young Draguta, as you might imagine, was terribly spoiled."

Ignacio kept his eye on the ceiling as he spoke. "Whatever she wanted was hers. If she failed to get her way, she would simply hold her breath in protest until her poor father eventually gave in. Miserable child. She could never be satisfied. At some point she stopped leaving the castle entirely, preferring instead to just sit in her room and pout. Her skin soon turned a ghostly white, as it never saw the sun, and dark circles grew under her eyes. She grew weak and one night, so the story goes, she held her breath just a little too long—"

"And she died," Abigail said bluntly, finishing the story for him.

"Sure enough. Just fell over, dead as a doornail."

A blast of cold wind rushed through the room.

"And it looks like her ghost has found its way here," the Ranger said.

The wind whipped around Ignacio and then swirled past Franklin, who swatted at it like a fly.

"Then again," Franklin added, "it could just be an unusual draft."

They settled in for the night, with Abigail helping Franklin prepare dinner and Ignacio tending to the damage done to Charlie's shoulder.

"Not bad if I say so myself. Just a couple of stitches popped," Ignacio said, tying off the latest stitch. "Now let's see that you keep 'em in this time." Ignacio glanced back over his shoulder at Franklin. "It was gallant, though, Charlie. Real Ranger spirit," he whispered. "Well done. Don't see enough of that these days, a true and heroic rescue. I'm sure young Abigail appreciates her new surroundings."

Charlie looked at Abigail as she stood next to Franklin, cutting turnips for a stew. She seemed tiny and out of place, and her demeanor had changed little since leaving the dock. But seeing her there in the lodge with them warmed Charlie; he felt as if the chill of the cold river had finally left.

They ate dinner together at the long table. Charlie sat beside Abigail, and as the meal progressed, he noticed that although there was food on her plate, she seemed content to just push it from side to side with her fork. He never saw her take a bite.

After dinner, Charlie wrote another letter to his mother while Ignacio and Franklin pulled out their charts and maps to discuss the journey ahead and to prepare their official dispatches for the Prime Minister.

"Here." Ignacio pointed to the great desert on the map. "The Rangers in the region say that Tok's main raiding parties come from this spot in the north and here in the west. With the weather turning, I am afraid another attack is imminent. They will want to get in one more run before winter."

"I wonder if a change in the seasons will be enough to

curtail the situation this time," Franklin said, finishing the last of the stew. "It's a long-standing dispute and one that this Tok puts squarely on the Council. I would just as soon not get involved in the local politics. I already regret letting the Prime Minister talk me into this *diplomatic* mission."

The wind picked up outside as a mixture of snow and sleet began to fall on the stone lodge. Franklin built up the fire and left with Rohmetall to check on the horses while Abigail and Charlie laid out their sleeping blankets. A furious gust of snow and ice blew in when Franklin opened the door and then seemed to remain in the lodge after they were gone.

"I wonder if the Baroness has chosen to join us again," Ignacio said, trying to focus on the gust, which whipped itself into a whirl and spun wildly across the tabletops.

Abigail dropped her bedding, climbed up on a bench, and held out her hands as if to embrace the wind. As Franklin's papers flew about the room, Charlie thought he could see the outline of a person begin to materialize. The crystallized vapors of the snow and ice seemed to cling to a shape in the center of the mist and then a little girl, smaller than Abigail Rose even, slowly appeared.

"Greetings, Baroness," Ignacio said, lowering his head and dropping to one knee. "Ignacio Santos, Ranger, Mountain Division. It is an honor to find ourselves in your presence."

The Baroness's shape became more evident as the swirling winds around her calmed. She was wearing a long, elaborate gown and a jeweled tiara that was tucked into her snowy white hair.

"We thank you for your hospitality. In your name we will be

sure to leave plenty for the next travelers who come this way," Ignacio said, though the Baroness's cold gaze remained fixed on Abigail.

"Cold, so cold," the Baroness Draguta Flori snapped as she approached the girl.

"Perhaps she is cold," Ignacio said to Charlie. "Are you cold, Baroness? We could build up the fire if it helps."

"I think she meant Abigail," Charlie whispered.

The Baroness turned to Ignacio. Her pale skin glittered in the mist like flecks of diamonds on fresh-fallen snow, and for a moment, she almost looked peaceful.

"Are you cold?" the Ranger repeated.

"No!" the Baroness shrieked. She spun around and shot to a high corner of the room. "No! No! No!" the Baroness cried again. She took a deep breath that filled her cheeks and held it until her face turned crimson and then a scarlet red.

"My, my. Such behavior. I suppose the stories are true, then," Ignacio said, bowing again. "Baroness, we only wish to pass the night here. We will move on in the morning—I promise."

The Baroness let out the long breath and dropped back down to Abigail.

"A question." The Baroness turned her attention to Ignacio. "Yes, if you wish to pass the night, first a question . . ."

"A question? Why, yes. Something been troubling you?"

The Baroness ignored the Ranger and continued, "What is a friend in summer but an enemy come winter?"

The Ranger looked at Charlie and Abigail. "Friend in summer, enemy in winter? I'm afraid I've never been good at riddles."

"Yes," the Baroness said. "Friend in summer. Enemy in winter."

"I'm not sure I know what she's talking about," the Ranger whispered.

Charlie thought about it. *Friend in the summer.* The summer is hot. *Enemy in winter.* The winter is cold. He thought about the hot summer days back home at Old Joe's orchard and the cold arctic air that rushed down from the mountains in the winter.

"It's the wind, isn't it?" Charlie blurted out, not entirely sure of the answer himself, but it was almost all that he could think of in the Baroness's blustery presence.

"Is this your answer?" the Baroness screeched, dropping down from the rafters to Charlie. "All of you?"

Charlie looked at the Ranger and Abigail. Abigail's expression remained blank. The Ranger shrugged.

"Yes, the wind. That's the answer," Charlie said, this time with more confidence. "It's the wind."

"The boy is correct," the Baroness shrieked, her words emphasized by a rush of sleet and snow. "A breeze is welcomed in the heat of a summer day but the same gust cursed in the dead of winter."

"Well done, Charlie," the Ranger said. "Well done."

"It wasn't all that difficult," Charlie whispered, brushing the Baroness's frost from his shoulders. "First thing that popped into my head."

"Another!" the Baroness cried. She circled just above Abigail's head and began to sing.

"I left my home, I am alone, and now I can't get back.

I look around, my face a frown, for I know not where I'm at . . .

There goes the sun, this day is done and yet I am still here.

Darkness falls, but no one calls, it's just me and all my fears.

So turn three times, and have a cry, and answer if you can.

The riddle's done, the song's been sung, now tell me what I am?"

Charlie ran the lines back in his head. *I left my home, I am alone, and now I can't get back . . .*

"What do you think, Charlie? I don't have a clue," Ignacio admitted.

"Me either," Charlie said, running through the next verse. *I look around, my face a frown, for I know not where I'm at . . .*

"We best figure it out. I would rather not sleep out in a snowbank if it can be avoided."

An agonizing moment passed as the room fell into an uneasy silence. Then Abigail stepped up from the bench to the table and after turning in a circle three times spoke.

"Lost," she said flatly. "You are lost."

"*Lossst,*" the Baroness hissed. "Is *thissss* your answer?"

"Makes sense to me," Ignacio said, looking at Charlie and then back at Abigail. "You sure?"

Abigail nodded.

"Yes," Ignacio Santos announced. "Lost is our answer."

"Correct . . . you may pass the night, and the boy. And this . . . girl." The Baroness paused before Abigail. "But not the creature."

"The creature?" Charlie whispered. "She doesn't mean Franklin, does she?"

"It would appear that way, wouldn't it?" the Ranger whispered back before responding to the Baroness. "But the creature, as you call him, is our friend. He is your friend, also—"

"No! It frightens me!" the Baroness shrieked again. This time Charlie had to cover his ears. "No! No! No! No! No! I know what *it* is! I can see all that *it* has done, all the horrors of *its* past!"

The Baroness floated back toward the ceiling, drew in another long breath, and was soon red again. Just then, the front door opened and Franklin entered with Ringo in a blast of winter air. The Baroness locked her eyes on Franklin and continued to hold her breath as Ringo jumped up on the table next to Abigail to bark at the apparition. Her face went from red to purple, then, perhaps just as the Baroness's life ended, there was a loud pop, and she was gone. A cloud of snow and ice fell from the ceiling, splattering on the stone floor.

Ringo leapt down from the table and sniffed at the puddle of slush.

"What was that about?" Franklin asked, brushing the snow from his cloak.

"We've had a visit from the Baroness Draguta Flori. I'm afraid she's not a fan," Ignacio said, slapping Franklin on the shoulder.

"What did I do?" Franklin asked.

Ignacio only laughed and turned to roll out his bedding before the fireplace.

"I doubt it's the last we've seen of her tonight."

Abigail, Charlie, and Ignacio slept around the hearth in

their bedrolls, but Franklin lay down on the other end of the room near the door, saying the fire was too hot for him.

Sometime in the night, Charlie woke up from his strange dreams and lay awake thinking about the letter he had written back home. He wondered how his parents and Old Joe were doing and if they missed him. He thought about Billy too, but that made him sad, so he turned to the encyclopedia to follow up on Rohmetall's report about ghosts, and soon found himself flipping through the pages to the entry for the undead.

As he turned page after page, learning about how they came to be, Charlie felt sorry for these lost souls. The book suggested that such beings were often shrouded in mystery and could arise from "a variety of factors." Usually it was something about unfinished business, or it could be as simple as an interrupted journey to the afterlife. But the worst cause of all, the one that stuck with Charlie, was that a being could be unaware of its own situation. It was possible for a death to be so unsettled that the soul failed to accept its fate. Charlie closed his eyes and wondered if this explanation could apply to the Baroness Draguta Flori. It was a lot to take in while trying to fall asleep.

The Baroness did return throughout the night but left almost as quickly as she appeared, usually at the first utterance or motion from Franklin. In the end, Charlie thought, the Baroness turned out to be more of a nuisance than actually frightening—though it was curious that even a ghost would find Abigail cold to the touch.

— *chapter 28* —

Down from the Mountain

THE STORM HAD blown over by morning, leaving the pine-woods covered in a thick blanket of snow. Charlie stepped out of the lodge and pulled on his wool cap and mittens, grateful that Mrs. Winthrope had thought to pack them for him.

It was quiet and still in the forest, except for a lone magpie that was sitting on a crooked branch, cracking pine nuts in its long, curved beak. Charlie took a deep breath, feeling the cold air burn deep into his lungs, and then addressed the bird.

"Good morning, Mr. Magpie. Slept well I hope."

But the magpie did not respond, nor did it give any sign that it was paying attention to anything other than its breakfast.

"You're not the first magpie I've seen here, you know," Charlie said aloud. He thought of Oscar and his rehabilitating pet and how that now seemed like such a long time ago. "We have magpies back home too, so don't think I'm impressed. I met a ghost last night, and I know a boy who is a werewolf and another boy who can turn himself into a fish—well, kinda.

What do you think of that?" Charlie asked, but the bird continued to ignore him.

Charlie shrugged and left the magpie, following the tracks to the stables, where he found Franklin brushing down the great horses.

"Quite a sight to awaken to," Franklin said, gesturing to their wintery surroundings.

Charlie stood at the open door of the stable at the edge of the snow and hay. "I like it. The snow," he said. "It's quiet."

"Yes, it is."

They stood, taking in the silence of the snow-laden trees until Franklin set down the brushes and gathered the horses' harnesses.

"Are we taking Abigail with us?" Charlie asked, stepping into the stable to help him.

"What would you suppose we do with her? Leave her here?"

"No. It's just, I wasn't sure. With where we're going . . ."

"If we even make it," Franklin added.

Charlie picked up a saddle blanket and handed it to the Monster.

"Regardless, I do not know of a suitable place to leave her along the way," Franklin continued. "I'd trust her to Mrs. Winthrope, but I am afraid at this point that is no longer an option. I suppose we will have to find a home for her with the Mumiya." Franklin threw the blanket up on Goliath's back. "You are wise to worry, Charlie. Some apprehension is healthy. But as your, who was it, your grandfather says, chin up. We will do all right, as will your Abigail Rose."

Franklin walked around the front of the horse, playfully punching Charlie as lightly as he could on his good shoulder as he passed. "Besides, there's plenty to keep our minds occupied—there's the upcoming talks, our cartography lessons, and then to find your cousin Billy, right?"

"That's right," Charlie said, starting to smile. He looked up at Franklin and said it again. "That's right."

Rohmetall joined them by the stables, pulling the cart out to harness the horses in the morning sun. Then with Franklin and Charlie, he brought them all around to the front of the lodge. True to Ignacio's promise to the Baroness, they cut plenty of wood to replenish what they had burned during the night and a little extra.

"You know, between the excitement of the trolls and then Miss Rose, I almost forgot to ask," Ignacio said as they finished stacking the logs. "When we first met, I was looking for a lycanthrope that's known to roam these parts. Younger, but no longer a pup; he's a bit of a lone wolf, really, goes by the name of Dwight York."

Charlie looked to Franklin, who was helping Rohmetall load their supplies in the cart.

"Just lookin' to consult him about these raids down below. He's green, but he's been useful in the past, talking sense into some of the more youthful packs. Wanted to see if he'd be willing to engage them in talks again. We could use all the help we can get."

"Ah, yes, Dwight York. We've seen him, back toward the river. But that was days ago," Franklin said. "I spoke to him about his duties, though. Under the circumstances, he may come around..."

"Much appreciated," the Ranger answered, turning his attention to his horse. "Well, I must get back to my tasks. Have the relief patrol to meet, anyway."

"I understand." Franklin added one more crate to their load and then approached Ignacio to bid him farewell.

"I'll more than likely see you below if I find him," Ignacio said, shaking Franklin's hand. "I'm afraid these impending troubles will bring us together again."

"And do not forget the dispatches..."

"Yes, yes, directly to the Prime Minister. I'll send an express rider right away," Ignacio said as he swung up into his saddle.

"Do you think you could mail this one for me?" Charlie asked, handing the Ranger the letter he had written to his mother.

"Of course. It's not an official dispatch, so can't guarantee the timeliness of the delivery, but I'll see to it."

Ignacio straightened in his saddle.

"Good luck with your search, and you take care of this big fellow, will you? Abigail, you take care of Charlie."

"I'll do my best," Abigail replied.

"Mr. Rohmetall, Ringo, well, huh, good luck to you too." Ignacio waved his hand, and stepping his horse back toward the river, he began to sing.

"From ghoulies and ghosties and long-legged beasties
And things that go bump in the night.

O Lord, won't you save us from the horrors that haunt us
And give us good dreams till the light.
For we are the Rangers, the hard-riding Rangers,
And we'll give all those nasties a fright!
Those ghoulies and ghosties and long-legged beasties
And things that go bump in the night."

"What's that he's singing?" Charlie asked, looking from Ignacio to Franklin. For a moment he thought the song sounded familiar.

"It's what the Rangers used to sing once upon a time," Franklin said, holding his head a little higher. He cleared his throat. "From an old Scots prayer, I believe . . ."

"So step up your horse, and set out your course,
For we Rangers protect what is right!
And be warned, all you ghoulies, you ghosties and beasties,
All you things that go bump in the night!"

Ignacio continued, whistling the tune as he rode off through the pine trees.

"Come on, boy," Franklin said. "We have a long ride ahead."

Franklin set Abigail next to Rohmetall on the bench of the cart, and they left the lodge, traveling up a long ridge that allowed them to see out to the Agrarian Plains. Despite their frequent surveying stops, they made better time on the descent out of the mountains. They spent the night in a rocky crag just below the tree line, and began the next day's journey before the sun had risen.

As the day wore on, the air grew warmer and drier; the trees were smaller and sprouted in wild spirals, and the ground cover changed from the thick carpet of the forest floor to jagged rocks. Abigail and Ringo slept in the cart as they rode, the horses ripping at the clumps of faded green and brown vegetation that sprang up from the cracks in the mushroom-shaped stones.

"They sense what is coming," Franklin said, pulling on Faust's reins to guide him back to the trail. "The aridness of this place concerns them. They know without water there can be no food."

Franklin leaned forward to stroke the side of the big horse's neck. And once more, Charlie thought he saw something in the Monster's eye. Again, just a flicker, but he could have sworn that Franklin almost smiled, this time in his admiration for the animal perhaps or the excitement of the adventure that lay ahead—Charlie couldn't say.

"This is their first journey to this place. Just like you. Prepare yourself, Charlie, because when we get there, you will not believe what the Mumiya have accomplished."

Franklin sat back in his saddle and rode next to Charlie as he spoke.

"They brought with them the practices of their ancestors and have built great aqueducts and canals. They channeled the river as it comes from the mountains, so they can now grow crops in the desert. It is truly a sight to see. There are fish farms and botanical gardens, spring-fed pools and machines with pulleys and cantilevers that can lift with the strength of a hundred men. They are impressive mathematicians, astronomers . . ."

The trail worsened in places and became steep, but Franklin kept their minds occupied, sharing with Charlie a brief history of the Mumiya. He spoke of them, of their great achievements, with a deep respect. He told with great enthusiasm of their roads and of course the pyramids, and he marveled again at the crops they were able to produce at the edge of the great desert.

"And their medical advances, well, they are truly second to none," Franklin continued. "But as a society, they are no different from most, plagued by such troubles, you will see. They grow gorgeous rows of corn, fields of wheat as far as the eye can see, and yet they rarely have the manpower for a proper harvest." Franklin shook his head. "It rots, Charlie. The crops actually rot standing in the fields."

"I don't understand," Charlie said, thinking about the orchards back at Old Joe's farm. He couldn't imagine Old Joe letting his apples rot.

"Well, it is simple, really. Along with the skills of their ancestors, they also brought with them their ancient caste systems, which no longer allow for a sustainable working class," Franklin explained. "The Mumiya are all royalty, or so they say. In their past lives, the great pyramids and such were built by slaves. But slaves had not the means for mummification. This was a privilege reserved for the upper class. Sure, some slaves were mummified along with their masters, pets too for that matter, but apparently not at similar rates."

"Mummified?" Charlie repeated. "Did you say mummified?"

"Well, of course they are mummified. They are known as the *Mumiya* after all, aren't they? Have you been reading that book or simply pretending to? The word is a medieval Arabic term, I believe, or *mumia* in Latin," Franklin said, shooting Rohmetall a look that further definition would be unwelcome.

"Nowadays, this society can no longer support itself this way. Made only of kings and queens, the hierarchical disputes are endless. Each one claims to have authority over the other. Their system was never properly designed for the realities of the afterlife. And let me tell you, a former king is hardly decent stock for a solid laborer, or a queen a scullery maid. After all, these are skilled positions and what would a king or queen know of that? And then there are the bog men. I wouldn't know where to begin; we haven't the time. They say some of them are almost seven feet tall . . ."

Charlie enjoyed listening to Franklin as they rode. He had become accustomed to his gruff cadence, but he also noticed that something about him had changed. Franklin spoke of the Mumiya with an energy Charlie hadn't seen before. Swept up in their history, he described the inner workings of their city-state with great excitement. Franklin, *the Monster*, seemed almost carefree. The small birds and butterflies that flitted from the scrubby underbrush must have sensed this too, because

Charlie noticed that they flew without fear from the branches, almost welcoming Franklin as he rode by, some even landing on his shoulders for a moment before darting back into the air to flutter around him.

Abigail had woken up somewhere along the way and held her hand out for them to land on if they cared to. When they did, she beamed and giggled, and so did Charlie, along with Ringo, who barked. Even Franklin now smiled as he spoke.

"Oh, and do the Mumiya hold a grudge. Always squabbling about some old family drama, past double crosses and the like. That's the reason for this diplomatic business. A brother and sister—can you believe it? I knew their mother and father, and I tell you they would not have stood for it. Not for a minute. They are a tough lot. We will have our work cut out for us the next few days to be sure."

Franklin spoke with a frenzied liveliness for the rest of the afternoon, stopping here and there to attend to his maps and dispatches. As the sun set on the horizon ahead, they found themselves back by the river. The flies were thick by the water's edge but did not bother Charlie or Abigail, preferring instead to collect at the jagged seams at the Monster's wrists and neck. They made a small fire, which helped with the flies, and had a good dinner of trout pulled from the river. Then they camped that night on a sandy shore among the scattered rocks.

Abigail seemed more at ease the farther they traveled from the dock where she once lived. She sat by the fire, rubbing her leg where the chain had been attached to her, stopping from time to time to stare into the flames. Rohmetall stayed at the edge of camp with the horses and cart, and Ringo curled into a ball in the sand, content not to move after the long day's travel. Abigail and Charlie laid out the bedding and were soon asleep.

But just a few hours later, Charlie woke to the quiet flow of the river. He looked around the camp, realizing that at some point Franklin must have left for his nightly wanderings.

Charlie rolled over on his side. Abigail was asleep with her back to him, and although partially concealed by the torn layers of her dingy clothes, he could see the welted line of scar tissue on her ankle where the iron cuff had been.

"Are you asleep?" Abigail said, startling Charlie.

"No, I'm awake."

The wind blew and the firelight danced around them, shrouding Abigail in shadow.

"I haven't thanked you for rescuing me. Thank you, Charlie," she said, her back still turned from him.

Charlie thought of her chained at the dock instead of here with their little group. He tried to answer, but his words were caught in his throat.

"Of course." He coughed. "It was nothing, really. You saved me too. I'm not sure what I would have done if I hadn't caught hold of your fish net."

"Well, thank you all the same," Abigail said. "And, Charlie..."

"Yes."

"I heard you're searching for something, looking for someone who got lost."

"Yes, my cousin. His name is Billy."

"He's lucky. To have someone willing to do that..." Abigail's words sounded distant, as if they were floating in the wind that blew across the sand.

"It is strange here," she continued. "The farther we go, the more I can remember. I can remember that just before that dock, I think I was wandering. I'm not sure where I was going before that man caught me, and now I wonder if there was someone like you out there, maybe looking for me . . ."

"I'd bet someone was," Charlie said. He paused for a moment and thought of his family back home, considering the possibility that despite his letters, his parents and Old Joe might be out looking for him too.

"I hope so. Good night, Charlie."

"Good night, Abigail," Charlie said, unsure of what else to say. "Sleep tight."

VOLUME III

— *chapter 29* —

The Land of the Mumiya

$\mathcal{H}$E WAS THERE again, looking out across the great desert plain, although he no longer had to shield his eyes as the sun had almost set. Charlie followed Billy's silhouette and the great crowd of birds that swirled around him, but this time his cousin walked hand in hand with a smaller figure. Charlie ran toward the horizon, toward their shadows, but lost them. He blinked and in an instant, they were gone, leaving him, once again, all alone.

Charlie sat up. It was dark. Sand was blowing around, stinging his face. A warm breeze from the river swept through their encampment. He looked out at the stars. They filled the sky, almost reaching the ends of the earth, and Charlie wondered if he was still dreaming.

"There have already been scouts about—better that we get moving," Franklin said. He was crouched by the fire, pushing sand over the embers.

"Scouts?" Charlie asked, wiping the sleep from his eyes.

"Up, Charlie."

Charlie threw back his bedding. He looked at Abigail, who was asleep, and then to Rohmetall, who was busy breaking down the camp.

"Come on, Charlie. No time to waste," Franklin said with his usual sternness. The excitement from yesterday's ride had clearly faded. "We have to get moving. I will not ask politely again."

"Yes, Ch-Ch-Charlie Cooper. No time to waste," Rohmetall clanged.

Charlie gathered his bedroll, then joined Rohmetall to hitch up the cart while Franklin carefully lifted Abigail up onto the seat. Soon they were back in the saddle again and heading on their way.

Franklin went ahead, leaving Charlie riding beside the cart with Rohmetall, Abigail, and Ringo. Just after dawn, they pushed up from the river and found the road lined with towering rows of corn and wheat fields, just as Franklin had described. They passed aqueducts and intricate, levied canals, and they knew as they rode that they were being followed.

Ringo barked anxiously at the cornstalks, and Franklin constantly scanned the crops around them for signs of movement. When she woke, even little Abigail began looking behind them from time to time.

"What is it?" Charlie asked. "The Mumiya?"

"Their scouts, at least." Franklin nodded. "More than likely from whichever faction has the run of these fields."

As they continued, the Mumiya scouts became bolder.

Charlie started to catch glimpses of them pushing through the great cornstalks that now lined both sides of the road. They rode on, though, until Franklin pulled back on his horse, halting the group with a gesture of his hand. Once stopped, they could hear from the crunching stalks that the waves of scouts stretched across the field in every direction. Their small party was surrounded.

"Look," Abigail said, pointing toward the parting crops. "There are so many . . ."

Charlie thought she seemed oddly calm under the circumstances.

"We will be all right. Remember, a lot of this is show," Franklin assured them.

The scouts followed one after the other out of the corn and crowded around them on the road. The mummies were all shapes and sizes and wore varied headdresses, some of Egyptian gold, others Peruvian jaguar cowls, and still others that were Celtic silver or shaped like Mesoamerican serpents made of polished jade and turquoise. Some of their linen bandages were falling off them, dragging on the ground as they moved forward, while others wore theirs tightly wrapped. But their eyes, their dead milky eyes, were all the same. It felt like hundreds of the fish-belly-white cataracts were locked onto them.

The mummies reached out toward Franklin and Faust, and the big horse reared back, kicking out his hind legs. This knocked several of the mummies to the ground, but it did little good. The ragged creatures immediately pulled themselves up to continue their task.

Franklin leaned forward to calm the big horse before dropping to the ground in the midst of the corpses.

"We have come here on behalf of the Prime Minister with official business from the Council," Franklin declared, raising his hands over his head. "We request an escort to your city center."

The mummies swarmed around Franklin, ignoring his words and pushing him away from the cart.

"Charlie, the girl!" Franklin shouted.

Charlie tried to turn Goliath, but the horse could not move and stepped sideways instead, stumbling on the mummies underfoot.

"Help!" Abigail screamed.

Charlie looked over and saw a swarm of ragged hands pick Abigail up and carry her from the cart off into the cornfield.

"Let her go!" Charlie shouted, feeling for his sword on his pommel.

It was too late. The sea of hands grabbed him too, passing him across the corn on an endless wave of mummified arms. He fought to look back toward the road, where a wall of mummies held Franklin and had engulfed Rohmetall, Ringo, and the cart. But he lost track of them as he was carried through the broken stalks that cut and raked across his face.

"Franklin!" he yelled, even though the Monster was already gone.

Moving along atop the scouts, Charlie wrestled his way closer to Abigail, reaching out to grasp her hand. It was still ice-cold, but she did not pull it away. She stared blankly at Charlie with her crystal-blue eyes as the mummies passed them overhead, across the endless fields of corn.

"Charlie! What's happening?" Abigail cried.

"We'll be all right. Hang on!" Charlie called back, trying to sound more confident than he was.

As they neared the edge of the cornfields, the Mumiya scouts set them down on the ground, and immediately organized themselves into straight lines with Abigail and Charlie between them. The mummies pushed them forward, and they ran through the long, narrow rows and then out onto a gravel road, where they continued until Charlie thought his legs might collapse. The sun was low when the corn eventually gave way to a collection of small earthen buildings and they could see the tops of the pyramids in the distance. To their other side was a vast desert. They ran down the road, passing farms with overgrown crops and more low earthen buildings. Mummified crowds in open-air markets parted as they passed, but then returned to their business.

The road widened as they ran past the first of the pyramids. Its heavy stone steps were steep and led to an open, flat peak, where there were carvings of round-eyed serpents with flared nostrils. The next pyramid's walls were smooth, with its sides joined at a sharp point. As they ran, they passed more pyramids in varying stages of construction, until they finally approached the largest of the pyramids. It towered high above them, growing higher the longer they ran.

When they reached the city center, Charlie and Abigail were herded into a large plaza, where a swarm of mummies surrounded them. Hundreds more arrived, each one a different size and shape, yet they all wore similar bandages and had the same dead white eyes. The mob converged before the main pyramid, and Abigail and Charlie were again lifted and passed forward, hand over tightly bound hand. Near the base of the pyramid, Charlie heard Ringo barking and saw Franklin in the midst of the melee. They were leading him away, along with Rohmetall and Ringo, but Franklin could not be moved. The Mumiya held him as he fought back, refusing to give up an inch of ground. Franklin pushed and pulled the pile, but there was nowhere for him to go. There were just too many.

"Where is the boy?" Charlie could hear Franklin growling to his captors. "The girl?"

Charlie wrestled the bony hands that held him and managed to pull his arm free.

"Franklin! Over here!" he shouted, and waved.

"Charlie!"

The Monster turned and pushed the pile toward them, roaring as he ripped at the mummified hands that tried to hold him back. Charlie kicked his legs and tried to stand so Franklin could see him but quickly fell, dropping to the ground amid the mob. The mummies were pressed so tightly against one another that Charlie found it difficult to breathe. Gasping for air, he reached his arm up, holding it as high as he could above the crowd. A cold hand took hold of Charlie's, and through the chaos, he could see Abigail, still in the Mumiya's grasp. Just as she did back at the river, she was trying to pull him up with all of her strength.

"Hang on, Charlie," she said. "I've got you."

Then a horn sounded from somewhere deep within the pyramid, and all of a sudden Abigail and Charlie were dropped to the ground. They fell to the cobblestone, and the mummies immediately backed away, leaving them at the base of the stairs in the center of the plaza. They were a few paces away from Franklin, who had just turned to face the circle, not trusting their retreat.

"Charlie, are you well?" Franklin hollered.

"We're fine," Charlie shouted back.

Franklin inched toward them slowly, his gaze fixed on the mummified horde. But the Mumiya were now completely preoccupied, staring up at the top of the pyramid, ignoring their captives as if they were no longer there. When Franklin was in reach, he grabbed Charlie and Abigail in a single swoop and held them at his feet.

"How is your shoulder, boy?"

Charlie pulled his coat over the splotches of blood that dotted his shirt. "It's good," he lied.

"And you, Abigail, they didn't hurt you, did they?"

"No, Mr. Franklin, I'm all right, thank you," she said, looking around at the plaza. Again she was oddly calm. Whatever fears she had, they were now replaced by apparent fascination.

Franklin's clothes were torn, and the stitch he had repaired at his neck had been pulled loose.

"How's this for a welcoming committee? What did I say?"

"All for show," Charlie gasped, trying to catch his breath.

The horn sounded again, prompting them to look up at the top of the pyramid, which shined gold in the setting sun.

"About time," Franklin growled. "There will be a few words about the start to this summit, I assure you . . ."

The horn sounded a third time, and the mummies dropped to one knee, bowing their heads almost to the ground.

"Come, Charlie, Miss Abigail," Franklin said, walking toward the base of the looming steps.

The stairs were so steep it was like climbing a ladder. At times, Charlie and Abigail had to use their hands to pull themselves up. When Charlie peered down behind them, he instantly felt dizzy. Down below, the hundreds, if not thousands, of mummies that had taken them from the cornfield were still on bended knee in a half circle at the bottom of the pyramid.

Franklin reached the top of the steps and turned to pull Abigail and Charlie to stand with him.

"Some show, eh?" the Monster said.

Charlie shuddered. It had all happened so fast, he had not had time to think about how he had just been carried on a wave of the dead. He could still smell the stench of their decay on his clothes.

"Straighten up, will ya?" Franklin said, hitting Charlie on his good shoulder. "Get your chin up. Show them who you are."

They stood at the open end of two long lines of mummified warriors, each one wearing a more elaborate headdress than the last. The warriors held long spears and flags that snapped and popped in the hot breeze that blew in from the desert. The guards ushered them forward onto a rug of thick oddly-spotted fur—then toward seven wide stairs that led to an even higher upper level. At the top of the stairs sat a large jeweled throne flanked by two smaller ones. Charlie could see the great desert behind the throne, which made him shudder again. The sight was intimidating and reminded him of Billy.

"We'll be all right, boy," the Monster said. "Quit your shivering."

When the horn sounded again, Charlie could feel it rumble in his chest. The warriors all dropped to their knees as a line of mummified royalty in capes of rich purple and burgundy appeared from a stone door. One of them held a sword out toward the setting sun.

"Her Majesty and Supreme Ruler, Nuit Khensa Tuya VII," the noble announced, dropping to one knee. The rest of the Mumiya followed, all kneeling on the ground. But Franklin remained standing, so Charlie and Abigail did the same.

The horns sounded and the stone door opened again. Then a tall, slender mummy with the most elaborate headdress yet stepped out, dragging the long train of her bloodred cape behind her. She looked out over her subjects and gracefully descended a few of the steps until she stood with her head a few feet higher than Franklin's.

"Do you not bow down before the Queen Nuit Khensa Tuya VII?" the ruler of the Mumiya asked.

Franklin clenched his fists at his side and breathed deeply before speaking. "What is the meaning of this? I demand an explanation for this disgraceful treatment."

Khensa Tuya extended her mummified hand, holding her

large ruby ring out to Franklin. "You may kiss the ring," she offered.

"I should think not," Franklin replied. "I feel I may be coming down with something. Would hate to pass it along..."

The queen drew back her arm. "Ah, the great Monster of all Monsters. Still with your vanity."

"Vanity? Come now," Franklin said, eyeing the extravagance of her court. "I am here on official Council business at the request of the Prime Minister. Please see that our property and livestock are returned so that we may address the matters at hand."

Khensa Tuya stood a bit straighter. "The Prime Minister? Is he here?"

"No," Franklin replied coolly. "But we should expect him shortly if you refuse to cooperate."

"I see," Khensa Tuya said.

She turned and climbed the few stairs to sit in her throne.

"I have papers," Charlie heard himself say. "Letters of transit from the Prime Minister himself."

"And what of this one?" Khensa Tuya said, pointing her tattered finger toward Abigail. "She bothers me."

"She is our guest," Franklin said. "And as such is also awarded the safeguards of the Prime Minister."

"Well then." The queen looked down at the ruby on her hand. "I suppose it would be an honor if you would consider yourselves my guests as well."

"The honor is ours," Franklin said, sneaking a wink to Charlie.

"You will be taken to your quarters, and then we will speak over the evening meal. But first . . ." Khensa Tuya stood to take in her vast lands and the mummified crowds who were still gathered below. "Will you look at this glorious sunset? Ah, to bask in the adoration of my loyal subjects."

She waved her hand at the throngs below and sat back in her throne. The last rays of the setting sun bathed her in a radiant golden glow as Charlie, Franklin, and Abigail were led inside the pyramid.

—— *chapter 30* ——

An Audience with the Queen

SURROUNDED BY MUMMIFIED warriors, Charlie, Franklin, and Abigail were roughly guided down the long stone passageways of the pyramid in what seemed like endless circles. Franklin had to stoop down most of the way to make it through the low, narrow tunnels. At the end of the maze, there was a short wooden door with lit torches mounted on either side. The mummies stopped at the door and parted, creating an even smaller path.

"What? You expect us to go in there?" Franklin asked, crouching down.

The door opened and Franklin leaned his head through the frame.

"This will be the end of me. All right, then. Come, Charlie."

Franklin reached out, gathered Abigail and Charlie in his big arms, and helped them through. He kept his eyes on the mummies the entire time, then followed, and they shut the door behind him.

"Welcome, Ch-Ch-Charlie Cooper," a friendly metallic voice said.

Charlie turned to find Rohmetall standing with his head just at the limit of the low ceiling. The room was large, but the height was oddly short. Ringo welcomed them as well, jumping up on Charlie first, licking at his hands and face.

"Hey, fella, how you doin'? You all right, boy?" Charlie was relieved to see his old friend, even in the captivity of the strangely squat room.

"Is this ol' Khensa Tuya's idea of a joke?" Franklin said. He stood bent nearly in half for a moment before dropping down to a knee. "You see this? You see her sense of humor? A general lack of respect is what it is . . ."

"*Respect. Pride.* 'Those who bow to Necessity are wise,'" Rohmetall said. "*Prometheus Bound* . . . Aeschylus, although authorship debated-debated . . ."

Franklin glowered at the steam man.

"That's enough! Who asked you, anyway? When we return to the Charnel House, there will be some adjustments made to you, my fine encyclopedic friend. This I guarantee." Franklin leaned back against the wall. "And what's become of our horses?"

"The horses are well taken care of. The stable hands here are more-more than capable. Your supplies and papers for Queen Nuit Khensa Tuya VII are on the table," Rohmetall replied.

"Why, thank you," Franklin said, looking around the room. There were two windows in one of the walls, but they were too small for any of them to fit through. "The Mumiya trust no one and therefore all are considered suspect. They take their prisoners first and then sort friend from foe."

Franklin set Abigail on the foot of a bed in the far corner, and pulled his sewing kit from his gear.

"Regardless, if we are going to meet with the *queen*, might as well look presentable," he said sarcastically. A sour mood had overtaken the Monster.

AN HOUR PASSED BEFORE THE QUEEN'S GUARD SUMMONED them to her official chambers. The room was large with open windows and wall-to-wall murals depicting all that was accomplished under Queen Nuit Khensa Tuya VII's reign. Older, bent, and stooped, the queen's statesmen welcomed them in and urged Franklin to begin the talks, as Khensa Tuya would join them shortly. Franklin looked stately as he laid out his materials and papers, having quickly repaired the stitches at his neck, as well as the rips and tears in his clothes. Abigail sat quietly in the corner while Charlie helped himself to the long table of food that was laid out for them. Fresh vegetables and fruits were mashed and whipped in bowls, and Charlie could barely identify the different kinds of strange fish and breads. The table was set up by the windows facing the desert and Charlie thought of Billy, wondering if he too had come this way, possibly even looking out across the same stretch of moonlit sand.

When he turned his attention back to his dinner, Charlie noticed that there was a magpie on the windowsill near the end of the buffet. The magpie was eating what looked to be some sort of dark cookie, and much like the bird that he had seen by the lodge, it seemed to have little interest in Charlie. He tried to scare the bird away but quickly realized his attempts were a distraction to the proceedings and returned to filling his plate.

Charlie ate as much as he could and then sat sleepily next to Abigail in the corner. He tried to concentrate on what Franklin was saying about the Council's proposed treaty, but found his eyelids heavy and soon slumped forward in his chair.

"How is one to think with this oaf snoring in the corner?"

Charlie woke with a start and looked up at Queen Nuit Khensa Tuya VII, who stood above him.

"Look at him. So young, so full of life . . ."

She seemed to examine Charlie enviously, though it was hard to tell with the dead, colorless reflection of her eyes.

"And whatever is he doing here?" Khensa Tuya asked, turning back to Franklin.

"Who, me?" Charlie said, wiping some drool from his cheek. "I'm looking for someone. My cousin. I think he got lost. His name is Billy."

"*Billy?*" the queen gasped. "What on earth is a *Billy?*"

"Please, time is of the essence. Let us stick to the subject at hand," Franklin said. He was standing over the table, his charts spread around him. "With the Council's treaty, you are all but guaranteed to see a dramatic reduction in your loss of production due to the insufficiencies of your workforce—"

"And thievery," Khensa Tuya added. She returned to the table and sat in a large chair at its head.

"Yes, and thievery, and extortion and broken treaties," Franklin continued impatiently. "We know all this . . ."

"You can't be serious," Khensa Tuya sighed. "You come here expecting me to believe that the marauders could be counted on as some sort of a what? A reliable workforce? Ha!"

"Not all," Franklin said. "Of course, some are beyond our control, but others will jump at a chance for peace and a guarantee that their cook pots will be filled come winter."

"Half the marauders are werewolves or other creatures of the night. They sleep most of the day and then go traipsing off at dusk, expecting to be excused, and returning only when it suits them!"

Franklin gripped the thick stone table and took in a deep breath.

"Then pay them a half day's wage. Anything is better than your current state. Would you not agree?"

"But they must be punished for their actions!" Khensa Tuya said, banging her fist down on the armrest of her chair. "The way they pillage the land, why, I should—"

"We have been through this," Franklin said wearily. "There must be amnesty. A fresh start . . ."

"Tucked away in your castle," Khensa Tuya scoffed. "You don't live among us. You have not seen the aftermath . . ."

"That is not the point."

"And what is your point?"

"That you and your brother, Tok, must sit down and negotiate if we are to establish a lasting peace."

"I beg your pardon, Your Highness." An older, stooped

mummified servant stepped forward. "But there is urgent news . . ."

"How dare you interrupt!" Khensa Tuya shouted.

"B-b-but, Your Highness . . ." The servant's voice quivered.

"I am losing my patience," Franklin growled. "We have been up half the night and are no further along than when we started . . ."

"You will not take that tone with me!" Khensa Tuya shrieked. "Who do you think you are?"

The Monster gripped the table tighter, and Charlie thought he could hear the rock crumbling beneath his fingers.

"Who am I?" Franklin said. "Why, we were just discussing that the other day, weren't we, boy? Ah, who am I? I have been called all manner of things through the years. Some kinder than others—I am sure you've heard a few of them. Would you care to see why?"

"Is that a threat?" the mummy queen hissed.

"P-p-please, Your Highness," the servant stammered, dropping to his knees. "It is a communiqué, from the P-P-Prime Minister . . ."

"The Prime Minister!" Khensa Tuya stood abruptly, almost knocking her chair over. "Is he here?"

"I-I-I do not know. But he has sent this," the cowering servant said, holding the Prime Minister's message above his lowered head. "Urgent news of troubles that brew in the desert."

Khensa Tuya snatched the envelope from her servant's hand, ripped it open, and read.

"Well . . . ," Franklin said.

"'Urgent news—Troubles brew in the desert.—P. M.,'" she read aloud.

"Urgent news? Is that it?" Franklin said. "We are all well aware of the situation—"

"Yes, as you say, *aware of the situation*, and yet you have refused to act!"

"Let us be fair," Franklin spat back.

"Fair?" the queen repeated with a snarl.

Franklin lowered his head. "I knew this was a waste of time and expressed as much to the Prime Minister—"

"Excuse me," Charlie interrupted. While he found the news from the desert fascinating, he could barely keep his eyes open after the excitement of the day.

"What's that?" Franklin said, turning to Charlie.

"I'm wondering if I . . . if we . . . Abigail and I . . . can we be excused?"

"Of course, my apologies, Charlie . . . Abigail, what was I thinking?" Franklin said, looking back at the queen. "We should table this discussion so that I can see the children to bed."

"As you wish. They will show you to your quarters," Khensa Tuya said, motioning to her attendants. She whispered something to one of them and then waved them all to the door.

This time, they were taken to a different room with more sensible ceilings. It was much more comfortable with two beds and an open door that led to another room with a third bed. There were large windows that overlooked a courtyard below and opened out toward the endless desert. As they entered the second room, they were surprised to find the Prime Minister standing at the open window. There was a magpie perched on his shoulder, which held a half-eaten cookie in its beak. They both stared out at the night sky, seemingly lost in thought.

"Well, well, well, look who we have here," Franklin said, interrupting their pensive silence. He stretched his long arms over his head, enjoying the new height of the space. "I see now why our situation has mysteriously improved."

"It is a pleasure to see you too," the Prime Minister said. He seemed to almost share a laugh with the magpie before it flew out the window, and then he approached the group. "And how are you, Charlie? You look well. I trust your travels have been educational."

"I'm good, sir. Thank you."

"Ah, yessssss," the Prime Minister continued, turning his attention to Abigail. "I had received word that your party had grown. And who might you be?"

Abigail extended her hand, which the Prime Minister shook gently. Charlie noticed he did not have the others' reaction to the coldness of her touch.

"Abigail Rose. I'm with 'em, as Charlie and Mr. Franklin here rescued me."

"Mr. Franklin?" the Prime Minister said, looking at the Monster. "A rescue. I see. Well, we have much to discuss, much to discuss indeed."

"I would say there is. What is the meaning of all this? If you could have come here in the first place, what am I doing here?" Franklin bellowed.

"The situation has worsened," the Prime Minister said. "There is news of impending raids and I understand the talks are deteriorating rapidly, no thanks to you."

"No thanks to me? I told you. I am not equipped to handle their mummified arrogance. I should have been sent to speak with the banshees or, better yet, the trolls or goblins. These are the negotiations that I am accustomed to. Not so much pomp, let alone circumstance."

"I am sure you have done as best you could. And now at least the egg is broken, so to speak. I am confident there will be an agreement by morning."

"And then that is it! I will return to Charnel House immediately following. Our agreement is hereby terminated. I am going home." Franklin pointed his gnarled finger at the Prime Minister. "I knew you were up to something, and this little sideshow is the proof. Her Highness *Queen* Khensa Tuya will come around now that you are here. There is no need for me. She will do your bidding. But we, we turn back tomorrow."

"Turn back?" Charlie cried. "We can't turn back now! We've come so far!"

"Now, now," the Prime Minister said, trying to calm them.

"No, look at the mess we're in," Franklin went on. "As I said all along, it is not safe. There is still so far to go, and the boy has already been injured."

The Prime Minister turned. "Charlie, are you injured?"

"I was. But I'm fine now. Franklin and the Ranger saw to it."

"See, what was it, *Franklin*? The boy is fine," the Prime Minister said, moving toward the door. "Come now. There is no need to cure all that ails us *thisss* evening. Charlie and Miss Abigail must sleep. We will assess that situation later. For now, Khensa Tuya awaits."

"Ah, yes. The queen awaits," Franklin said angrily, following the Prime Minister out of the room. "The queen awaits . . ."

They locked the door behind them, leaving Charlie and Abigail standing in front of the immense windows. Looking out over the desert, they could see the sky was clear and dotted with bright stars.

"It is beautiful," Abigail said.

"It is," Charlie replied, but his mind was elsewhere. He was thinking about what lay beyond the desert. He was thinking of the vast, open plain that haunted his dreams—and of Billy.

Abigail turned and stared blankly at Charlie. "Strange fellow, this Prime Minister. His hands felt as cold as ice."

— *chapter 31* —

Just Past Midnight

CHARLIE WAS FAST asleep when he felt a heavy hand nudge his shoulder. He slowly opened his eyes to find Franklin standing over him. The Monster held a candle and did not seem to notice the wax that dripped down his hand and onto Charlie's bedroll.

"I am sorry, Charlie. I see now we have made a mistake. You should not be here. We have gone too far as it is. It's too dangerous, plain and simple. This valley is no place for a boy . . ."

"But, Franklin," Charlie sputtered, sitting up, "I'll be good. I'll do what you say. I can't go home now."

Franklin towered over him, the shadows of his face flickering in and out of the candlelight.

"The Prime Minister's plan is too risky. I have been responsible for enough pain and misery in my life. I will not add your name to the list."

"But, Franklin—"

"Enough."

"Well, I'm still going. I won't give up, Franklin, I just won't."
Charlie rolled over, turning his back to the Monster.

"No, Charlie, we leave tomorrow. This is not open for debate. Go to sleep."

Franklin blew out the candle, and Charlie could hear his heavy steps echo across the darkness of the room. He laid back on his bedroll, pulled out his photo with Billy, and looked at it in the moonlight. *No,* he thought. *We can't turn back. We've come this far.* He had to find Billy—he just had to. And there was nothing that Franklin could do or say to change his mind.

— *chapter 32* —

Out on the Open Plain

$\mathcal{W}$HEN CHARLIE WOKE up, Abigail was back at the window staring out over the desert. He dragged his tired body out of bed and joined her, looking up at the clouds gathering in the sky above them.

"Seems a storm is coming," Abigail said.

Like the desert in his dreams, the wind from a black cloud blew the dust up, turning the sky a brownish orange.

"The Prime Minister came by while you were sleeping," Abigail said. "He left for urgent business in the east but said he would be back this evening, so to call out if you need him. He also said we're free to come and go as we please, now that the treaty is almost in place. You can wash up down in the court- yard if you like."

Charlie gathered his things in his pack, and they left the room, finding their way through the maze back to the main hall. Mummified attendants averted their eyes and bowed before them as they passed now. They found Franklin at the doorway of the stateroom, where he informed them that the talks had gone well in the end, even better than he had imagined.

"Amazing how receptive a queen can be in the presence of the Prime Minister," Franklin said. "Do not stray from the courtyard, though. I hope to have this wrapped up in time for us to leave this afternoon."

Charlie did not answer and could not look at Franklin. His anger was building, and he was afraid if he did, he might say or do something that he would later regret. Although he couldn't blame Franklin for wanting to turn back, how could they after they had already come so far? Old Joe wouldn't, Charlie thought. Billy certainly wouldn't—

"Quitter," he snapped, no longer able to control himself.

Franklin glanced down at Charlie with a surprised look on his face.

"What did you say to me?"

"You heard me," Charlie said, turning his back on the Monster. "Quitter."

"Hey, come back here," Franklin ordered, but Charlie was already gone.

He stormed away with Abigail close behind. They wound down another series of passages until they found themselves in the courtyard. As he walked, he counted each step, trying to calm himself and forget the disappointed look he saw on Franklin's face.

In the middle of the courtyard, there was a well with a gate that stood directly behind it. While the storm was still in the distance, the dark clouds above told them it had grown closer.

There were mummies by the well, who urged them to drink, and then slowly shuffled about the courtyard among themselves. Some filled pitchers with water or attended to odd chores, but for the most part, they just walked this way and that, which left Charlie wondering what they were actually doing. And there were cats and some dogs around the courtyard as well, even a few monkeys, all mummified and lounging about.

After they had washed and had enough to drink, Charlie and Abigail sat in the shade against the side of one of the low buildings and looked out again at the vast desert beyond the gate.

"I wonder what's over there, across on the other side. I suppose it could be something splendid," Abigail said, lost in her own words. "It almost calls to you, doesn't it?"

"Something special, but who cares? We'll never know. Besides—" Charlie began, but was interrupted by a small mummy who had come right up to them.

The mummy was so small it looked like it could be a toddler. It stared at them with its dead fish eyes and picked at Charlie's clothes. At one point, it poked at them with a stick, which Charlie promptly grabbed and broke in half. This sent the little mummy running, and they watched until it disappeared back inside the pyramid.

"Peculiar behavior," Abigail said.

Charlie wondered if she was talking about the mummified child or him. She was sometimes hard to read that way. Then a long shadow fell over them, announcing the appearance of the mummified remains of a girl a little bit taller than Abigail.

The girl stood silently, waiting for Charlie and Abigail to stand up. When they did, she stared at them for a moment before speaking.

"I am Urbi Zalika Khensa Tuya," the girl said. "*Urbi* means 'princess' in my language."

"Yes, uh, Urbi," Charlie said, cutting her off; he was already annoyed. "I've met your mother. I'm Charlie. This is Abigail."

"Zalika will suffice," the princess replied, extending her hand to him. Charlie grasped it in his, opting to shake her hand rather than kiss it.

"I saw what my younger brother did to you with the stick. I found it amusing when you took the stick from him and broke it in half," Zalika said without any emotion. "Very amusing. I almost laughed."

Charlie felt himself flush a bit and looked over to Abigail, who just stared back at Zalika with her cold blue eyes.

"You are not from here, are you? I apologize, but the longer I have been here the harder it is to tell," Zalika said to Charlie.

"No," Charlie replied. "I'm not from here."

Charlie turned to walk back toward the well, remembering that he had forgotten to brush his teeth. Abigail and Zalika followed.

"If you are not from here, where do you come from?"

"I'm from the other side of the mountains. We're not sure where she's from," Charlie said, pointing back to Abigail.

"Over the mountains? Is that possible?"

"I suppose. I'm here, aren't I?" Charlie said.

Charlie drank from the well but kept his eye on Abigail.

She had stopped a few paces away and was staring at the desert again. The skies were getting darker overhead and the wind was growing stronger as it blew in from the plain.

"Why did you come here? Why did you come over the mountains?" Zalika asked.

"I was looking for someone," Charlie said, opening his backpack to pull out his toothbrush.

"This girl, here. In the rags?" Zalika gestured toward Abigail.

"No. It wasn't her," he said, still trying to find his toothbrush. There were his extra socks, his hat and mittens, the rubber werewolf mask, but no toothbrush.

"Charlie, come. Come look at this," Abigail called. "It is truly amazing..."

Charlie abandoned his search but stuffed the mask in his pocket thinking that he would scare Zalika's brother if he saw him again.

"You see?" Abigail said, pushing the tattered bonnet back on her head.

Walking toward the gate, Charlie followed her gaze out to the desert. A huge wall of sand was approaching them from across the plain, stretching as far as he could see. The storm was almost upon them.

"Sandstorm, I guess," Charlie said.

"No, Charlie," Abigail said. "Look closer."

He looked into the storm again and saw what had caught Abigail's attention. On the fringes, Charlie could see odd-shaped silhouettes that grew larger as the storm grew closer.

There were winged creatures, witches on broomsticks, and a line of werewolves, trolls, and hobgoblins, all pushing forward alongside horses with headless riders and ogres with heavy clubs.

"That is not just a storm," Zalika said, turning back toward the pyramid. "Marauders! It is a raid!"

As she said the words, sand from the storm began to whip across their faces in heavy sheets. They stumbled blindly back toward the well as the first of the witches made her descent. The witch flew hard, buzzing the courtyard just above their heads in a cackling black blur. A second witch followed, and then there was an explosion.

"Charlie!" Abigail cried.

Charlie reached out for her, but Abigail wasn't there. He could barely see a foot in front of him through the thick wall of sand.

"This way!" a voice called.

Charlie stumbled forward and fell into Zalika, who had pulled her wrappings up like a scarf to protect her eyes.

"We have to get inside. They will take us, Charlie!"

"Take us?"

"For ransom!" Zalika shouted over the storm. "Come on!"

"I can't leave Abigail out here," Charlie called back, but Zalika had already disappeared. Suddenly, a horse burst forward from the storm, its chest knocking Charlie to the ground. He heard Zalika scream in the chaos, and there were more hooves. Then a thick leather-gloved hand dropped from above, lifting Charlie and throwing him across the pommel of the horse. The horse spun sideways and leapt forward into the storm.

"Franklin!" Charlie screamed, though he knew it was no use. With the surprise attack, the Monster was more than likely in the midst of his own battle.

The sand continued to beat down on Charlie as they rode. All he could do was cover his face with one hand and hold the horse's long, tangled mane in the other. They rode for what felt like hours before Charlie sensed them drop down the far side of a hill, where the wind still blew but they were somewhat sheltered. The gloved hand grabbed Charlie roughly by the collar and jerked him down from the saddle. He looked up at his captor but turned away horrified and as quickly as he could. There was no skin on its face. No repaired flesh, like Franklin. No bandages or werewolves' cowls, just pure bone against a dark hood—nothing else—a skeleton.

The tall, sticklike creature dragged Charlie to the back of a crude wagon, where it picked up an empty canvas sack.

"All right. No troubles," it shouted over the storm. "In you go."

Charlie struggled against the creature's grip as it stuffed him in the sack. He fought to get his head out, and for a second he thought he saw Abigail, but he was pushed back into the sack before he could be sure.

"Quit your squirming," the skeleton ordered, punching the sack. "And up you go."

Charlie felt himself fly through the air and land with a heavy thud in the back of a wagon. He tried to get out of the sack again, but the skeleton had done a good job with his knots.

Charlie felt other sacks land next to and on top of him, and then the wagon lurched forward.

"Abigail! Can you hear me? Zalika!" Charlie called, but the storm drowned out his words.

Charlie couldn't tell how long they traveled, so he was relieved when he heard the storm die down and, eventually, felt the wagon rocking to a halt.

"Okay. We've reached the rendezvous, so a wee little break," a sniveling voice said. "I'll let you little piggies out of your sacks, but don't even think about running. There's nowhere to go anyway."

Charlie was lifted from the wagon to stand in the sack, but when he stood, he realized that his entire right side had fallen asleep during the journey, and he immediately fell sideways.

"Aw, this little piggy's had a rough ride."

Charlie could hear the voice more clearly now. He knew that it sounded familiar. He had heard it somewhere before.

"Here ya go . . ."

Charlie was jostled again as the canvas opened, and he stood up out of the sack to take in the fresh desert air.

"You!" the voice said, though Charlie could not make out the face. His eyes had not yet adjusted to the harsh sunlight. "I should have known we would cross paths again!"

The rest of the canvas sack was pulled back, and Charlie was pushed toward the voice.

"And where's the big fella and his claptrap companion? And your friend, the kid with all the wolves?"

The haze was starting to clear, and Charlie could just make

out the outline of an *X* on the man's pockmarked cheek. Then he recognized the voice. It was the traveler Lester Mortlock, who had attacked them with the ogres.

"I see. They ain't around, are they?" Lester Mortlock said, looking over his shoulder as if he expected Franklin to jump out at any moment.

Charlie swung blindly at the man, shouting, "You let us go. You let us go now!"

"Let you go? Ha," Lester spat, pulling a long knife from the sheath on his belt. He slashed out with the knife, and Charlie fell back, covering his head with his arms. "You're lucky I don't fillet you like a fish!"

Charlie looked down at his arm and saw the wet red welt that was rising across his forearm underneath the fresh rip in his coat.

"You like that? Huh? Want some more?"

Charlie crawled backward, thinking about Franklin's warnings and reluctance to continue. He wondered, staring up at the knife, if maybe Franklin was right, maybe they should have turned back, gone home. But then his thoughts quickly turned to the man standing over him and, more optimistically, to what Franklin would do to this Lester Mortlock if he were here.

"No, I didn't think so." Lester returned the knife to its sheath. "Now, get down there. And be glad the lot of you will fetch me a pretty price once the ransoms come in . . ."

Lester turned to a one-eyed ogre who lumbered from the front of the cart. "You. Keep an eye on this one."

"You hear him?" the ogre said, pointing a grotesque finger toward its face. "I've got my eye on you. Now, move."

Charlie still had trouble seeing in the harsh desert light and stumbled down the sand dune toward a small, muddy well. He was handed a wooden bucket, which he eagerly accepted and drank as fast as he could, letting the dirty water splash over his head when he had his fill. Out of breath, he fell back against the well, rubbing his eyes, and as they slowly adjusted, he saw Abigail Rose.

"Abigail!"

"Hello, Charlie," she said in her typically understated fashion. "Well, here we are in the desert."

"Yep," Charlie said, breathing heavily but happy to see her. "Here we are . . . and he's right. There's nowhere to run. Are you okay, Abigail?"

"I'm fine, Charlie. I got pretty scared, but I'm fine."

"Yeah, I was scared too," Charlie said, looking out on the great expanse. It was flat as far as the eye could see, with a few windblown dunes of sand. He looked to the horizon and recognized this place—it was the desert from his dreams. But now he wondered if Billy had been calling him this whole time or warning him to stay away.

"Your arm, Charlie. You're bleeding," Abigail said, kneeling beside him.

Charlie glanced down at his arm, where blood was seeping through his coat sleeve.

"We need to find a way out of here." Charlie looked back at the wagon. "Before it is too late."

"Another little piggy," Lester said, handing a third sack to the one-eyed ogre, who threw it over his shoulder and carried it to the well. "This one will be worth a pretty penny . . ."

"Not to get out," the ogre said to the contents of the sack. "Just the head."

The ogre dropped the sack to the ground and pulled open the string at the top. Zalika thrust her head forward and began to yell.

"How dare you!" she cried. "I demand that you untie me at once! Don't you know who I am?"

The ogre looked over at Lester.

"Go ahead," Lester spat. "Where is she going to go?"

"Okay. Then I build a fire?" the ogre asked.

"No, you don't build a fire. There were very implicit instructions against fires." Lester turned away and mumbled to himself as he returned to the wagon. "Over and over, the same things. I'm constantly repeating myself."

"So, no. No on building the fire?" the ogre said, a puzzled look on his face.

"Yes!" Lester cried.

"Yes?" the ogre repeated, scratching his large bald head.

"No! No! No! No! I'm saying yes to the *no* on the fire! You would think after a while it might . . . just might sink in!" he yelled, disappearing over the dune.

"Yes, to the no to the no to the yes to the no on the fire," the ogre said, trying to work out the logic. "Okay, I will look for wood," the ogre concluded, dumping Zalika out of the sack and onto the sand.

"That beast will find his head on the end of a spear when my mother hears of this!" Zalika rolled to her knees, gritting her teeth beneath her linen wraps.

Charlie handed her the bucket filled with water.

"We do not require water, but thank you," Zalika said, her voice returning to its calmer state.

Charlie set the bucket down. He was dizzy and leaned against the side of the well to regain his balance.

"Charlie, you are injured," Zalika said, grabbing ahold of him.

"That horrible man cut him pretty good." Abigail moved to help.

Charlie could feel warm blood dripping under his sleeve. A few drops landed in the sand at his feet.

"Yeah, he got me pretty good, all right."

"I see," Zalika said. "We can heal your wound."

Zalika unwrapped a series of bandages on her arm and removed a small blue vial that was tucked against her bones.

"Pull up your sleeve," she instructed as she ripped a bandage from her linen wrappings. She splashed water on the bloody cut and removed the blue crystal stopper from the bottle. "We all use this from time to time, as things tend to come undone. It is similar to cauterizing. It will seal the wound."

"What is it?" Charlie winced as Zalika leaned forward and cleaned the area.

"Many things—bitumen, herbs, spices, minerals. It will sting a bit and then mummify the trauma to stop the bleeding."

"Wait, did you say 'mummify'?" Charlie exhaled.

"Yes. Now, hold still."

Zalika tilted the bottle, and a few tiny drops fell into the jagged cut on Charlie's forearm.

"Ahhh," Charlie cried. He could feel the liquid burn his skin as it seeped into the cut. Then the wound began to close and itched horribly for a moment before going numb.

"There, how is that?"

Charlie unclenched his teeth. "Uh, it's fine," he said, surprised. "Doesn't hurt anymore."

"And the bleeding has stopped. Here, you hold on to this. I have plenty." She handed Charlie the small blue vial.

The newly healed skin looked gray and dead, and the jagged line made by Lester's knife felt as hard as a rock, as if the wound had been filled with a line of concrete. He thumped the area with his finger and found he could not feel a thing. However, the blue solution had stopped the bleeding.

"Thank you," Charlie said, taking the vial and shoving it in his pocket along with the photograph of Billy. "Now what?"

"Now what?" Lester repeated. He was walking down the dune toward them. "Now you sit, and we wait until the others join us. Then we will take you to Mr. Tok, and that is when I can wash my hands of this business."

THEY SPENT THE AFTERNOON FOLLOWING THE SLIVER OF shade around the well and watching the ogre as it looked in vain for firewood among the drifting dunes. Lester rarely took his eyes off Charlie and occasionally motioned to the knife that he now wore on the outside of his coat. At dusk, they were joined by another group of marauders, their wagons and carts also filled with captives and other bounty. A witch circled overhead on her broom while the other beasts killed an old mule behind the well, tearing at its flesh with their fangs and claws.

"Looks like it's almost payday," Lester announced to his captives when his fellow marauders started moving back to their horses. "Drink up, then it's back in the sack."

The ogre tied the sacks over Abigail's and Zalika's heads, hoisted them over his shoulder, and threw them back into the wagon, where the ghouls and goblins snorted and pulled at the bundles.

"Hands off, hands off!" Lester shouted, beating back the beasts. "Valuable cargo here! Ransoms await!" He then turned to Charlie. "Now, little piggy. Your turn," Lester taunted. "Got to keep moving. Wouldn't want your big fella and that wolf pack riding up on us, would we?"

"You better hope he doesn't," Charlie said as they pulled the sack over his head and tossed him into the back of the wagon.

The wagon lurched forward, and Charlie lay listening to groans and grunts of the marauders who now traveled with them. At some point, they were at an incline and Charlie rolled with the other cargo until he hit the side of the wagon. Once there, he sat up in the sack, feeling his way up the boxboards with his elbow through the canvas. He then let his arm slip over the top as far as the material would allow and pushed off the bed of the wagon with his feet. Though he couldn't see, he felt himself leaning over the edge of the wagon box. *If I could just,* Charlie thought, and then he pushed again—

Charlie hit the ground with a thud and began tumbling head over heels in the sack. He rolled to the bottom of the incline and then lay there a moment to make sure the marauders' wagons had passed. When he could no longer hear them, he wrestled with the bag and pulled at its heavy seams, biting the tiny exposed threads until they frayed. It took some time, but eventually Charlie pulled back the sack and stood.

The moon was up high in the night sky; its light shimmered on the white sands, illuminating the surrounding desert in an eerie glow. It was cold, so he wrapped the canvas sack around his shoulders and found his way back to the wagon tracks. He studied their trail and was able to determine which direction they were headed. Charlie knew he needed water, so he checked the tracks again before heading back toward the well.

Looking to the stars to mark his direction, as Franklin had taught him, Charlie followed the trail up over the dunes and across the flat, open expanse. As the night wore on, Charlie began to count his steps, noting that the urge to do so had not been as strong here in Monsterland. But he counted them anyway—it helped somehow—with the growing fear and dread that he felt weighing down on him. Near dawn, he could see that a circle of vultures had already found the dead mule from the previous day. Just beyond, he saw the muddy well.

Charlie drank from the well eagerly and then sat again in

the shade at its base. The sun was higher now and burned hot. He looked out over the desert, watching the vultures pick at the remnants of the mule. After a while, he emptied his pockets on the flat stone beside him. All he had were the werewolf mask, the fangs, the vial from Zalika, and his photograph with Billy.

What am I doing here? Charlie pondered, looking down at the photograph. Alone and lost in the middle of the desert, a desert in the midst of this forgotten land. Where was he going and what was it he had to know? Why did he have to see Billy again? And what if what they said back home was true? That Billy was just gone? Charlie shuddered and turned his thoughts to Abigail and Zalika, to Franklin, Rohmetall, and Ringo. He hoped that they were all okay. Then he thought about his parents and Old Joe. He wondered what they were doing at this very moment, and what they would say to him if they were here.

"Chin up," he said out loud. *That's what Old Joe would say,* he knew it. *That's what they'd all say, even Franklin.* "Chin up . . ."

Out of the corner of his eye, Charlie saw something streaking across the sky and ducked down behind the well. It was a witch, more than likely out looking for him. *The werewolf mask*—Franklin had said it might work from a distance. Charlie pulled the mask on, waited until she passed, and then swung his leg over the side of the well and lowered himself just below the rim. No use pushing his luck. He held on to the muddy walls with the tips of his fingers as the witch circled back, which sent the vultures flying into the air. Charlie could feel his fingers slipping but held on as the witch made one last pass. When he was sure that she was gone, he counted to twenty and climbed out of the well.

"She didn't see me," Charlie said, pulling off the mask. Proud of his quick thinking, he stood up. "Ha-ha, she didn't see me! Take that!" he shouted after the witch. "I'm going to find Billy, and no one, not you, not anyone, is gonna stop me!"

Then he thought he saw the witch turn around and, with the moment broken, quickly jumped to the far side of the well to hide again.

Breathing heavily, he leaned back into the shadow at the base and looked out over the vast plain. He thought about Billy once more, but he did not see him or anyone else out in the distance. When his breathing had calmed, he dropped the wooden bucket back into the well and pulled up some more muddy water. Charlie drank from the bucket and then soaked the canvas sack. He draped the wet canvas over his head and walked over to the dead mule. The original wagon tracks from their abduction were covered in the storm, but the marauders' trail from the previous day could still be seen.

He followed the tracks, hoping that they might lead back for help or maybe even to Franklin. The sun was hot overhead and the canvas soon dried. After some time, he was thirsty, so he sat down at the bottom of a dune to look back at the well and wondered if he would find any other water out there, out there all alone. If this was the only water, it might be better if he just stayed at this dune. He had to be careful now that he was on his own, and from here, he could watch the well from a distance and sneak back for water when he deemed it was safe. And then, he thought, cheering up a bit, if Franklin was looking for him, maybe he would come this way too. That is—Charlie shuddered—if Franklin survived the attack.

Charlie climbed to the top of the dune and peered over the ridge. He scanned the horizon, and again there was nothing, so he pulled the canvas down to shield his eyes and slept.

He was soon there again, out on the open plain. The sun was lower than it had ever been in the dream before . . . and there was something else that was different. While the birds were there, whirling and swirling overhead, it was all in reverse. He was standing on the low dunes where Billy usually walked, whereas Billy and the smaller silhouette next to him stood at the edge of the shadows. Billy was shouting something, but Charlie could not hear him over the screeching birds, and then, just like that, Billy, the small figure, and the black cloud were gone, and Charlie was once again left all alone.

When Charlie woke up, the sun was high overhead. His mouth was dry and his lips cracked. Trying to shake the dream, he climbed to the top of the dune and scanned the horizon. It again seemed empty, but when Charlie looked back toward the Agrarian Plains, he was sure that he saw a flash of light in the distance. The light flashed again, and again, becoming more frequent. After a while, Charlie could make out two, maybe three, riders and a cart and thought he had a fifty–fifty chance that this could be good or bad. He was patient as he watched the riders slowly move closer, and he soon thought he recognized the approaching party. Charlie put on the werewolf mask just to be safe, then stood up on the dune and waved.

"Over here!" he shouted.

Franklin rode in front with Ringo running at the heels of his great horse. The Ranger was next, followed by Rohmetall and Dwight York, who rode in the cart trailing Goliath.

"Ch-Ch-Charlie!" Rohmetall called.

Charlie removed his mask as he ran down the dune, and Franklin rode up to meet him.

"Charlie!" Franklin said, swinging down to the sand and pulling him into a hug. Then he grabbed both shoulders as if he could assess any damage. "Are you well? You okay? I thought we lost you, boy . . ."

"I'm good," Charlie said. His voice was dry and cracked.

"And the girl? Abigail Rose?"

"She's gone. That Lester Mortlock was with the marauders, and they took her and the queen's daughter, Zalika, too. He said he was selling them to Tok for ransom!"

"Lester Mortlock," Franklin spat. "I should have taken care of that miscreant when I had the chance."

"They rode in from the desert and took all of us! They had me tied up in a sack, but I fell out of the wagon."

Franklin handed Charlie a water flask, which he eagerly accepted.

"I know the way they went, though," Charlie gasped as he drank. "We can follow their tracks."

Franklin looked out, past the well.

"Yes, as long as this weather holds."

"Oh, Franklin," Charlie said, trying to catch his breath. "It was horrible."

"There, there . . . you're all right now." Franklin threw his big arm back around Charlie's shoulders. "I didn't realize it was this bad out here." He sighed. There was a genuine look of apprehension on his face as he studied the rough terrain ahead of them. "I wish I could tell you it was almost over, Charlie, but like I've been saying, this nightmare has really just begun."

— *chapter 33* —

In Pursuit

*T*HEY LET THE horses have their fill at the well and rode hard after the marauders, following their tracks through the sand. Charlie was glad to be back in the saddle atop Goliath and in the company of Franklin, Rohmetall, Dwight York, Ringo, and the Ranger. As they galloped through the desert, he told them more of his ordeal, and then Dwight shared the details of the marauders' attack in exchange. The Agrarian Plains had been hit from all sides, he said. Crops were burned, stores looted, and Khensa Tuya had been seriously injured. When they left, her medical staff was fearing the worst.

"They attacked when they did because *he* was called away," Franklin added, referring to the Prime Minister. "I am sure that was always their plan. I doubt they would have tried it otherwise."

When they heard of the marauders' attack, Dwight York and Ignacio had joined the defense with a company of Rangers in the southern fields. After a short battle, they managed to drive the marauders back into the desert.

"Not much of a fight, really. They'd snatched what they had

come for and fled. We were fortunate to catch up with the big fellow here in time to join in the search," Ignacio Santos said as they rode.

Late that afternoon, they came to a point where the marauders' tracks split in the sand. Unsure which set to follow, they dismounted to consult Franklin's maps.

"It looks from the horsemen's tracks like the wagons went in that direction. Possibly toward this outpost here, at the base of this ridge," Franklin said, tracing their route on the charts he had laid out on the back of the cart.

"But they may have transferred their captives from the wagons to horseback knowing we would be in pursuit," Ignacio countered as he scanned the horizon.

"It is possible," Franklin said. "We should split up. I will follow the wagons west, and you two follow the horsemen to the east." Franklin pointed to a dot where the desert met the water. It was at the edge of the map; the area beyond was marked *unknown*.

"Rohmetall, you will take the cart and the boy and go to the north, here . . ."

"Ah, yes. There's a port of sorts," Ignacio said, examining the map.

"Taking Ch-Ch-Charlie Cooper," Rohmetall repeated.

"No," Charlie said, looking up at Franklin. "I want to go with you."

"It is out of the question. The last thing we need is another rescue on our hands." Franklin rolled up the maps and slid them back into the leather case.

"But, Franklin, you can't go out there alone," Charlie pleaded.

"Ha."

"But you'll need my help . . . you'll need—"

"Enough." Franklin started toward Faust but caught himself, and after a long sigh, he turned back. Dropping to a knee, he placed his heavy hand on Charlie's shoulder and motioned out toward the desolation with the other. "Look. Look around you. You're not supposed to be here. You understand that, right? Do you forget what's waiting for me out there? Just think of all you've been through, the horrors you've already seen. I told you, I won't be responsible . . . I can't be."

Franklin stood. The conversation was over. "Please, Rohmetall, take him."

"Come, Ch-Ch-Charlie Cooper," Rohmetall said. He was holding Goliath's reins.

"It is for the best." Dwight York offered Charlie a hand with the stirrup. "We'll all see one another again soon, I bet."

"But you don't even have a horse," Charlie added as he was hoisted up onto Goliath's back.

"I have faster ways to travel." Dwight York winked with a grin. "Let's hope this ol' Ranger can keep up."

"We'll see about that," Ignacio shot back, already in the saddle.

Rohmetall climbed aboard the cart still holding Goliath's reins.

"This way, Ch-Ch-Charlie Cooper," Rohmetall stuttered, pulling Goliath with the reins in his hands. The cart lurched north, away from where the tracks had split. Ringo barked from the bench seat as they left.

"But, Franklin...," Charlie called back.

"Go, Charlie. Like Dwight said, we will see each other soon—I promise."

Charlie watched as Franklin rode off to the west and Ignacio and Dwight York headed to the east.

"We are riding north, Ch-Ch-Charlie Cooper, north to the Vast Inland Sea . . . ," Rohmetall announced, passing Charlie Goliath's reins. "Please follow me."

"Yeah, that's what they told us to do. Ride north," Charlie said. He was still looking back, trying his best to keep Franklin in his sights. "But," he muttered under his breath, "I'm not so sure..."

When they neared a flat of loose sand, Charlie slowed his horse to a few paces behind the cart and tightened the straps holding his sword and other gear to the saddle. With his things situated, Charlie took a deep breath. He looked back over his shoulder once more; it was just in time to see Franklin disappear over the last dune on the horizon.

"You ready?" Charlie whispered to Goliath. Then he spun him around and shouted, "Sorry, Mr. Rohmetall, I gotta go! I think Franklin may need me!"

"No, Ch-Ch-Charlie!" the metal man cried.

The great horse bolted ahead quicker than Charlie had anticipated, but he held on and urged Goliath to go faster. Ringo leapt from the cart and followed close behind, and they ran as fast as they could and didn't stop until Charlie was convinced that they were far enough away from Rohmetall and his instructions to go north.

"We'll take this break, but we better keep moving," Charlie said, slowing Goliath to a trot. They could still see Rohmetall in the distance. He was struggling to turn the cart in the sand. "I'd hate for Franklin's tracks to get covered in another storm."

Charlie and Ringo reached the spot where their party had split just as the wind started to pick up, and then went west, following Franklin's trail. At sunset, Charlie could see Franklin cresting the rolling dunes before them, so he spurred Goliath faster, worried they would lose the Monster in the night. They continued, but as they moved forward, the tracks abruptly turned, heading into a trough between two dunes.

"Ringo," Charlie whispered, calling him to his side. "Come on. Just a bit farther and we'll show ourselves."

They rode as the trough narrowed until Ringo let out a low, guttural growl. Charlie pulled back on Goliath's reins, stopping to look up at the dunes above him.

"What is it? You hear—"

Charlie did not finish his sentence. All of a sudden a huge rotting hand appeared from the dark—it covered his mouth and then pulled him down from the horse. Charlie landed in the sand at the base of the dune, with Franklin hunched down at the horse's feet over him.

"What did I say, Charlie?" Franklin whispered, barely able to control his anger.

"I know," Charlie mumbled, wrestling himself free from behind Franklin's hand with a quick turn of his head. "Stay with the cart, but how could you just leave me? I want to help. You'll need my help, won't you?"

"*Quiet.* You almost rode on top of them," Franklin whispered more forcefully, his gaze shifting to a spot beyond the dunes.

"Who? The marauders?" Charlie whispered back.

"A small group of them, yes." Franklin made a clicking sound through his decayed teeth, and Faust appeared from the darkness. "We will discuss your insubordination later. For now you will stay here with the horses. Do not come over the dune until you hear me call."

Franklin grabbed Charlie roughly by the chin. "You listen to me this time, Charlie. For your own good, you understand? This is no game, boy."

Charlie nodded.

"Not until I call you," Franklin reminded him, handing him the horses' reins and heading off into the dunes.

Charlie sat crouched at the horses' feet with Ringo whimpering at his side. He saw the moon peeking over the dunes and thought that at the very least, they would be able to see better soon. Then he heard the first scream, which was followed by a roar and a shrieking yelp. Charlie tightened his hold on the reins and inched forward. He heard another scream and decided that despite his instructions, it couldn't hurt to climb the dune so that he was closer when Franklin called.

From the very top of the hill, Charlie could see a little camp below with a wagon off in the shadows of a fire. And in the midst of the commotion, there was Franklin, wrestling a large black werewolf to the ground. There were already two ogres lying in the sand, moaning, and a hooded man running up the dune toward Charlie.

Charlie pulled his sword from its sheath on the saddle and ducked down below the ridge. When he heard the man approach, he leapt out, brandishing the blade.

Caught by surprise, the man screamed and fell back down the hill, rolling in Franklin's direction. Ringo took off after the man, catching the tattered ends of his coat in his jaws just as Franklin secured the werewolf in a headlock.

"You will transform now or this will be your last breath!" Franklin growled. "Do you hear me?"

The werewolf fought and clawed but could not break free, so he gave in, slowly changing back to his human form. Franklin stood and threw the half-beast over near the fallen ogres.

"Charlie, come bring the rope," Franklin called, turning his attention to the hooded marauder at his feet. As Charlie pulled the horses over the ridge, Franklin reached down and took hold of the man by the collar of his coat.

"I should have known I hadn't seen the last of you!" the man cried as his hood fell back, revealing the sinister but familiar mark on his cheek. It was Lester Mortlock. "How in all this great desert!" he exclaimed.

"Your misdeeds leave a trail that is far too easy to track," Franklin said, tightening his grip. "Where's the girl? Where is the queen's daughter?"

"They're gone," Lester shrieked. "I don't have them. They were sold and taken farther west."

"*Sold?*" The Monster shook with anger.

"Ransomed, really, to Tok. He wants them as leverage, for the negotiations . . . Their tracks should be easy enough to follow, though." Lester cowered. "They have a day's ride on you. That's all I know, please, please!"

"There was a time when I would have ripped you to pieces and ended your miserable life right here. You are fortunate it is no longer that time," Franklin said, dropping Lester Mortlock in disgust. "Charlie, hand me the rope and put out that fire."

Franklin tied Lester and his cohorts back-to-back in an odd assortment of knots and set them in the wagon. Then he freed their horses and tied the one-eyed ogre to the front.

"You," Franklin said, grabbing hold of the ogre's jowls. "You keep that one eye of yours pointed that way, you hear me? I don't care what this fellow tells you. You understand?"

The ogre nodded.

"Now go."

The ogre stepped forward, pulling the wagon.

"Hold on, you can't send us back there!" Lester cried. "Not after what just happened—"

"I can't?" Franklin called back.

"You and your fire!" Lester screamed at the one-eyed ogre. "I'd bet he spotted us a mile away. I fall asleep for five minutes and all hell breaks loose!"

Charlie stood next to Franklin, and they watched the wagon as it inched away in the moonlight.

"Do you know? Do you know what they'll do to us?" Lester shouted. "Please, I beg you!"

Ignoring Lester's fading pleas, Franklin turned and suddenly grabbed Charlie by the shoulders.

"What did I tell you?"

He shook the boy and then lifted him off his feet so that they were eye-to-eye.

"I said to go with the cart, stay with Rohmetall. And what did you do?"

Charlie could feel Franklin's grip tighten as the Monster's glare deepened.

"You've put me in a bad spot. If I turn back with you, we lose more ground and maybe our only chance to save Abigail, let alone the mummified royalty. What do you have to say for yourself?" He shook the boy again, his anger building. "Out with it!"

"You're hurting me," Charlie gasped, barely able to breathe. He thought his arms might be crushed at any moment.

"What? Speak up!" the Monster roared.

"My arms, you're hurting me!" Charlie cried.

Franklin's eyes widened in horror. He immediately loosened his grip and lowered the boy gently to the ground.

"Charlie, I'm sorry," Franklin said, his voice barely a whisper. He reached out, but Charlie stepped back, clutching his sides. "I . . . I was trying to protect you . . ."

Franklin knelt down with a pained expression on his face.

"Did I . . . did I really hurt you?"

Charlie took a long moment before he answered. "No. I'm all right. But you scared me."

Franklin fell back to sit against the dune.

"I must control myself or I am no better than this scum we sent packing," he sighed.

Charlie rubbed his arms and looked down at his feet. "That's okay. I know I made you mad."

"It is no excuse," Franklin said softly. "I am truly sorry, Charlie. I will find it difficult to forgive myself."

"But I should have listened to you. I'm sorry too, Franklin. Sorry I called you a quitter, sorry I got you into this—"

"Into what?" Franklin interrupted. "This place? Our journey? You didn't get us into this. We all did."

Charlie sat down next to Franklin in the sand.

"And I am no quitter," the Monster said after a while. "Thanks to you, perhaps, as now we cannot turn back."

"What about Abigail and Zalika?" Charlie asked.

Franklin looked out at the night.

"The marauders have a healthy start on us, but we are fewer in number and without wagons, so let us hope we catch them soon. An opportunity to rescue the children will present itself. And this time—"

"I'll listen to you," Charlie said, finishing the sentence. "I will. I promise."

"And I," Franklin promised, throwing his arm around him, "I will listen to you too."

"Deal." Charlie smiled. He was glad to have his friend back.

They followed the marauders' tracks for the rest of the night, the freshness of the trail telling them that they were getting close. Near dawn the terrain quickly changed; the sand gave way to broken rock, and they rode up onto a low ridge that looked out over the endless salt flat below.

"They say this goes all the way to the Vast Inland Sea," Franklin said, taking a measurement with his sextant. "But not many dare to cross this wasteland. There are no wells, no water that we know of out here."

Thinking of Abigail and Zalika, they rode on, following the tracks, and the ridge dropped them down to the hard, cracked earth of the flat. Ringo seemed distressed and the horses were hesitant out on the salt flat, but Charlie and Franklin eased them along, stroking their manes and pushing them forward.

In the afternoon, when the sun was high, they came to a rise of loose, fragile stone that jutted out like a narrow finger across the scorched earth.

"A reef from another time," Franklin said, pulling the brass telescope from his saddlebag and scanning the horizon. "Look there. You see?" Franklin raised the telescope again, his gaze focused on a tiny shifting line—the only sign of movement in the distance. "It's them."

He handed Charlie the telescope.

Charlie adjusted the lens, trying to bring the marauders into view. "I don't see them. Oh wait, yes, I do. There they are!" Charlie exclaimed, giving the telescope back.

"Yes, there they are. Looks like they have the children tied up on horseback in those ridiculous sacks," Franklin said, refocusing the lens. "They're led by a rope, one sack on one horse, a second on the other, one for Abigail and one for the queen's daughter, I would reckon." Franklin adjusted the telescope again. "And maybe fortune is smiling upon us. Their party appears to be splitting."

Charlie shielded his eyes from the sun and could just barely make out their movement without the telescope. A group of horsemen were breaking off, turning south and leaving the main party.

"At least they're fewer in number now," Franklin said. "With these witches about, it's only a matter of time before they spot us from the air, so this may be our only chance."

Franklin looked back at the boy.

"You and the dog, you'll have to join me now, Charlie. I see no other way. This place alone is dangerous. I cannot leave you here," Franklin said, his eyes shifting back to the marauders in the distance. "You ready?"

"I'll be all right." Charlie took a deep breath and nodded firmly.

They dropped down the loose rock, back to the dried mud of the flat, and rode up on the caravan's flank with the sun at their back and purposely in the marauders' eyes. When they were within a few hundred yards, Franklin slowed the horses to a trot.

"I will ride straight into their midst—"

"Franklin, you can't. There are too many," Charlie pleaded.

Franklin eyed the line before them and tightened the cinches on his saddle. "Half of them are cowards. They will turn and run as soon as they see me coming. A quarter will hold their ground until I am upon them and then do the same."

"But, Franklin, that still leaves the rest of them . . ."

"Yes, the real monsters. They won't be able to resist taking a crack at an old Ranger. They will charge, and when they do, they will meet the aberration that gave them their name." Franklin pulled loose the ties on the battle-ax and hefted the heavy weapon in his hand. "Put the dog across the pommel of your saddle and ride with me—single file. We will angle toward their rear, cutting off this open space and the captives from the front of the line. Then I'll free the rope on the string of horses, and you will lead them out here onto the flat. If we are hassled, keep riding. I'll take on whoever dares to try to stop us. You understand?"

"I understand," Charlie said, following Franklin's example and tightening his rigging.

"Now, there are ransoms involved, so they won't give up easily. But I will be watching. You just keep moving. Except for the werewolves and the witches, the rest will have trouble catching Goliath." Franklin turned and almost grinned. "As for the witches and werewolves, Charlie, leave them to me."

Franklin rode ahead at a slow clip, and Charlie, with Ringo balanced on his pommel, followed behind. The marauders in front of them continued to ride without breaking or turning back, so Charlie wondered if they had been seen. Almost in answer, a witch floated up from the marauders' line and flew straight at them just a few feet above the ground. They had been spotted.

Franklin spurred his horse faster, glancing at Charlie and calling back to him. "Here we go!" Franklin shouted. "Hold on, and stay with me!"

Franklin pushed forward, swinging his crossbow from his

back and bringing it up to his shoulder. The witch was almost upon them when Franklin's arrow struck its target. She was still for just a moment before tumbling off the broom, hitting the dried lakebed below, and disappearing in a cloud of dust. A second witch dropped in from somewhere above, but Franklin already had her in his sights. When he shot this time, though, the witch veered to the side and the arrow flew wide. The Monster slung the crossbow back across his shoulder and lifted the heavy battle-ax. The witch swooped down again, and Franklin stood in his stirrups to meet her, swinging the heavy ax down as she passed. The blow splintered the broomstick, sending its cackling pilot head over heels to join the other witch sprawled out on the desert behind them.

When the second witch fell, the line of marauders broke apart, spreading out as Franklin rode straight toward them. He let out a roar, and half of them, as he had said before, simply turned and ran. But Franklin only rode faster.

"Now, Charlie! Now!" Franklin shouted, leading his horse toward the back of the broken line and the captives.

Charlie and Franklin rode straight into the chaos of the scrambling marauders, meeting little resistance amid the confusion. When they reached the string of horses, Franklin caught hold of the lead rope that tied them together and cut it from the wagon. He handed the loose end to Charlie, and then spun around in his saddle to bring his heavy ax down on a hobgoblin who was biting at Goliath's and Faust's legs.

"Run, Charlie, run! Don't look back! You keep riding. I will catch up to you," Franklin shouted. "I promise!"

Charlie gripped the rope and pulled, but the second horse stood scared and refused to move. Franklin retrieved his ax from the hobgoblin and slapped the broad side of it across the flank of the horse, making him jump forward to follow Charlie.

"Go, Charlie, go!"

He held the rope as tight as he could, and Goliath ran, the other two horses struggling to keep up. As they broke clear of the turmoil, Charlie looked back despite what Franklin told him. The Monster was holding his line, taking on any creature that dared to try to follow. Then Charlie heard that familiar roar again, the earth-shattering cry that seemed to say, *I am ready to die out here today. Are you?* But it did not frighten Charlie as it had in the past, perhaps because of the other howls and screams that could be heard, or because Charlie knew that no matter how angry he was with him, Franklin would still be there to protect him.

Charlie let Ringo drop down to run beside them, and he rode across the flat as fast as he could, pulling the horses along with him. He couldn't tell how far he had ridden, but reminded himself to keep going until he could no longer see the cloud of dust that was Franklin and the mob on the horizon behind them. Twice he glanced back to see Franklin break from the battle and try to join them, but both times he had to stop to push back marauders who had caught up to him. The next time he looked back, Charlie had lost sight of him completely.

Finally, he slowed the horses and jumped down from his saddle. Ringo immediately lay down, settling into the shade provided by the standing horses, and looked up at him.

"What?" Charlie said as he untied his sword from the pommel and moved over to the first horse and his canvas cargo. "No water yet. Better to see what Franklin thinks when he rejoins us."

"Charlie?" Despite the muffled sound, he recognized Zalika's voice from inside the canvas. "Charlie! Is that you?"

He quickly cut the rope that held the large sack and pulled it loose. Zalika, her bandages a mess, struggled free as Charlie helped her down from the horse.

"Charlie!" she cried, throwing her arms around him. "Oh, it was dreadful, just dreadful! We kept riding and riding. I thought we would never stop . . ."

Charlie rushed toward the other horse.

"I thank you, my mother will thank you," Zalika went on with relief. "She will reward you handsomely."

Charlie reached up to cut loose Abigail's sack, but something wasn't right. It felt different, lumpy. He yanked at the rope, and the sack slipped forward and fell. It landed with a thud, throwing itself open, and they were both surprised by the potatoes that rolled out onto the hard, parched earth.

Charlie kicked at the potatoes with an alarmed look on his face.

"Where's Abigail?" Zalika asked.

"I don't know," Charlie said. "We saw the horses with the sacks. We figured one was you and the other was Abigail."

"But it is not."

"I can see that." Charlie kicked another potato. "We should go back. We have to tell Franklin before we get farther apart."

"Go back… for that common girl?" Zalika exclaimed, barely able to conceal her shock beneath her loose wrappings.

"Yes." Charlie swung back onto Goliath's back. "That's what I'm doing."

"But it's not safe! We should wait here for the Monster," Zalika pleaded.

"Franklin," Charlie said. "He likes to be called Franklin. And he needs to know about Abigail."

"But if we waited…"

Ignoring her protests, Charlie turned Goliath back to where he had left Franklin in the melee. With little choice but to follow, Zalika jumped onto the marauders' horse, and with Ringo running behind, they rode with the third horse trailing them for the better part of an hour before Charlie thought he saw the speck of a lone rider.

"I'll go ahead. Any sign of trouble, run back the way we came," Charlie said. "Franklin said if you ride that way, you'll eventually hit the water."

As Charlie rode on, he kept his hand on the hilt of his sword until it was clear that this hulking rider was Franklin.

"Charlie!" Franklin called as he rode up. He was covered in dirt, and some of his seams had come undone, but he appeared mostly intact. And there, sitting on the pommel in front of him, was Abigail Rose. "Looks like we forgot something, eh? Almost missed her on my second pass. They had her in a wagon with their other contraband."

"Hello, Charlie," Abigail said, again with little emotion, even with the ordeal they had just been through.

"Ha, and I see you have recovered the queen's daughter," Franklin continued as Zalika rode up to meet them.

"And a sack of potatoes . . . ," Charlie said.

"Potatoes? Well, at least we have something to eat," Franklin said, turning his horse to look back behind them. "No time for celebrations, though. We have to keep moving. They will regroup and follow soon enough. More than likely joined by that party that left them earlier."

"I'm sorry, Franklin."

"Sorry? Sorry for what?"

"Well, I didn't keep riding, and I missed Abigail . . ."

"Nonsense, Abigail is here," Franklin said, "and you have rescued the queen's daughter. If Tok had gotten ahold of her, we would've had an all-out war on our hands." Franklin playfully hit Charlie in the shoulder, practically knocking him off Goliath's back. "Your bravery might have saved hundreds, if not thousands, of lives."

"You think so?" Charlie said.

"Without a doubt." Franklin smiled at him and rode on at a trot. "But come now. We are not out of this yet."

Zalika rode after Franklin and Abigail, but Charlie sat on his horse looking back across the flat. *The marauders will follow,* he thought, *but let them.* He and Franklin could handle it. They beat them once, they could do it again. And now that they had Abigail and Zalika, they could get back to finding Billy.

chapter 34

The Salt Flat

$\mathcal{F}$OR THE NEXT two days, they rode hard across the salt flat, trying to avoid the heat of the desert sun by traveling at night. At dawn on their third day, Franklin thought he saw movement on the horizon behind them, so they pushed on even as the sun rose high overhead. Ringo ran out in front of them as the day started, but as the miles wore on, he trailed behind, sometimes by several hundred yards, his tongue dangling almost to the ground. Franklin would circle back and place him on the pommel in front of Abigail to rest, then, an hour or so later, he'd set the dog back down, and the whole cycle would start again. By the end of that same day, they had run out of water, so Franklin took them off course to the north to search.

After a while, they came upon a shallow indentation, a dried puddle, really. Franklin suggested the area might have been a small oasis at one time and dropped down from his horse to examine the ground, which was covered in jagged cracks. He explained that when the surface water evaporated, large sections of parched clay had been pushed up in these platelike pieces.

"Look," Franklin said, removing several large sections, digging with his hands into the damp earth that was exposed beneath. Charlie marveled once again at the Monster's strength and the ferocity of his work—he soon had a hole about half his size cleared, and his arms were covered in wet, sticky mud. Charlie dropped off his horse to help but found that the Monster had already reached water. They watched as it seeped into the small pool that Franklin had made and drank all they could before filling their waterskins.

"We should rest here," Franklin said, surveying the surroundings and marking the area on his map. "Then we will take what water we can carry and continue. It's safe to assume these marauders are suffering from the same problems that we have encountered, but it would be wise to keep moving."

Exhausted as they were, Charlie, Zalika, and Abigail agreed. They gathered their strength and pushed on, though Ringo was now content to ride on Charlie's pommel exclusively.

Around noon the next day, Charlie noticed that Franklin was looking behind them more often. There were clouds of dust on the horizon in that direction, and as the day wore on, they seemed to be moving closer. Late that afternoon, Franklin stopped and pulled out his telescope.

"It is what I have feared. They are tracking us and they have hounds with them. They will find us, sooner or later, no use pretending otherwise."

"I don't understand," Abigail said. Her face was shadowed beneath her bonnet. "Why do they keep coming?"

"For me," Zalika replied. "I am afraid that I have brought these troubles down upon you all."

"Nonsense," Franklin said. "We are all in this together. Now, not another word about that. Besides, I won't allow you all the credit. I am sure that there are a few who'll remember me as well."

The Monster looked to the north through the telescope.

"There are rock formations ahead, looks like the flat craters a bit, even. Maybe the end of this torture is near. If we can make it there, perhaps we can fortify ourselves somehow, or hide among the stone."

They rode toward the rocks at a steady pace. They were an odd collection of sandstone spires with windblown alcoves; some stood jutting up from the crater's floor while others lay broken where they had fallen.

"We have to time this. If we take the horses out too fast they will never make it. It's still too far, you understand, Charlie? They'll wear out," Franklin said, glancing back behind them with greater frequency. "So when I tell you, not before, you run. Make it to that crease, there. Hide up in the rocks with Zalika and Abigail. You hear me?"

"Yes, I hear you." Charlie had to shout over the commotion of the horses. He paused and took a deep breath. "Franklin . . ."

"What is it, boy?"

"I'm pretty scared," Charlie admitted.

"There's no time for that now," the Monster said. "All we can do is ride."

So they rode on, and near dark Charlie noticed that Franklin looked uneasy. It was the hounds. The first had appeared in packs, and in no time the mongrels that raced forward were almost even with them on both flanks—with more trailing directly behind. The hounds were running with large wolves, rabid-looking hyenas, and bulldogs, some with two heads that bit and snarled at each other as they ran.

Franklin eyed their progress warily; swinging his crossbow across his shoulder, he took the horses to a gallop. But the rabid pack followed, increasing their pace. Then the dogs were gaining. Franklin spurred Faust forward as the pack closed in, and the other horses started to run with his pace.

"Now, Charlie, now!" Franklin cried, aiming the crossbow at the closest beast. "Run! Get to the rocks!"

It was a race. Charlie put his head down and rode Goliath hard, but the hounds were close behind, forcing them into a shallow alcove at the base of the rock formation. Franklin drove the horses to a narrow crevice and pulled them around so they faced the small opening.

"May be able to defend this," he said as he surveyed their position, though Charlie could sense the hesitation in his voice.

"They're almost here!" Zalika screamed.

Franklin pointed to the slick rock above them. "Charlie, there, the ledge . . ."

"I see it!" Charlie shouted as loud as he could.

"Climb up, all of you, and stay there," Franklin ordered. Then he looked Charlie in the eye. "Promise me, boy. You're no good to me down here."

Charlie nodded as Franklin lifted Abigail from the front of his saddle and set her on the ledge. "Take the dog, Abigail, and hold him," he said, handing Ringo to her before helping Zalika up as well. "Climb, and then climb higher!"

Franklin caught hold of Goliath's reins.

"Go on, Charlie, you too, now. Just leave the horses. Unfortunately, they have seen this before—" Franklin began, but he was cut short as a large werewolf leapt at him. He managed to knock the first wolf back just as another took its place, pouncing onto Faust and ripping into his flesh. The horse spun wildly and fell, but Franklin leapt out of the saddle and, in a single fluid motion, brought his heavy battle-ax down on the creature. Still it was no use; the moment he struck down that wolf, two more mongrels were already upon him, snapping at the Monster and sinking their teeth into Faust.

"Franklin!" Charlie screamed. Ignoring his promise, he pulled his sword and turned Goliath away from the rock to face the snarling beasts.

"No, Charlie!" Franklin cried, but the boy rode forward in a blind rage, slashing down at the dogs that now surrounded them. Screaming and shouting, Charlie hacked at the fiends, but it did little good as more and more mongrels joined the pack from the darkness of the desert.

In the chaos, Franklin fought his way to Charlie and forced

him down from Goliath, who had already been set upon by the wolves.

"No, Charlie. You will listen to me," Franklin said, grabbing the boy by the shoulders. "You promised. Please, you must go."

With tears in his eyes, Charlie shook his head. He tried to throw his arms around Franklin's sutured neck, but the Monster pushed him up to the ledge.

"Climb, Charlie, climb!" Franklin ordered, just as the wolves came at him again.

Charlie watched as the beasts pulled Franklin to the ground below. Looking out into the darkness, he could see the marauders coming closer, riding forward with more hellhounds at their feet and torches in their hands.

Franklin saw them too, but holding his ground, he stood in front of the remaining horses with his back to the rock wall. The Monster let out a furious roar, and with the battle-ax in one hand and the sword in the other, he fought off the horde as best he could.

"Franklin!" Charlie cried, feeling helpless.

Franklin swung his battle-ax and fought the pack back, but as the last of the rabid dogs lay dead at his feet, the marauders arrived and they attacked the Monster in a fury of claws and fangs, heavy clubs and blades. Franklin punished the ones in the front, but there were too many. As he drove a hobgoblin back on one side, an ogre would bring down a heavy fist from his front. And witches flew in and out from the darkness, dropping low to pull at Franklin's hair or to hit him with their clubs.

"Charlie . . ." A cold hand touched his shoulder. "Franklin told us to climb," Abigail said softly, pulling Charlie up. Turning away, Charlie felt himself stand and follow her. They climbed until they found Zalika huddled with Ringo in a crevice of rock.

"I thought they had you!" Zalika bawled, forcing Charlie into an embrace.

Over her shoulder, Charlie looked down from the ledge and could see that Franklin was hurt. An arrow stuck out from his back, and one of his wrists was dangling from its torn stitching, leaving the bone exposed. But Franklin fought on and no matter what they tried, the marauders could not bring down the Monster of all Monsters.

Charlie stepped forward, but Abigail and Zalika held him back.

"They're killing him," he cried. "We have to do something!"

"What are you going to do?" Zalika yelled, tears soaking the wrappings around her eyes. "You are just a boy."

"But look what they're doing. They're ripping him to pieces!"

Charlie stood up from their hiding place on the ledge. *No, he thought. It can't end like this.* Franklin deserved more. Not to die out here all alone, not after all they had been through. And it wasn't even his fault. Charlie knew that he was the one who had gotten Franklin into this . . . and the Prime Minister. Charlie's mind was racing . . . *The Prime Minister* . . . He looked down at the hilt of the sword . . . *The Vampire* . . .

Charlie took a deep breath and held the sword out in front of him. The firelight of the marauders' torches below shone bright off its blade.

"Stop!" Charlie shouted. Tears stung the corners of his eyes.

"Charlie, what are you doing? They will see us!" Zalika cried, but Charlie continued.

"Stop, I said! We travel under the protection of the Prime Minister!" Charlie shouted as loud as he could. A few of the marauders looked up at him while the rest continued their attack on Franklin and the horses.

Charlie held the sword high over his head and brought the blade down against the rock with a heavy clang.

"I—SAID—STOP!"

Sparks shot out when the metal hit the stone, and the sound, which was louder than Charlie expected, echoed against the rock, reverberating down into the mayhem.

Stunned, the mob, if only for a moment, did as they were told and stopped.

"We travel under the protection of the Prime Minister!" Charlie shouted again, this time gasping for breath.

The mob burst out in laughter mocking him, and a witch, torch in hand, flew up toward the ledge. Charlie raised the blade, readying himself for an attack.

"Aye, it's the boy, the Monster's boy," the witch cackled. "And the princess, the queen Khensa Tuya's child!"

"No, Charlie! Climb!" Franklin growled from below.

The witch lifted her torch to the ledge, illuminating the

children. The mob continued to mock them, their calls and screams growing into shrieks of laughter.

"We travel under the protection of the Prime Minister!" Charlie shouted again with more conviction. He pulled the documents from his coat. "I have papers! Signed papers! Papers with the Prime Minister's official seal!"

"Ha!" the witch cackled.

She swooped down and snatched the documents from Charlie's hand.

"He has papers!" the witch screamed.

"He has papers!" the mob roared back.

The witch flew down and dropped the papers to a tall, cloaked figure who sat on his horse near the front of the mob. A mummified hand reached out from the long robe and caught the roll.

"The Prime Minister's seal!" the figure scoffed. "His powers granted from a fraudulent Council!"

The crowd cheered enthusiastically as the figure stepped his horse forward, holding the papers over his head.

"I am Tok and these are my lands!" he roared. "The lands that, with the Council's blessing, Nuit Khensa Tuya stole! Your papers are worthless here in the desert! As worthless as the government that gave away what rightfully belongs to me!"

Charlie could barely see Franklin through the mob below, but he could tell that he had dropped his heavy ax and was having trouble holding his sword out to keep the circle of beasts at bay. A troll and a goblin skirted around him and were already climbing the smooth stone toward their ledge. They did not have much longer.

"They are papers of safe transit!" Charlie shouted.

"Worthless!" Tok hissed. "I do not honor the Council, nor their empty words and promises!" The marauders jeered and howled their approval as Tok spun his horse in a triumphant circle.

"Kill them!" he ordered with a wave of his arm. "Kill all of them!"

"No!" Charlie screamed as the beasts converged again on Franklin. He tried to climb down, but Zalika and Abigail pulled him back.

"Wait, Charlie," Abigail said, her voice just above a whisper. "Look . . ."

Flapping its wings out in the distance, there appeared to be a single bird, just one, a black bird with white markings. Then there were two, then three, four, five, until soon there were hundreds and the sky was covered in a dark cloud of them, fluid almost as they swept down just over the marauders' heads.

"They're magpies!" Zalika shouted.

The flock descended upon the mob, beating the hideous creatures back with their wings and sharp beaks until the marauders were forced to stoop, kneeling on the ground with their arms raised in defense. Then, just like that, the flock swirled into a whirling vortex, and with a deafening screech that sounded like an explosion, the magpies were gone.

As an eerie hush fell over the stupefied crowd, all the

marauders were now focused on a single figure draped in a long, hooded cape who walked casually through their midst, humming the final verses of an old nursery rhyme.

> *"Eight for a wish,*
> *Nine for a kiss,*
> *Ten a surprise you should not miss,*
> *Eleven for health,*
> *Twelve for wealth,*
> *Thirteen beware it's the devil himself . . ."*

The figure paused to pull back the hood of his cape. It was the Prime Minister, and never had Charlie been so happy to see someone so dead.

"The boy speaks the truth," the Prime Minister said, dropping his lyrical tone. "He does have my safe conduct. And therefore you all have borne your trespasses against me."

The Prime Minister passed Tok and, without even looking at him, plucked the papers from his hand.

"*Trespassessss,*" the Prime Minister continued, "that I do not take lightly."

"Who are you to dictate what goes on out here?" Tok shouted. "Out here, a place you have forgotten, a place that even your maps label a wasteland?"

"Who am I?" the Prime Minister asked. "Shall I remind you?" The Prime Minister turned back to the mob, pulling his long cloak around him. *"Shall I remind all of you?"*

Tok stepped his horse back and lowered his head. The rest of the marauders followed, giving the Prime Minister a wide path.

"Is this the only rule you know? *Fear?*" the Prime Minister yelled at the crowd with a flourish of his cape.

The marauders edged farther away from the Prime Minister, averting their eyes from his icy gaze.

"I pity you," the Prime Minister said. "Your only answer is violence. After all that *we* have suffered . . . this your response . . . *pathetic.*"

The crowd shuddered, cowering in shame.

"Disgraceful." The Prime Minister shook his head. "Make no mistake, *we will* deal *with* your lack of civility at a later date, as I have more pressing matters to attend to. *You,*" he said, his stare fixed on Tok. "You *will* leave. And you *will* leave now. You *will* give thanks to *w*homever you give thanks to and you *will* remember the kindness I have shown you . . ." The Prime Minister turned back to the mob. *"Shown all of you!"*

"This is not right!" Tok cried. "It is not fair what you and your government have done here!"

"Then it is a matter to be brought up before the Council," the Prime Minister said. "As their elected representative, I will see to it personally that your grievances are heard, but I promise you—*all of you*—it *will* not be settled here, not now, *with* claw, club, nor blade." The Prime Minister smiled, exposing his long white fangs. "This, I guarantee."

"Then we will speak again," Tok said.

"Of that much I am sure," the Prime Minister answered. "Do *we* have an understanding?"

The marauders looked to Tok, who answered by bowing low and swinging his horse around to retreat.

"Now. Be gone with you, all of you, before I lose my patience," the Prime Minister snapped.

"There are others who will hear of this, and you know of whom I speak," Tok replied coolly as he rode past the Prime Minister. "Those who do not fear your ravenous kind."

The Prime Minister stood completely still, unfazed by Tok's words.

"And to you," Tok added, his glare turning back to Franklin. "This is not over, Monster! Do you hear me? If you make it through this night, we will also see each other again. And next time, your beloved Prime Minister may not be there to protect you!"

Spurring his horse forward, Tok let out a bloodcurdling screech and rode off into the night. The rest of the marauders gathered their wounded and followed, disappearing into the darkness as quickly as they had come.

The Prime Minister watched as they left, then turned and walked toward the rock formations and Franklin. "Now, what have you gotten yourself into, my fine friend?"

"Friend? Friend indeed," Franklin said. His voice was cracked and weak. He dropped his sword and fell back against the rock.

"Come now, what kind of talk is that?" The Prime Minister knelt down beside him to survey the damage.

"That was quite the entrance," Franklin gasped. "Tok's rabble seemed impressed."

Charlie dropped down from the ledge and landed in the sand, rushing over to Franklin's side.

"Franklin...," he said, kneeling next to the Prime Minister.

"Charlie." Franklin coughed, barely able to hold his head up. He struggled to pull the knotted rope that he prayed with from his coat. "Abigail and Zalika, are they safe?"

"Yes, they're safe. See, here they are," Charlie said, pointing over to where Abigail stood at the base of the rock, helping Zalika down. Ringo whimpered nervously at their feet.

"Ah, good... good. Well done, Charlie, well done," Franklin said.

"But I didn't do anything," Charlie said, his words catching in his throat.

"Sure you did, boy, sure you did." The Monster's voice now barely a whisper. "And the horses... how are the horses?"

Charlie's heart sank. Without looking over, he knew that Faust, Franklin's big black Clydesdale, was dead. Goliath and the horses they had taken from the marauders were pinned back against the rock. Wild-eyed, they stamped in place nervously, some cut and still bleeding, but thanks to Franklin they had survived.

Charlie gestured to the other horses first. "And where is Faust?" Franklin tried to sit up, but dropped back against the stone when he saw his horse lying still where he had fallen.

"Such a magnificent creature," he said with a gasp. Then his head rolled back, and he let out a long, labored breath.

"Franklin," Charlie said. But the Monster didn't move. His breathing was faint.

"Come now. There is work to do." The Prime Minister put his arm around Charlie. "And we must work fast."

The Prime Minister instructed Charlie to get the sewing kit from Franklin's saddle. With some difficulty, they managed to move the Monster to a flat stone, laying him out with a saddle blanket rolled under his head. They relit some of the marauders' discarded torches, and Charlie watched as the Prime Minister, assisted by Zalika, went about stitching and repairing Franklin's torn and ripped flesh. They used Zalika's blue potion to mummify what they could, sewing up his other joints by following the jagged edges of his seams. They continued to work as a storm with thunder and lightning blew in; the rain that followed fell in large droplets, washing the blood from Franklin's wounds. Near dawn, the rain moved on, and the Prime Minister and Zalika wrapped Franklin's remaining cuts with strips of her borrowed linen, and then covered him with a tattered blanket.

"Now we wait. Unlike mine, his blood will cherish the sun," the Prime Minister said, looking out at what remained of the night. "We will see what tomorrow brings, but I think you will be surprised as to what a day of rest will do. His creator had the foresight to inlay remarkable properties of regeneration."

Charlie nodded, unable to take his eyes away from Franklin.

The Prime Minister stood, gesturing to the approaching dawn. "After I see to the horses, I will find a cave up above. You will not be bothered, I promise, and I will rejoin you at sunset."

He turned to the rocks. "Keep watch over him. If he regains consciousness, see that he rests."

Charlie looked up to watch the Prime Minister go, then shoved his plastic fangs into his mouth and went back to sit with the Monster. With Ringo curled up in the sand at his feet, he bit down on the fangs and held his picture with Billy like a talisman while he waited.

chapter 35

The Monster of All Monsters

*A*T DAWN THE sun rose, casting odd shadows on the aftermath of the attack. Broken spears and turned carts dotted the landscape, and vultures descended to see what the marauders had left in their hasty retreat. Charlie watched the Monster closely, but throughout the long morning his breathing was still faint. The only improvement was that his fingers would twitch from time to time. As the day wore on and the sun rose higher in the sky, Zalika urged Charlie to join them in the shade, where they could still watch over Franklin yet were shielded from the harshness of the desert. But Charlie refused. With Ringo at his feet, he continued to sit at the Monster's side, sometimes staring at his picture of Billy for hours on end.

At midday, Abigail joined him with wreaths that she made from the wildflowers that grew in the pockets of rock. She strung them around the Monster's head as he slept. The sun dropped as the afternoon labored on, and Franklin seemed to be gaining strength. He groaned from time to time, and his breathing became more pronounced. The Prime Minister joined Charlie just after dusk and seemed pleased with Franklin's progress.

"He has taken what life the sun had to offer. More rest and you will see. I am sure he will be up and about before you know it."

The Prime Minister examined the horses' injuries and saw that they had also improved. He gathered the rest of Franklin's rigging from Faust and loaded the saddle into a wagon the marauders had left behind. They buried Faust as best they could in the loose rock and then built up the fire.

As night fell, howling cries rang with the wind that rose off the desert, but the Prime Minister assured them that they were safe. He saw that Abigail and Zalika had blankets so that they could sleep warmly around the fire, and then the Prime Minister sat with Charlie at the Monster's side and they talked late into the night. They spoke of the battle and of Franklin's strength and bravery. And they spoke of the impending war.

"I am afraid," the Prime Minister said, "that this is not the last we have seen of these troubles. I am not sure this Tok is willing to engage in talks that will truly lead to a lasting peace."

The vampire looked tired. The many years spent as Prime Minister seemed to weigh heavily on him.

"It saddens me, Charlie, that it has come to this, but I would think it was somewhat expected. This noble experiment that we have engaged in with your government may have been doomed from the beginning, and I fear that if we do not resolve these issues soon, all parties will lose patience."

"I don't understand," Charlie said. "If they lose patience . . ."

"Then, I would imagine, there will be war in this valley, an all-out war of the like we monsters have never seen," the Prime Minister said. "And if war does not resolve the conflict, then I am afraid that your government would have little choice but to terminate our agreement and dissolve the Council, essentially putting an end to all of this."

"Put an end to it? What does that mean?" Charlie asked, thinking about all the terrible stories that Old Joe had told him about war.

"I am afraid that without this place, well, where else would this modern world allow us to be?" The Prime Minister sighed. "The price we will end up paying for, to put it simply, *not getting along.*"

The conversation fell silent. It was all too much, Charlie thought. After everything that had happened, he couldn't bear the idea that a war could put an end to Monsterland, leaving Franklin, the Prime Minister, and all of this land's many inhabitants with nowhere to go. He tossed and turned that night, eventually falling into a troubled sleep. He dreamed of Billy. Franklin, Abigail, and Zalika were there too, but the dream was muddled and confused, fragmented with the recent horrors that clouded his memory.

When he woke, he was curled up in a saddle blanket in the sand at the base of the flat rock. It was morning, and Franklin and the Prime Minister were gone, Abigail's wreath of flowers lying where the Monster's head had been. Charlie stood and saw Abigail, Zalika, and Ringo still asleep around the fire.

He climbed into the odd rock formations and found Franklin on a ledge looking out over the salt flat. The Monster knelt in prayer facing the rising sun, his head hung low. Charlie was quiet as he approached, and then stood against the rock, watching Franklin, waiting for the Monster to raise his head.

"You're back," Charlie whispered after some time, unable to hold in the tears that had welled in his eyes.

"I am." Franklin coughed, standing slowly and wrapping the knotted piece of rope around his hand. "And you, no worse for wear?" he asked, turning to face Charlie.

"Just a few cuts and bruises—" Charlie started to say, but then he broke away from the rock and threw his arms around the Monster.

"Now, now," Franklin said awkwardly, patting the boy on the back. "What is all this?"

"I thought you were gone," Charlie cried. "Gone for good..."

"Come now, from the likes of them?" Franklin scoffed playfully. "Have you forgotten who I am?"

"You're Franklin," Charlie said, fighting back his tears. "You're Franklin Prometheus—the Monster of all Monsters..."

"That's right, and don't you forget it," Franklin replied with a half grin.

"There were so many, Franklin. It was horrible. They just kept coming," Charlie said.

"Ah, but it is over now and we are here. Are we not? Our

chins up, still standing," Franklin crouched down to Charlie's level.

"Yep," Charlie said, collecting himself. "Chins up, still standing."

"Then let us see to what is left of the horses. We are not to the safety of the coast yet, are we?"

"No, sir, not yet."

"And let's hope that the Ranger and young Dwight York did not encounter the troubles we found here. Not to mention what's ever become of Rohmetall, that overblown bucket of bolts." With that, Charlie and Franklin walked back to the camp to join the girls by the fire.

They packed their things, and Franklin thanked Abigail for her wreath of flowers.

"First thing I saw when I woke, a glorious sight indeed," he said. She gave him a nod and a small smile in return.

Charlie helped Franklin fasten a harness and tie the horses they liberated from the marauders to the scavenged wagon.

"You should ride in back," Charlie offered. "Continue to rest."

"Nonsense," Franklin said, pulling himself up onto Goliath. Compared to riding Faust, he seemed to dwarf the smaller Clydesdale. "You drive the wagon. I would think I have enough left in me to sit in a saddle for a ride to the coast."

Charlie smiled and climbed up on the bench seat with Abigail next to him. Zalika sat beside Franklin's saddle in the back of the wagon, letting her mummified legs dangle from the bed as they bounced back onto the salt flat heading north.

THEY RODE SLOWLY THROUGH THE MORNING, AND AFTER A few hours the flat broke and turned to rocky sand. Franklin led them at a slow trot with Ringo walking along in Goliath's shadow. From time to time, Franklin's head slumped forward, and he seemed to sleep most of the day as they rode.

They drank the last of their water at midday when they stopped to take a compass measurement, pulling their cloaks over their heads to shield them from the relentless sun. Gulls and other seabirds appeared in flocks on the sand, and soon they could sense moisture in the air, even though they still could not see the water.

They rode on and on, and as the sun hung low late that afternoon, Charlie could see a shimmer in the distance when he stood on the wagon's bench.

"Look, there it is!" Charlie shouted. "Could it be a mirage?"

"No. Not a mirage. Look at the horses," Franklin said with a laugh. "They can smell the water. We have made it, Charlie, we made it!"

The horses quickened their pace, and soon they reached the low dunes and the hard, packed sand of the beach. Franklin rode at a gallop and did not let up on the horse until Goliath was chest-deep in the small waves that lapped the shore. Franklin turned to Charlie, who followed close behind, letting the marauders' horses pull the wagon until they stood with the water up to their bellies. Charlie dropped the reins and fell off the seat to land with a splash at Goliath's feet.

"Well done, Charlie, well done," Franklin said, then slid

from Goliath's back and landed next to the boy with a giant splash of his own.

Abigail stayed seated on the wagon along with Zalika and Ringo. But Charlie and Franklin could not see them. They were floating on their backs, looking up at the last of the day's fading light, watching the sunset on the water at the end of the great salt flat.

—— *chapter 36* ——

Port

$\mathcal{T}$HAT NIGHT THEY slept on the beach, and in the morning they rode up the coast. Franklin was still weak and rode slumped in the saddle with his crossbow laid over his lap. At midday they passed the rusted hull of a steamship, then the wrecks of wooden schooners, cutters, and sloops—their skeletal ribs exposed and bleached white by the desert sun. They rode through the debris, following the coast until they came upon a cluster of low buildings made of salvaged wood, eroded metal, and stone. A jetty of heavy rock harbored a rotted dock that jutted out from the beach and stood over a few boats, some of them sunk. They made their way down the row of ramshackle buildings to an inn with a carved wooden sign that swung on rusty chains. The sign read, THE BANSHEE'S BOOT.

"Hello," Franklin called. He turned his horse and steadied his crossbow. "We seek lodging."

Ringo jumped down from the wagon, ran up the steps, and stood at the shuttered doors, whimpering.

"Aye, what is with all this shouting?"

The doors swung open, and a skeleton-thin man with one arm and a wooden leg stood in the doorway, propped up on a driftwood crutch. A black leather patch covered his right eye, and he wore a greasy captain's hat that was heavy with salt.

"What is it? Who goes there?" he called out.

"I am Franklin, Franklin Prometheus. We seek lodging."

"Franklin, what? Pro-me-tot-toes...heh...heh...Pro-me-tat-toes?... My, my, that's a mouthful." He chuckled to himself, adjusting the patch. "Ah, yes, Captain Alfred Dedmon at your service."

The captain stepped out on his crutch. His face was marred with burns and his skin was tight and pulled back around his good eye.

"I'm proprietor here and the harbormaster for what it's worth, only permanent resident, actually. Your man, the metal fellow, told me you'd be by. I've prepared rooms. Only rooms in Port, but well priced nonetheless," he said with a one-eyed wink. "I've got a chowder on if you're hungry."

"Good. We will see to the horses first, and thank you for your hospitality," Franklin said.

"He's round back with them other fellows, the metal man, that is...," the captain added.

They found Rohmetall, Dwight York, and the Ranger Ignacio Santos at the horse stables and were greeted enthusiastically. Rohmetall informed Franklin that he had secured lodging, and Zalika relayed their ordeal, noting Franklin and

Charlie's exceptional bravery, to which Ignacio Santos replied, "I would expect nothing less."

As it turned out, the Ranger and Dwight York had been in a skirmish themselves.

"We found some stragglers from the marauders you met, a nasty lot. They told us what happened out there on the flats . . ."

"After some persuasion, mind you," Ignacio added.

"We feared the worst," Dwight York continued, "so good to see you all still in one piece. All that being relative, I suppose."

"Yes, you should rest, big fellow," Ignacio said, slapping Franklin on the back. "We'll check those bandages and tuck you in for the night. Sounds like you've earned a good night's sleep."

They settled in around a wood-burning stove and ate the chowder offered by the captain. As usual, Abigail seemed indifferent to the meal, but Franklin ate several helpings after Ignacio and Zalika saw to his bandages. It could have just been the fire, or maybe the big pot of the captain's chowder that sat on top of the old potbelly stove—Charlie wasn't sure. But he knew he felt a certain warmth about him as he looked around the room. A shared sense of what they had accomplished and the feeling that they were finally safe, for the night at least, after what they had all somehow survived.

When the embers of the fire had begun to fade, Franklin excused himself and retired to his room. After Charlie ate all he could, he left Ringo with Dwight York and headed up the creaky wooden stairs too. Everything had happened so fast Charlie hadn't realized just how tired he was. He drifted off the moment his head hit the pillow and slept soundly that night with the window open and the wind whistling through the old ramshackle building. While he did not wake, Charlie did dream, but there were no deserts, or shadows or clouds of swirling birds. He did dream of Billy, though. He was there with him in the woods by Old Joe's house. They were running through the high trees in the sunshine, and in this dream, they were laughing.

In the morning, Charlie found Franklin with Abigail, Ringo, and Rohmetall on the beach. The Monster sat in the sand with his arms draped over his raised knees, and a short distance away, Abigail was untangling fish from the net that Rohmetall held in his steel hands.

"I never minded the fishing," Abigail said with a shrug.

Charlie sat down next to Franklin, and they watched as Abigail and Rohmetall moved farther down the beach to cast the net. Ringo ran next to them, unsuccessfully snapping at seagulls.

"There is something strange about this girl," Franklin said once they were out of earshot. "Have you noticed it too? How peaceful she seems here with us, and yet, she does not seem of this place."

Charlie dug the heels of his feet into the sand. "Back when we left the river, she told me she was just starting to remember, remember before that dock."

"And?"

"Well, she said she thought she was going somewhere, but

that was it. She wasn't sure where, or why even." Charlie looked up at Franklin. "She just wondered if anyone missed her, really."

Franklin let out a long, labored sigh. "There are far too many lost souls in this valley, but it feels wrong to see one so young," he said.

Charlie stared out at what lay on the far side of the water, thinking back to the night they met Draguta Flori. Rohmetall and the book had said something about the confusion of lost souls, those whose paths were unsettled or interrupted. Charlie turned the idea over in his mind as he watched Abigail wrestle with the nets.

"I was wondering from reading the encyclopedia," Charlie said, pointing past the small harbor, "if maybe she's from over there. Or headed there, you know. She's lost, kinda like Billy."

"Could be. Either way I am hoping that someone or something there may know. I would like to see her find a more permanent peace." The Monster lowered his head toward Charlie. "What about you? Are you ready for the next part of our journey?"

"I'm ready," Charlie said. There was no question in his mind, really. He was still afraid, no doubt about it, but he was learning here in Monsterland to live with his fears. And that no matter what he read in a book or how well he prepared and planned, the unknown would always be waiting for him. It was how he handled what scared him that mattered. He might be afraid of what lay ahead, of what they might encounter next, afraid for Franklin and Abigail even, but somehow he was still ready.

Charlie looked up at the Monster. "And you? Before the marauders, you said we were turning around—"

"As well we should for your safety. As you've seen, even I cannot always protect you here." Franklin dropped his arms and leaned back in the sand. His bones cracked as he moved, and Charlie could hear his skin pulling tight at his many seams. "But we have come this far, and now we have the girl to think of. Something tells me we should continue. Besides," Franklin added with a half laugh, "it seems we can't go back even when we try."

The Monster turned to the boy. "So, you are sure of yourself? Your mind is made up to continue, even after all you have seen?"

Charlie looked out over the water again. The sky was overcast and hung low on the horizon, although there were hints that the sun would eventually find its way through.

"Yes. I need to find Billy. He could be lost, like Abigail. And like you said, we've come this far."

"That we have, Charlie," Franklin said, slapping him on the back. "That we have."

—— *chapter 37* ——

The Lost Island

*F*RANKLIN AND CHARLIE returned to the inn and ate breakfast with the captain. Over steaming grits and black coffee, he told them of the strange goings-on across the water, and of the ships whose wrecks were strewn about this section of the shore.

"It's the maelstrom that haunts these waters," the captain explained more than once. "And the devils who live within . . ."

Earlier that morning, Dwight York had volunteered to take Zalika back to the Agrarian Plains. To avoid the wastelands, he had purchased a small boat from the captain, which he was already outfitting for the journey back along the coast. When Charlie went to say good-bye to Zalika, she kissed him on the cheek. He was surprised to find that beneath her wrappings, Zalika's lips felt warm and alive like his, unlike the touch of Abigail's cold hands.

"Oh, Charlie," she said, kissing his other cheek. "Who knows what we will find upon our return, but you are always welcome among the Mumiya. Safe travels, and please be careful."

"You too," Charlie said, waving good-bye.

"I have a feeling our paths will cross again," Dwight York called back as he pushed their boat away from the pier. "And good luck. I hope you find what you are looking for."

Once they were gone, Franklin arranged with the Captain for the use of a similar ship, a small sloop with a fixed sail, and it was decided that Rohmetall would stay at the port with Ringo and the horses until they returned. The Ranger asked to join them, and Franklin agreed. With all they had encountered, he said he would be grateful for another set of hands. They spent the rest of the day checking the rigging, stocking the ship with food and water, and loading Franklin's arsenal of weaponry.

"None of that'll do ya no good, not there, not where you're going," the captain said. And repeated his warning the next morning on the pier as Franklin was double-checking his crossbow, adding, "But don't take my word for it . . . You'll see."

Franklin thanked the captain for his hospitality and assured him they could handle themselves before shoving off. "We'll be fine," he said, helping Abigail into the boat. "Won't we, Charlie?"

"Sure will," Charlie replied, joining her in the bow. He was actually feeling good about the day.

The ship was sound, and once Franklin and Ignacio raised the sail, it cut across the water at a silent speed that surprised Charlie. They did not say much as they headed out over the water, distracted as they were by thoughts of what might be waiting for them on the other side. There were no signs of life out there other than the long, tubular body of a scaled serpent that snaked on the waves alongside them, swimming with the ship but never showing its head. It followed them for the better part of an hour, and then came so close to the ship that Abigail reached out and touched it.

They sailed on past sunset, and when the stars appeared in the night sky, Franklin took out his sextant and charted their progress on his rolls of maps. Charlie and Abigail slept under the stars in the bow with Franklin and Ignacio alternating time on the rudder.

In the morning, they spied land on the horizon, and by late afternoon they were sailing along a coast with thick forests that towered over narrow gravel beaches. The shore opened to a small cove, where Franklin dropped the sail, letting the boat drift in silence toward the pebbled shore.

Before Charlie even heard the crunch of the bow on the beach, Franklin had let go of the rudder and leapt overboard into the waist-deep water. He pulled the boat as far as it would go, securing it to the exposed roots of a towering redwood tree. Charlie jumped off into the clear, cold water and helped Abigail down from the bow. He tried to carry her the few paces to the shore, but she slid from his arms.

"Thank you, Charlie. I can make it all right," she said, running her fingers across the surface. "These waters are wonderful. They feel so alive."

As she waded to the shore, Charlie thought she looked peaceful here, almost as if she could continue walking into the deep wood to become part of the wilderness that lined the beach before them.

"Hey, how about a hand?" Ignacio asked, breaking Charlie's gaze. He splashed over to take the heavy cask of water that the Ranger was holding out from the bow.

"You be careful with yourself, now. I'm told these trees hold many secrets," he whispered to him.

Charlie helped Ignacio and Franklin unload the rest of the boat. When they were done, the Ranger headed down the beach in one direction and Franklin in the other, Charlie presumed, to scout the island for what the night could possibly have in store. Abigail returned from the trees with an armload of firewood, so Charlie decided to do the same. He wandered toward where he had last seen Franklin, picking up odd bits of driftwood and listening as the island settled in for the night.

Walking deeper into the woods, he soon found that the thick forest floor beneath the trees was just as tiresome as the sands of the beach behind him. He heard movement ahead and walked forward until he found himself at the edge of a large clearing. Franklin was there, kneeling in a circle of uneven trees, staring up at the sky as it turned with the setting sun from gold and red to purple, blue, and black. Charlie crept closer but stopped when he heard tree branches cracking at the other side of the glade. The crashing sounds were made by a large bear.

The bear looked like other bears that Charlie had seen in the mountains above Old Joe's orchard, except that its coat was a yellow-ivory color and there were snow-white patches around its eyes and haunches. The bear cautiously entered the clearing, smelling the air and pawing roughly at the ground. Franklin stood up to face the bear, which stood in kind, letting out a low growl that turned to a roar. Franklin did the same, but with a ferociousness that frightened Charlie, just as it had in the past. Then the Monster spread his arms, leaned his head back, and howled. The birds and other creatures of the trees went silent. The bear growled again, but then Franklin did something that surprised Charlie. With his arms still out, he knelt down to the ground once more and, unlike their first meeting with the queen of the Mumiya, he lowered his head and bowed low.

A deep, rumbling growl came from somewhere within the bear as it dropped down, and with all four paws on the ground, he lumbered a few steps closer to Franklin. Franklin remained where he was until the bear reached him. Then they both turned to look directly at Charlie.

Charlie stumbled back, tripped over a log, and dropped the armload of firewood that he had collected. Franklin had raised his head and now seemed to be in some kind of conversation with the bear. Charlie hurried back to the beach, wondering what he had just seen.

When he returned, Ignacio and Abigail were throwing chunks of driftwood onto a fire that roared in a pit they had dug in the pebbles and sand.

"Was that all the wood you could muster?" Abigail asked flatly when Charlie entered the ring of firelight empty-handed.

"I guess we know who'll be doing the dishes," Ignacio added, tossing a good-sized log onto the blaze.

A short while later, Franklin returned from the woods

carrying the quartered shank of a moose over his shoulder. "A gift," he said. "He's allowed us to stay." As they roasted the meat over the fire, Charlie asked the Monster about the bear and its odd coloring.

"They're known as Kermode," Franklin explained, "or the Spirit Bear."

"The Kermode?"

"Their kind is from over the mountains. I suppose there used to be others here, but they must have passed or moved on because this one is on its own now."

Franklin turned the moose shank on the spit, and Charlie wondered if the Monster felt a sort of kinship with the bear. After all, they were both alone in this valley.

When they were done eating, they gathered back around the fire and laid out their bedrolls. Abigail and Charlie settled in, but Franklin and Ignacio sat on stumps nearby and talked.

Charlie took out his photograph with Billy, propped it up against his pack, then drifted in and out of sleep, a whirlwind of images racing through his head. The rainy Halloween night in the graveyard and his first visit with the Prime Minister, his ride with Mrs. Winthrope, and meeting Franklin in the stables back at his treasured Charnel House. Though he shuddered at the thought of their first encounter with Lester Mortlock and his wayward band of ogres, he recalled that this was when they were introduced to Dwight York. He thought the same of the cold night in the rain when the trolls attacked, but found comfort thinking of their meeting the Ranger Ignacio Santos, and then was proud that he, Charlie, had freed Abigail Rose from the dock on the river. His thoughts turned back to Billy, his parents, and Old Joe. He hoped they were well and couldn't wait to tell them where he'd been and all about the many wonders that he had seen. When Charlie did dream that night, his dreams were filled with birds, dark birds with white markings. There were huge flocks of them, swirling in black clouds, screeching just above his head.

— *chapter 38* —

Time to Go

SOMETIME NEAR DAWN, Charlie woke. The fire had burned to coals. Franklin and Abigail were gone, but Ignacio still sat on a stump across from him, although he was now beside the Prime Minister.

When Charlie looked up, the Prime Minister turned to him and said, "It is almost time." There was a lone magpie perched on his shoulder, and Charlie could see the reflection of the dying embers in its eyes.

"Time?" Charlie asked, happy to see that the Prime Minister had rejoined them, but wary of the magpie.

"Time to go," he replied, "into the *woods*." Then he whispered something to the magpie. The bird took to the air and flew out over the water.

Charlie watched the bird grow smaller in the distance and spotted Franklin standing at the water's edge with Abigail. They were looking at the last of the moonlight that bounced off the gentle waves that lapped the shore, the Monster's silhouette dwarfing the small girl.

"We must hurry. The closer to morning, the more agitated the strigoii will become."

"What's a strigoii?" Charlie asked, reaching for his rucksack and the encyclopedia.

"Leave that," the Prime Minister instructed, turning away from the fire. "As you will soon see, the time for that book has passed."

Ignacio remained seated as Charlie stood and collected himself; he was poking the fire with a long stick.

"Aren't you coming?" Charlie asked, shoving his picture with Billy back in his pocket.

"Me? No, I have no business there," he said. "Not at this time. Good luck, though, Charlie. I sure hope you find what you're looking for."

Ignacio dropped his eyes back toward the fire, and Charlie went to join Franklin, Abigail, and the Prime Minister at the edge of the woods. To Charlie's surprise, the bear appeared as they left the beach and they followed his hulking figure deep into the forest. They walked for what seemed like hours, though there was little sign of the approaching dawn through the trees that towered overhead. They were quiet as they walked on, going farther and farther into the eerie thickness of these peculiar woods, and they continued until they came to a clearing littered with giant slabs of rock, which appeared to have fallen or were somehow thrown about. The stone relics were overgrown with tangled vines and mosses; in certain places, you could only see their outline beneath the matted vegetation.

"We are almost there," the Prime Minister announced, breaking the uneasy silence. "This is the threshold. Stay close to me. There is danger here at the edge. The strigoii will be there trying to intercept those who are going the wrong way."

"Strigoii?" Charlie whispered, realizing that his hands were trembling. "I don't get it. What's a strigoii?"

"They are the true dead," the Prime Minister explained. "They are my dead. My fate as this is what awaits me."

"They're dead? Dead vampires?" Charlie asked.

"Yes," Franklin said. "They are not to be trifled with."

Within moments, the strigoii appeared on the edges of the clearing, just as the Prime Minister had warned. They were small, almost naked creatures. The little hair they had stood up in red sprouts on the very tops of their heads or was clustered in tufts on the ridges of their long, tattered ears. Their ribs stuck out above their swollen bellies and they hung from the immense trees by long claws that glistened in the darkness. The strigoii watched them with a curious look in their eyes; they gnashed their fangs, which made a clicking sound that sent a shiver up Charlie's spine and he wondered if Billy had encountered these creatures here too.

"*Dorim să trecem*," the Prime Minister declared.

Charlie and Abigail looked at Franklin.

"He tells them we wish to pass," Franklin explained.

"*Noi nu dorim să treceți*," the creatures hissed in response.

"But they do not wish us to pass," Franklin continued.

"*Nu-ți cer permisiunea. Stiti cine sînt. Declar că voi trece,*" the Prime Minister said.

"He is telling them that he does not need their permission and that we will pass," Franklin continued.

"*Îți onorum viata lungă a dumneavoastră. Dacă trebuie să treceți, treceți. Dar să nu stați mult. Cât mai mult stați, cât mai mult rămâneți,*" the strigoii replied.

"They say that they honor his long life and that if he must pass, pass. But they warn us to not stay long. *The longer you stay here . . . the longer you must stay here . . .* or something to that effect. Hard to tell with this dialect," Franklin said, visibly frustrated with the task of translating.

"A bit rusty perhaps, but close enough," the Prime Minister said, turning his back to the creatures. "Now, let us continue before they change their minds."

Franklin took a moment to thank the bear, bowing low again before him in gratitude. The bear nodded in return and watched as they followed the Prime Minister deeper into the woods. The strigoii moved in behind them when they passed, and Charlie couldn't help but feel sad for the creatures. It was the wistful, longing look in their eyes.

They walked for some time more, and Charlie noticed that faint signs of dawn were finally beginning to make their way through the upper canopy of the trees. As the early-morning mist cleared, the ancient forest was soon bathed in a glorious light.

"These trees will protect me to a certain extent, but I

cannot stay long," the Prime Minister said, looking up to the inevitable sunrise. "Quite a sight to see, though ... quite a sight."

The Prime Minister continued, and the farther they walked, Charlie began to feel a warmth wash over him like he had never felt before. His head was clear and he was somehow lighter.

"We are almost there," the Prime Minister said, quickly ducking his head to avoid a heavy branch. Franklin, distracted by the change in the air, walked straight into it.

"I don't understand," Charlie mumbled, slipping on the moss of a wet log. He was disoriented and stammered to himself, suddenly uncertain of his words. "I-I-I don't ..."

Charlie took a deep breath, and then steadied himself by leaning against the trunk of a towering tree. He looked up at the branches above and instantly felt connected to this place; he did not know how, but he could see and smell and was somehow touching everything that was around him. With his hand resting on the great tree's thick bark, he understood its workings and could actually feel its long roots as though they were his own fingers digging deep into the rich soil of the layered forest floor. There were flowers among the trees with butterflies fluttering from their petals, and Charlie could feel what they felt as their tiny, humming bodies were energized by the rich plants' nectar.

"This way," the Prime Minister called back, and Charlie stumbled forward, following his voice, which now sounded distant.

With one look, Charlie could tell that Franklin was affected by this place as well. He walked ahead with his eyes turned to the sky and his arms outstretched so that he could touch every fern, tree trunk, and branch that he passed too.

"It is unbelievable," Franklin said. "All my studies, my books and travels, yet I have understood more in the last few steps..."

"You are feeling them. The spirits," the Prime Minister explained. "Understanding all that they ever knew."

"And you?" Franklin asked.

"I do not share your experience. And what of our Miss Rose...," he said, slowly turning to her.

"It is beautiful here." Abigail giggled. "And peaceful, if that's what you mean..."

"Yes, it is indeed that." The Prime Minister smiled, satisfied with her answer. "And, I might add, I think we have brought you to the right place."

Dust particles danced on the rays of sunshine, sparkling like flecks of gold as they fell all around.

"Do you see them, Charlie?" the Prime Minister asked.

"See them?"

Abigail turned in the light and laughed. "I see them. They're everywhere!"

The floating dust seemed to thicken.

"See who? Where?" Franklin said, turning about and looking in all directions, his actions almost mimicking Abigail's, though far less graceful.

"Ghosts... spirits... souls. Whatever you call them." The Prime Minister smiled again. He walked with his hands slightly raised, and there was an unfamiliar lightness about him. "They're always around us, leaving traces of what they once were and all they had hoped to be . . ."

The Prime Minister stopped and the dust seemed to cluster next to him, where Charlie could start to make out a human shape taking form.

"Not just beneath these trees, but everywhere, all the time. They are just easier to see here, where so many have gathered."

A mist emerged from the form almost like a hand and touched Charlie lightly on the shoulder. It was cold at first, like the Prime Minister or Abigail Rose, but then a warm, peaceful glow washed over him. It was so sudden that he lost his balance and stumbled sideways again before catching himself. When Charlie looked up, he could see the spirits, all of them, and he could feel them. Pushing his way through the crowds, the mist of their cold, clammy skin rubbed against him. He was cold and shivered as some forms passed, while others filled him with the same warmth that he had experienced with his hand on the tree. Some smiled peacefully, others wore maniacal grins, but most just carried a solemn look and went about their day.

"It is special here, so many," the Prime Minister continued. "As I said, this is a gathering place."

"What are they doing here?"

"Waiting, Charlie. Waiting to hear if their lives were worth living. Some do not stay for long. Others will remain here for years. You see, some lives are not appreciated until well after they are gone. Still others linger because they are not missed, or they are forgotten. Lives unlived, perhaps, but it is not for us to judge."

Even from his studies with the encyclopedia, Charlie had no idea that ghosts were everywhere, all the time. He couldn't shake the old notions he had of ghosts, that they looked like bedsheets and could appear or disappear, maybe walk through a wall. But now that he could see the souls of the dead here in Monsterland, he realized he could not have been more wrong. These ghosts, these spirits, were all over and moving about constantly. Turning, bumping, bouncing into one another, going about their business just like the rest of us, although much like the Mumiya, it wasn't entirely clear what their business was; it was almost like they were on a crowded train, but this mass of dead went on through the trees for miles, as far as Charlie could see. There were just so many. It was endless.

"It's fantastic," Abigail gasped. It was still hard to tell, but even she seemed impressed.

There was a sudden flash of light, and Charlie saw one of the spirits fade away into the mist.

"See," the Prime Minister pointed out. "That one has just moved on."

"And how do you know so much about this place?" Franklin asked, still looking around suspiciously.

"How do I . . . ? As I thought you *were* aware, my old friend, I am dead," the Prime Minister answered. "I have been to this place before but left quickly. Torn away from these trees, I *was* brought back, tied by tainted blood to this body and its cursed infection . . ."

With another flash of light, a second spirit moved on as the Prime Minister turned to Charlie.

"There are others who are trapped, Charlie. Still bound, chained, and cursed like I was to their past lives, and to the wreckage of those they left behind."

"That is enough," Franklin barked. "You will scare the boy." He shifted and his shoulders shook as the spirits brushed by him. "This is all too much. Too much for me, even ..."

"Ah, yes. No doubt some former owners of your parts have passed under these sacred trees," the Prime Minister said, raising an eyebrow in Franklin's direction.

"A strange presence is about me to be sure," Franklin grumbled. He was wrapping his knotted rope around his hand. "What of it?"

The Prime Minister glanced up at the Monster. "Leaves one to wonder if one day, when your earthly form has finally given out, if what remains of you might somehow find its way here ... or somewhere like it ..."

"Yes, makes one wonder," Franklin said softly.

Charlie looked up at him and into his dead black eyes. Again, he thought he saw something, faint but glowing, behind the darkness. But this time, in this place, it burned differently. This time, Charlie could sense Franklin's fear of this unknown.

"I thought you should see it," the Prime Minister said to Franklin. "I know my fate. We have seen the strigoii today with our own eyes, but your fate may still remain unwritten ..."

The Prime Minister slowly led them away from what

appeared to be the spirits' main thoroughfare and assembled them under a large tree.

"You should all wait here," the Prime Minister instructed. "As I said, there's no guarantee your Billy is here, Charlie. But word should get out that you are looking for someone. I need to find a crevice or cave before the sun gets much higher. But I will see you again soon."

They watched as the Prime Minister turned and left. He walked back the way they had come and the swirling spirits parted as he passed, as though even they were afraid to touch him.

—— *chapter 39* ——

Summers Should Last Forever

*O*NCE THE PRIME Minister was out of sight, Franklin, Charlie, and Abigail sat at the base of the large tree among the ferns. With Charlie and Abigail on either side, Franklin put his heavy arms around them, pulling them in close as they watched the ghosts mill about. From time to time, Charlie thought he had recognized someone from back home, someone from his side of the mountains. At first it was hard to tell, but then he was sure that he saw their old mailman, Mr. Jenkins, as well as a face he recognized from a black-and-white picture that hung in the hallway back at school: a Mrs. McGowan, whom the gym was supposedly named for. But when Charlie called out to them, the spirits ignored him, choosing instead to linger around Abigail, hovering briefly over her before drifting away. Abigail was enjoying the attention; she smiled as the spirits approached and seemed happier than she had been their entire journey.

As they sat there beneath the tree, Charlie lost track of time. Minutes could have been hours; it felt as though they had been there for days, and yet it also seemed like they had just arrived in this strange wood. He shoved his hands into his pockets and could feel the rough, bent, and folded edges of his photograph with Billy. Then he closed his eyes and leaned back against the trunk of the tree next to Franklin. He closed them to shut out all the faces that drifted past. As Franklin said, it was too much. There was only one person who Charlie really wanted to see, and that was Billy.

Even with his eyes closed, Charlie could still feel the warm glow of the woods around him. He thought about Billy, picturing the tree over the river where they played and the day Billy dove into the cold water. Charlie remembered diving in after him and swimming down to the bottom over and over again, looking for Billy until he felt like his eardrums were about to burst and his lungs were burning. He remembered how he ran, tears streaming down his face, back to the barn to get Old Joe and how, after shouting up to the house to call for help, they both ran back and dove into the water to continue the search. The sheriff and the fire department joined them. But they never found him. They never found Billy.

Charlie shivered at the thought, but as time passed, he felt the warmth wash over him again and let his mind wander to other things. To the good times he had with Billy that he had almost forgotten. He remembered when Billy first came to live with them, and how they played in the woods and camped in the mountains. He remembered long bike rides and fishing and the river, and summer afternoons spent in the sun in the branches of the great tree. Charlie and Billy would climb up together and sit among the leaves, catching their breath before they jumped in to swim, again and again.

The sun shone bright as he sifted through these memories, and when he opened his eyes, the shafts of sunlight that found their way through the trees held the forest in a similar light. Franklin and Abigail were asleep, with Abigail tucked in under the Monster's arm, and despite the stark contrast in their appearances, he thought they looked peaceful together. Charlie looked up at the trees. He noticed the dust in the air again, which continued to fall and swirl in the sunlight. As it danced this way and that, it seemed to cluster in a ball that was brighter than the rest. Charlie watched as it moved closer.

"What are you doing here?" a voice called out, and Charlie felt something kick his foot. The warm glow rushed over him again, even stronger than before, and he turned to see the swirl of dust forming what he could just make out as a human form—a boy maybe, just a few years older than Charlie.

"Billy?" Charlie asked, but the form moved closer to the other spirits, drifting deeper into the woods. Charlie quickly stood, trying to see where it went.

"Billy, it's me, Charlie!"

But the form only moved farther away, so Charlie ran after it, calling, "Wait for me, Billy, wait!"

Racing ahead, he quickly lost sight of it and soon found himself standing alone in a small clearing that was covered in ferns and wildflowers with trees that towered higher that he thought possible.

"Billy!" Charlie called again. "Billy!"

"Yes, Charlie . . . why are you shouting?"

It was Billy, but his voice sounded distant, haunted.

"And I'll say it again. What are you doing here? What are you all doing here?"

"It's because of me, Billy! We've been looking all over for you!" Charlie couldn't believe it. He glanced around frantically. "But where are you? I can't see you . . ."

The dust was settling down in front of Charlie, and he could slowly see Billy's form shining brightly underneath. Still long and lanky, his hair a mess, he looked the same as the day he left, the same way he looked in the picture.

"Billy, it is you!" Charlie exclaimed on the verge of tears.

"Yeah, it's me," Billy said, smiling. "And you? You're okay?"

"Yes, I'm okay . . ."

"I was scared when I saw you, Charlie. You look different from the rest of us, but I thought maybe—"

"No. I'm not here the way you are," Charlie said, barely able to contain himself. "We came a different way, Billy. You won't believe where I've been . . ."

"I might. It's something, this side of the mountains, isn't it? Right there all that time. But why, Charlie, why are you here?"

"I had to find you, that's why . . ."

Charlie felt as though he was going to burst. It was really Billy. After all this time, it was really him.

"Oh, Billy, I don't understand. Where did you go? Where have you been? Back at the river, you were there, then . . . then you were gone."

"I don't know what happened," Billy said. "I dove in. I

remember hitting the water. It was cold and there was this weight—like I was getting pulled down—after that I was floating, kind of like I was swimming, but I wasn't. I wandered around for a while and then saw others like me and followed them here."

As Billy spoke, he drifted closer to Charlie, taking on a more human shape.

"I should have known. The river was too cold that day. I shouldn't have jumped in . . . I guess it's pretty obvious now . . . I didn't make it, Charlie. I drowned."

Billy knelt down to look his cousin in the eye.

"But you knew that, didn't you? You've known it all along."

"Yeah," Charlie whispered. "I guess I did. I just hoped . . ."

Unable to hold back any longer, Charlie threw his arms around his cousin and finally let himself cry. He cried for Billy, letting go of the tears that had haunted him since that cold October day on the river.

"It's not fair, Billy, it's just not fair," Charlie sobbed. "I miss you so much and I never even got to say good-bye . . ."

Billy waited awhile and then stood with his ghostly arm around Charlie's shoulders.

"It'll be all right, you'll see. Let's go for a walk."

Billy led him farther into the woods.

"You know, it's not too bad being this way, actually. I mean, sometimes it's just kinda boring. Walking back and forth, the same thing day after day. It's a little like school, to be honest, but it's fine, especially here in these woods. And the craziest thing is that now I'm somehow a part of everything—"

"Don't you miss us?" Charlie coughed.

"Of course I do. But I can still feel you. It's a bit like wandering around the house when everyone else is asleep. You wish you were asleep too, instead of all alone, but at least it's a comfort to know someone's there."

"But we miss you, Billy. Nothing's the same since you've been gone."

"Of course it's not the same, Charlie. Things change. That's what life is all about, change. Some good, I guess. Some bad. Who knows what's next—for any of us . . ."

Billy stopped and turned to his cousin.

"But you, you've got to let go. Your life back there has to go on."

"I just wish . . . I wish that day we had done something else," Charlie said, tears streaming down his face. "I wish we hadn't gone to the river. I wish that I could have—"

"Come on, you couldn't have done anything. It was an accident. If there's one thing you learn here, it's that accidents happen. They happen a whole lot."

"But, Billy—"

"No, Charlie. Don't you see?" Billy said. "There's nothing you could have done. And you feeling guilty, being angry about it, it's holding you back—Charlie, it's holding me back too. It's like what I felt pulling me down at the river. Your guilt, your anger, it's all a part of my unfinished business."

"But I could have—"

"No, Charlie. You couldn't have," Billy said, pulling his cousin into his arms.

Remembering summer days in the tree, Charlie felt the warmth wash over him once more. That cold day in October seemed to leave, and he suddenly felt lighter, as though the weight, the guilt and confusion that sat in the pit of his stomach for over a year, had been lifted.

"I know you couldn't have done anything to save me that day. What happened wasn't your fault. You've got to try to accept that, Charlie . . . do you understand?"

Charlie nodded his head.

"You sure?"

Charlie took a deep breath. "I'm sure."

"There, that's better." Billy stood up a bit more and straightened himself. "You know what Old Joe would say here—"

"He'd say chin up," Charlie said with a small smile. It was good to feel his cheeks pushing up the sides of his face again.

"That's right, chin up. Now, come on. We don't have much time, and I'd like to hang out with that goofball cousin of mine, not some old sad sack." Billy shoved Charlie playfully. "Let's go find the others too. It's been a while since I've spoken with anyone from the other side. Wouldn't want to waste the opportunity on the likes of you!"

Charlie wiped the last of his tears on his sleeve and pushed Billy back.

"It's good to see you, Charlie."

"It's good to see you too, Billy."

Billy shoved Charlie again as he walked ahead. "We can climb a few trees on the way too."

Charlie watched him for a moment before he followed.

"Okay."

"And you won't believe how much faster I am here," Billy said.

"Oh yeah, I could catch you," Charlie replied. "You know how fast I am."

"We'll see about that! You couldn't catch me before. What makes you think you can now?"

Charlie raced a few steps toward Billy, but he was already gone.

"Not even close!" Billy said with a laugh. He was now standing behind Charlie. "You run like a turtle."

"A *turtle*?" Charlie turned to lunge at him, but Billy dodged him again, and they ran this way, laughing and stopping to climb the towering trees, all the way to where they left Franklin and Abigail.

chapter 40

Abigail's Departure

When Charlie and Billy found Franklin and Abigail again, they were still sleeping at the base of the tree. Abigail woke as Billy and Charlie approached, which startled Franklin.

"Charlie," Franklin said. He sat up and looked around suspiciously. "Any luck?"

But Abigail had already answered the question by reaching out toward Billy, who took her hand and pulled her to her feet. When he touched her, Billy's form fully appeared.

"I'd like to thank you," Billy said, now extending his hand to Franklin. "Thank you for watching out for this knucklehead."

"Ah, yes, of course." The Monster accepted the offer and climbed to his feet. "Franklin—"

"Prometheus," Billy said, smiling, with no reaction to Franklin's gruesome appearance. "I know who you are. Everyone knows the Monster of all Monsters. I'm Billy."

Billy turned back to Abigail, who was awash in his glow.

"But, tell me, who is this?"

"This is Abigail Rose," Charlie started, and with Abigail's help, he relayed the story as to how she came to be here with them in the trees. He also told Billy what he had read concerning the lost in the book that Franklin had given him, about the confusion of those whose paths are interrupted, or sometimes unsettled.

"We thought, perhaps, this is where she is meant to be?" Franklin offered.

"Abigail Rose, I believe we've been looking for you," Billy said, confirming their theory.

"For me?" Abigail replied. She seemed to blush at Billy's attention.

"You should return to the beach," Billy suggested. "I'll ask around about Miss Abigail and find you there tonight."

"But, Billy—" Charlie began.

"It'll be fine, Charlie. You'll see. I'm not going anywhere just yet."

Billy walked them back toward the strigoii and held the cursed creatures at a distance until they passed over the fallen rocks and were on their way toward the beach. Charlie felt better as they walked, as if the warmth of the strange woods had stayed with him.

It was almost dark and a heavy mist was drifting off the water when Charlie, Franklin, and Abigail finally left the woods. Down the beach, they could barely see the fire from their camp through the fog.

"It will be good to see Ignacio," Charlie said as they approached. But they all stopped at the edge of the firelight. Their little campsite had changed.

Now there was a shelter of stones and driftwood, as well as other structures made from lashed timber and branches to protect their stores from the weather. The Ranger sat huddled by the fire, seemingly unaware of their arrival.

"I see you have been busy," Franklin called out to him.

Ignacio turned abruptly, as though awoken from a sound sleep.

"Busy?" he called back.

"Yes. With the shelter . . . You made good time," Franklin said as they stepped closer to the fire.

"Good time? Why, I would imagine! I've only had, what's it been, a week?"

"A week?" Franklin said with a laugh. "Don't be absurd. Why, we only left this morning."

"*This morning*, that's a good one. After a few days, I thought you'd abandoned me." Ignacio pulled back his hood. "Went in for a look when you didn't return but saw nothing. Some amazing trees back there, but no sign of you. No tracks, no trail . . . nothing—it was like you just disappeared."

"But it's true! We've only been gone a day," Charlie insisted, although he noticed that the Ranger's beard was fuller than he remembered.

"I'm afraid not. I've been sittin' here the whole time," Ignacio continued. "You all look well, at least. Glowing, actually. Must be the fresh air."

"And the Prime Minister?" Franklin asked, looking a bit wary at the Ranger's perplexing news.

"Haven't seen him, been a few birds about, otherwise just me and that bear friend of yours. Gave me a scare on more than one occasion, I'll tell you that much."

"A whole week?" Charlie repeated to himself, wondering how many trees he and Billy climbed while they were there.

Franklin looked up at the few stars that had broken through the settling mist. "I suppose anything is possible after what we have seen."

"It was glorious," Abigail sighed, stepping closer to the fire.

"Well, a day or a week, I would bet you're hungry by now," Ignacio pointed out.

Charlie heard his stomach growling in agreement and realized that he was definitely hungry, as hungry as he had ever been, maybe.

"I'll throw something together for you," Ignacio said, adding some wood to the fire. "I've had some time to forage and was pleasantly surprised at the findings."

They ate leafy greens and roots that the Ranger had found among the trees around the coast and fish that he had spent the week smoking. As they ate, they told Ignacio of what they saw—the strigoii and the strange sensation of being in the woods. They told him of the swirling dust and Billy. Abigail again wasn't hungry but sat near them in the sand by a gnarled root and hummed to herself as she fiddled with her ragged clothes.

"So, what now?" Ignacio asked, offering Franklin some tobacco for his pipe.

"We will see what this night brings and decide in the morning," Franklin said, accepting the pouch. "I am not sure that we have seen the last of what this island has to offer."

WHEN THE SUN FINALLY SET, THE MIST CLEARED TO REVEAL the stars high overhead. A short time later, a flock of magpies appeared from the woods and flew out over the water, followed by the Prime Minister, who slowly walked up the beach and approached their camp.

"May I join you?" he asked.

"Always a question worth considering," Franklin said. "But, of course. Please, warm yourself by our fire."

The Prime Minister sat with them, and Franklin and Charlie recounted their experiences once more. The Prime Minister was not the least bit shocked by the time that had passed since their departure for the woods.

"Just a day to you all," Ignacio said. "While I sat here in the rain all week."

"I saw Billy," Charlie said.

"I can see that," the Prime Minister replied. "I can see in your eyes that a burden has lifted."

"He said he would be back tonight."

The Prime Minister looked over to Abigail. "This much I have gathered."

They sat around the fire and spoke well into the night. As the hours wore on, Abigail curled up in a blanket to sleep. A low, heavy rumbling soon said the same of Franklin and the Ranger.

But Charlie did not sleep. He was simply too excited by the day's events. He sat with the Prime Minister, listening to the sound of his friends sleeping until the vampire broke the silence.

"You know, Charlie, I knew when we met what ailed you. I could see it in the way that you carried yourself. I could see the anger, the sadness in your eyes . . ."

"I guess so," Charlie admitted. "At least, that's what they said back at school."

"I cannot speak for them, Charlie, but I could see it, because I understand. I too was like you. Out of love, I held on to someone after they were gone."

"You did?"

"Yes . . . she was my love, my one true love . . ."

Charlie remembered the last portrait of the Prime Minister that hung at the foot of the stairs in his castle. He pictured the girl standing next to him and her warm smile.

"A long time ago but to me, like this place, a mere blink of the eye," the Prime Minister said. "My love was there, there the night when this happened, the night I was turned. Only she did not survive . . ." The Prime Minister seemed to lose himself in thought as he stared deeply into the fire. "I held her hand as our attackers left us for dead," he said, his voice just above a whisper. "I can still see her there, covered in her own blood as I was covered in mine."

The Prime Minister turned to Charlie; he could have sworn there were tears in his sullen eyes.

"But then moments later, we were here, here in these woods, Charlie. And she looked magnificent. She was no longer hurting, no longer in pain. Her hideous wounds were healed, and I will tell you, she lit the forest. Truly, a vision . . . a thing of beauty . . . but then, as quickly as we were here, reunited, I was gone again. Pulled back to this world, back into the pools of our blood, able to rise but cursed to rise alone . . ."

The Prime Minister clicked his long fangs, but this did not frighten Charlie as it had when they first met.

"I held on to her, Charlie, and with my anger I swore a path of vengeance. Vengeance that I saw served, but that ultimately hurt her more than the brutality that saw to her end. My rage is what held her here, Charlie. It held her, until I was able to find some semblance of peace . . ."

The Prime Minister looked away, out toward the open water.

"Did you see her again? Here in the woods?" Charlie said.

"I did," the Prime Minister replied. "And now she is finally able to move on . . ."

It was Charlie's turn to stare at the fire.

"Is that why you helped me? To get here for yourself?"

"No, I could have come at any time like I am here now. But I recognized that part of myself in you, Charlie, the anger, the pain. I knew then what I had done and knew that if I could help you, I should. In turn, you inspired me to do what I knew I had to do all along . . . and now I have." The Prime Minister threw a small piece of driftwood on the fire. "I thank you, Charlie. As I am sure my true love thanks you and Billy thanks you. And soon so shall young Abigail."

"Abigail?"

"Those chains were what held her, Charlie. They interrupted her journey. The chains were Abigail's burden. And you helped her find her way here. You freed her, as I gather you have now freed yourself."

Charlie's thoughts turned back to what he and Billy had talked about under the towering trees. He thought about what his parents and Old Joe and Ms. Hatchet and the counselors back at school had all said, trying to help him over the course of this particularly long year. And he thought about Abigail.

"What happens to her now?" Charlie asked softly.

"You know, Charlie. Just as you knew but couldn't accept about your Billy."

The Prime Minister turned, and the firelight danced in the pearly white of his pointed teeth.

"Abigail is home now. Though we may never know what happened to her, we can rest knowing that she is now where she belongs."

Charlie looked over at Abigail. She did look happy as she slept.

"Let us all take solace in that..."

Charlie and the Prime Minister walked down to the shore and stood looking out at the moonlight that danced on the water. It was cold away from the fire, but Charlie did not mind. They stood there until they felt a sudden shift in the wind and then turned to face it as it blew heavily from the woods.

There was a glow to the trees that whirled onto the beach and spun toward them near the water's edge. Charlie felt the warmth wash over him again and saw Billy's shape form in the swirling light. But as the whirl subsided, Charlie saw that Billy was not alone. There was Abigail Rose, also aglow, standing next to him, holding his hand.

"I checked. No one is sure how she lost her way. Maybe it was those chains," Billy said, echoing the Prime Minister's words. "Either way, it's good she finally made it."

Standing there, next to Billy, Abigail looked as happy as Charlie had ever seen her.

"Thank you, Charlie," Abigail said, leaning forward to kiss him on the cheek. This time, her touch was not cold. Instead, warmth spread from his cheek to his fingertips as she pulled away.

"Of course," Charlie said with an awkward grin.

"I'll never forget you, Charlie." Abigail smiled. "Not ever."

The Prime Minister stepped forward. "Billy, before you depart, a question."

"Sure."

"The Monster of all Monsters, the newly named Franklin Prometheus. With my own predicament I have always wondered, does he have a soul? A spirit of some sort, as we have seen here?"

Billy thought for a moment.

"It's kinda cloudy with that one. Might be up to him," Billy said with a laugh. "Who knows? You keep helping kids like you did Charlie, and maybe you'll make your way back here as well."

The Prime Minister straightened. "A generous thought, but I have accepted my fate."

Billy looked at Abigail, and then squeezed her hand tight.

"All right, we'll see you around," Billy said.

"Thank you," the Prime Minister returned, adding a slight bow. "Safe travels to you, Miss Rose."

"Why, thank you, Prime Minister," Abigail said with a curtsy.

Billy turned to his cousin. "I'll see you too, Charlie. You hear me? Checking in, you know, on what we talked about..."

Charlie looked up at Billy and felt the tears gathering in his eyes again.

"Hey, hey, no more of that," Billy said, letting go of Abigail to walk closer to his cousin.

"I think it's because I'm happy," Charlie explained.

Billy got a good laugh out of that and wiped the tears from Charlie's face.

"Come on, I'm not going anywhere, so don't worry so much."

"You're not? I thought after all this you'll be moving on," Charlie said.

"I might. But there are others like Abigail out there, so I may just hang around a little longer, see if I can help 'em out. Besides, it'll give me something to do." Billy tousled Charlie's hair. "Now, you better remember, just because you can't see me, it doesn't mean I'm not there."

Charlie smiled. Billy *had* been there, he thought. Even though he'd disappeared that day at the river, Charlie still had his memories—the good times they'd spent together, even the worn photograph he kept in his pocket. Billy might be gone, but he was still Billy. And all that they had together, both happy and sad, would stay with Charlie forever.

"I know," Charlie said. "I'll remember."

"See ya, Charlie." Billy laughed as he ran backward to Abigail. "Keep that chin up." He took her hand in his and waved before they turned and walked away. Charlie watched them until a swirl of dust rose up, hiding them from view. When the dust settled, they were gone.

"See ya, Billy," he whispered.

The Prime Minister placed a hand on Charlie's shoulder. It was warmer than he remembered, and Charlie could not help but wonder if what Billy had said was true. Perhaps the Prime Minister's fate, like his and Franklin's, was still unwritten—what came next was up to them, up to all of them. And Charlie decided right then and there that he for one was going to make the most of it.

—— *chapter 41* ——

Lost Angel No More

THE FIRST HINTS of morning were just streaking across the sky when Charlie and the Prime Minister returned to camp. They found Franklin sitting cross-legged with Abigail's tiny body cradled in his arms. Ignacio stood over them with a blanket to cover the girl.

"She's left us," Ignacio said softly. "Sometime in the night."

"Did they come for her?" Franklin looked up. His face was taut and his eyes looked even more sunken in than usual. "This was their plan, right?"

"Yes, she went with Billy," the Prime Minister explained. "She's home now. Abigail will be just fine."

"You're sure?" Franklin gasped.

"Yes, my old friend," the Prime Minister said, doing his best to console the Monster. "Quite sure."

The Prime Minister left at sunrise, and they wrapped Abigail's body in the blanket, found a spot on a bluff above their camp, and buried her at the base of a tree that looked out over the open water. Franklin dug the grave by himself, and dug it deep. He laid heavy rocks on top and carved ABIGAIL ROSE— LOST ANGEL NO MORE into the largest of the stones. He set the marker against the tree's twisted roots and, with Charlie, planted clustered sprigs of wildflowers in the small pockets of the rock.

"A fine spot," Ignacio said. "A fine spot indeed."

When they turned to drop back down to the beach, Franklin did not follow. Instead, the Monster knelt, weaving the knotted rope through his swollen and misshapen fingers, and bowed his head.

"Come on," Ignacio said. "Just let him be . . ."

The Ranger saw to the ship's rigging as the Monster stayed at Abigail's grave for most of the morning. When Franklin came back to camp, it seemed his usual gruffness had returned with him. He found Charlie packing up their gear and sat on a tree trunk to light his pipe.

"Well, Charlie, what now?" Franklin asked. "Would you say we have completed this task?"

"Yes, Franklin. I think we have," Charlie said. He was rolling up a heavy canvas tarp.

"Though this was never part of the original agreement," Franklin began, "I suppose you would like me to see you home?"

"I'd hope so, Franklin. I'd sure hate to go it alone," Charlie replied, looking up at him with a smile.

"Well then." The Monster stood up, took the rolled tarp, and secured it with their other bundles. "The same rules apply. You will help with the camp. You'll do as I say. The trip back will not be any easier."

"I understand," Charlie said.

"There will be the usual—goblins, trolls, and ogres, more marauders. Witches, werewolves, wendigos, could be warlocks, even. Who knows what we will encounter?"

"To be expected, I guess," Charlie replied, handing Franklin one of the crates of supplies.

"And then there's those cursed charts, *the Prime Minister's maps*, much to be done on that. I will expect your help with those as well, you know."

"I can help," Charlie said.

"Who's to say what the weather will do?" Franklin patted the boy on the back. "Especially in the mountain passes . . ."

They continued like this for the next few hours as they broke down the rest of the camp and loaded the boat. Charlie thought that Franklin must be feeling himself again with the return home before them. It was something he could plan and look forward to executing. Perhaps they both needed it to occupy their minds after all they had been through.

When their supplies were loaded, they joined Ignacio at the ship and set sail. Charlie sat in the stern facing the island and watched as it grew smaller and smaller on the horizon behind them. He would have guessed he might be sad as they sailed away from Billy and Abigail Rose, but he wasn't.

Instead, as he thought about the great adventure they had undertaken together, he felt satisfied. He turned to the bow, glancing at Franklin and Ignacio, and imagined the trip back, looking ahead to whatever they might encounter on their long journey home.

—— *chapter 42* ——

The Long Journey Home

*T*HEY SAILED THROUGH the night with Franklin carefully consulting and making notations on his maps and charts. The next day, they rejoined Rohmetall, Ringo, and the horses at the ramshackle port. Rohmetall greeted them with open arms, but Ringo was leery at first. Though he seemed to recognize Charlie, Franklin, and Ignacio, he barked at their approach, then whimpered and pulled away when Charlie reached out to pet him. After some playful coaxing, the dog eventually came around, though, and was soon back to his old self.

They slept that night at the Banshee's Boot, and then at first light struck out again, with Franklin riding Goliath alongside Ignacio, while Charlie, Rohmetall, and Ringo followed in the cart. Like Dwight York and the princess Zalika, they avoided the desert and the salt flat by following the coastline until they reached the mouth of the river that would eventually take them back to the Agrarian Plains. They secured a broad, flat boat there and, after loading the cart and horses, were off again, the horses now resting as Franklin, Charlie, and Ignacio pushed the craft upriver with long poles that were thrown in at no extra charge. They took turns sleeping on the barge and on more than one occasion were forced to fend off a few curious predators who needed reminding that Charlie and his friends were not the easiest of prey.

They finally arrived at the Mumiya trading ports and were greeted with much fanfare and celebration. Their reunion with Zalika was bittersweet, though, as they learned her mother, the queen Khensa Tuya, had passed on from wounds sustained in the marauders' raid. But there was already talk that Zalika would soon be crowned, and she promised that after her experiences in the desert, she would sit down with the Council and come up with a plan for a more permanent peace. They were treated to a banquet and given gifts of gold, silver, and jewels, and Franklin was presented with a magnificent horse. Like Faust, it was a large midnight-black horse of a sturdy breed that proved to be both strong and fast.

"A fine horse," Franklin concluded, inspecting the stead. But behind the Monster's gracious smile, Charlie could still see how sad he was at the loss of his beloved Faust.

Though Zalika implored them to stay, they moved on at dawn, riding through the great rows of corn and wheat toward the snowcapped mountains that loomed in the distance. With snow now in the passes, it took them longer to cross the mountains. Along the way, they encountered trolls, wayward ogres, and, on one occasion, a particularly ornery set of banshees, which is within itself a whole other story. Despite these set-backs, they plodded forward, surveying their route as they rode and seeing to the completion of the Prime Minister's maps. Much to Franklin's frustration, Rohmetall spent most of the journey pointing out all he could as they traveled. They met Dwight York near the spot on the river where they rescued Abigail Rose. He traveled with them as they dropped down from the mountains to the woods and the road that would eventually lead them back to Franklin's Charnel House.

They camped in the woods that night, and in the morning, the Ranger Ignacio Santos and Dwight York said their good-byes. They promised that they would see Charlie again some-day and then bounded off, the Ranger on horseback and Dwight York running as a wolf, into the high, heavy line of timber. As far as Charlie knew, the issue with Dwight York and the Ranger School was still unresolved, but that did not stop the two from singing a few choruses of the Rangers' song before they left.

Franklin, Charlie, and Rohmetall traveled on with Ringo running at their heels, only stopping once more for Franklin to reflect at the roadside shrine in the high trees by the small mountain stream. Later, as they passed through the village's narrow streets, they happened upon Lester Mortlock and his one-eyed cohort, who were locked in a pillory in the cobble-stoned square. Lester begged for his freedom, but Franklin refused to get involved with local politics, so they left him there, shouting after them, as children of various monstrous descents pummeled the ne'er-do-wells with rotting fruits and vegetables.

They rode on, making good time now that they were in previously mapped lands, and late that day they came to the crossroads that pointed to the Charnel House. Franklin paused for a moment before turning his horse in the direction of the Prime Minister's castle.

"We'll see you on to the tunnel, Charlie," he said, spurring the new horse forward. "After all this way, it just wouldn't be right otherwise."

It was dark and raining when they started up the long, winding road to the Prime Minister's castle, and Charlie could hardly believe it when they crossed the bridge and pulled the horses to a stop. He turned Goliath toward the tower that housed the observation deck and remembered the night when he first looked out over Monsterland. The time was so jumbled in his head . . . It all seemed so long ago.

He watched as Franklin dismounted and Rohmetall began to unload their belongings. He thought of the time they'd spent together, all they'd seen during the course of their great journey, and he wished he didn't have to say good-bye. But he also thought of his parents and Old Joe, and how he missed them—and now that he was thinking about it, how he even missed school and Ms. Hatchet. It was over, he thought. It was time to go home.

Mrs. Winthrope rushed out to meet them at the door and held Charlie in a long embrace as he slid down from his saddle.

"My, my, to look at ya!" Mrs. Winthrope said. "Oh, I am happy, so happy to see you. Ya made it! The Prime Minister will be thrilled!"

Franklin handed Rohmetall the reins, and the metal man pulled the cart and horses around the drive to the stables.

"And you, sir," Mrs. Winthrope went on. "Why, yer the talk of the land—the two of ya! Such stories. Such adventure."

Franklin moved stiffly as he stepped forward to greet Mrs. Winthrope. As he passed, Charlie noticed that one of his shoulders was hanging lower than the other again; his right arm was dangling loosely from its stitching.

"Not to worry," Franklin said, adjusting the loose joint. He patted Charlie on the top of his head. "Nothing a needle and thread and a little rest can't fix."

Mrs. Winthrope took Franklin and Charlie by the hand and led them up the steps and out of the rain.

"Come now," she said. "Let's get ya cleaned up, and then we'll have something to eat. The moon is already on the rise. We still have some time, but we mustn't dillydally."

"Ah, yes," Franklin said, looking at the sky. "With the weather moving on, I'd bet you will be heading to the tunnel tonight."

"Tonight?" Charlie said. As eager as he was to get home, it was still somehow disappointing.

"Come on, Charlie." Franklin sighed. He looked a little downcast too.

As they walked across the immense foyer, Charlie looked over the Prime Minister's line of portraits, and he slowed when he passed the painting at the bottom of the stairs. The young girl's smile seemed brighter to Charlie now; feeling better, he returned her smile before heading upstairs.

Charlie changed back into his old clothes, but his jeans and sweatshirt felt strange to him now, as though they were no longer his. He hurried to get ready, stuffing his werewolf mask into his pocket with his fangs and photograph.

He was pleased to see the Prime Minister when he came down the stairs to join him and Franklin for dinner, even if he felt underdressed now in their company. But Charlie quickly forgot his discomfort as they gathered around the table to enjoy another splendid meal. Though Franklin, Dwight York, and the Ranger knew their way around a campfire, there was not much that could compare to Mrs. Winthrope's superb cooking.

When they were finished with the last course, they retired to the Prime Minister's study, where Franklin presented him with their maps.

"These are rough, of course. I have some corrections, and then I'd like to make them more presentable, but as an idea . . ."

"Ah, yes." The Prime Minister spread the roll out on the table in front of him. He studied the maps for a moment. "And what is this?"

The Prime Minister removed a small set of spectacles from his vest pocket as Franklin sat back in his chair and lit his pipe.

"Well, I certainly appreciate the gesture," the Prime Minister said, motioning for Charlie to come closer. "Have you seen this?"

Charlie stood beside the Prime Minister and looked at the roll. Taking in the vast areas that had previously been unmapped, he was proud of the work he and Franklin had done.

"See there, down in the right-hand corner." The Prime Minister leaned over him, pointing with a long fingernail to the bottom of the map on top.

Charlie found the key and read out loud what was written below it in Franklin's hand.

CARTOGRAPHERS: FRANKLIN PROMETHEUS
AND CHARLIE COOPER

COMMISSIONED BY: THE HONORABLE PRIME MINISTER
OF VAMPYREISHTAT AND
SURROUNDING PROVINCES

"Lovely, is it not?" the Prime Minister said. "Well done. Congratulations are in the highest order to the both of you."

"It was Franklin, really," Charlie said, smiling from ear to ear. "I just kind of helped him where I could." Franklin grunted softly from behind his lit pipe. He seemed impressed by Charlie's humility.

"Ah, I wish there were more time." The Prime Minister glanced out the window at the evening sky. "But I am afraid we must cut the pleasantries short if we are to catch the moon at its fullest. It is a short walk from here, but the incline is steep and takes some time."

Mrs. Winthrope came in with Oscar, who was carrying a tray. Ringo followed, nipping at their feet, and Oscar's magpie trailed Ringo, fluttering around the room and nipping at the dog's tail.

"I've wrapped a pie for ya, Charlie," Mrs. Winthrope said.

Her voice cracked when she reached his name. "You can eat it if you get hungry on yer way."

"I'm not sure I've met anyone who's been to the wilds and made it back to tell the tale," Oscar added, looking from Franklin to Charlie with great admiration. "And now I know you both. Take care of yourself . . ."

"I will," Charlie said, leaving Oscar in the study to try to collect his flustered magpie. "You too."

Following Franklin and the Prime Minister across the foyer, Charlie grabbed his pack and they walked outside to the bridge and the grand landing. The rain had cleared and Rohmetall clanged up the drive toward them, his casing sparkling with a metallic sheen in the moonlight.

"Hello, Ch-Ch-Charlie Cooper," the steam man called. "Hello."

"I am afraid it is not hello," the Prime Minister replied, looking up at the full moon.

"Good-bye to Charlie Cooper?"

"Yes, Mr. Rohmetall. This is good-bye."

"'The pain of parting is nothing to the joy of meeting again.' Charles Dickens, 1812 to 1870. See chapter three, *Nicholas Nickleby*." The steam man whistled. "Do not forget us. No matter what they say. Do not forget, Ch-Ch-Charlie Cooper."

"I won't," Charlie said, and then turned to Mrs. Winthrope. "Thank you again, Mrs. Winthrope. Thank you for everything."

"Oh, but I should be thanking you," she said.

"Why thank me?" Charlie asked.

"For yer bravery, of course," she said, and hugged him tight. "You've shown us all something. Not many would have dared cross the threshold to this place, let alone travel where you've been. And you did it all for someone else. It's something to be proud of, to say the least."

The Prime Minister and Franklin started walking again, so Charlie followed, waving back to Mrs. Winthrope and Rohmetall as he crossed the bridge. Ringo ran ahead to where Franklin and the Prime Minister turned off the cobblestoned drive and onto a long, narrow path that wound up the side of the mountain. Charlie climbed the jagged stone steps after them, and the trail grew steadily steeper. In places, it became so narrow that they had to cling to the sides of the exposed rock for fear they would be blown off by the cold gusts that rushed down from above. They continued well into the night with the Prime Minister keeping a watchful eye on the moon as it slowly climbed with them. They went higher and higher, and when Charlie was so tired that he thought he could not take another step, Franklin was there to help him. The Monster picked the boy up and put him on his shoulders and carried him that way until they reached the tunnel entrance at the very top. Once there, he set him down gently next to Ringo, and they stood with the Prime Minister, looking out on all of Vampyreishtat.

"When you think about it, Charlie," the Prime Minister said, "you have seen more of this land than most of its own inhabitants."

It was true, Charlie thought, gazing out over the valley. But the lands below seemed so vast and wide that it was hard for him to believe how far they had traveled. He took a long, deep breath; the mountain air was cold and burned as it filled his lungs.

"And now these few final steps," the Prime Minister said. He turned to face the wall and ran his fingers over the runes that were carved into the stone. Then he nodded to Franklin, who lowered his shoulder and pushed against the rock. There was a loud cracking sound as the hidden door opened on unseen hinges.

"After you," Franklin said, stepping out of the way. The Prime Minister removed a flickering torch from the wall and started down the dark tunnel. "And you next, boy."

Before stepping through the door, Charlie had to stop and persuade Ringo to come along. The dog stood whimpering at the threshold with his tail between his legs and would not budge until Franklin gave him a gentle push with his foot. Franklin followed, stooping down until he could stand again in the great mausoleum at the end of the long tunnel.

When they entered, the Prime Minister had already crossed the room and was busy with the carved runes on the last door. Charlie looked up at the murals and stone carvings, feeling light-headed in the stale air of the crypt. As he thought back to the last time he was in this room, one of the carvings that he recalled seeing stood out to him. He realized now that the carving was of Franklin—the Monster of all Monsters. In great, dramatic fashion, it showed him charging forward on horseback in his armor, battle-ax in hand.

"It was never as glorious as all that," Franklin called back to Charlie as he helped the Prime Minister with the final door.

"I thought they *were* *w*ell commissioned," the Prime Minister replied. With a grunt, Franklin took hold of the heavy stone. "Charlie," the Prime Minister said, calling him over. "Are you ready to go home?"

"I think I am," Charlie said. "My mom's probably pretty worried by now, right, Ringo?"

Just then, Franklin pulled back on the rock and pried open the mausoleum door. The cold, fresh air of the forest rushed in and filled the crypt with its subtle sweetness. Charlie looked out and pictured his parents and Old Joe waiting for him, and took the first step up the stairs into the overgrown cemetery. The gravestones looked wet, but the sky was now clear and a full moon shone bright overhead. Franklin and the Prime Minister followed Charlie and Ringo a short distance into the graveyard and then stopped.

"*W*ell, Charlie," the Prime Minister said. "Here *w*e are. *W*here *w*e first met . . ."

"Yes, it is," Charlie replied, his hands twisting the straps of his pack.

"I suppose I should hold on to that," the Prime Minister suggested. "I do not think you *w*ill need it. I have heard that swords and ancient esoteric reference books are frowned upon at school these days . . ."

"Yeah, I don't know how I would explain the Roman gladius," Charlie said, swinging the pack off his shoulders and handing it to the Prime Minister. Then again, Charlie thought, how would he explain any of it?

"For safekeeping," the Prime Minister promised. "You never know when you may need it again…" The Prime Minister looked up at the moon and then back at Charlie. "It is getting late. Well, Charlie, there is always more to be said, but for now…" The Prime Minister extended a long, slender hand. "I thank you again."

"I don't know what to say," Charlie said.

"*Precisssely*," the vampire hissed.

Charlie took the Prime Minister's hand, noticing yet again that it seemed a little bit warmer, just as it had on the rock beach with Billy. And Charlie could also see that, like Franklin, there was the slightest hint of a glow twinkling somewhere in the shadows that were his eyes.

"Farewell, Charlie," the Prime Minister said with a bow. He patted Ringo on the head and then turned back to the mausoleum.

"The Prime Minister. Ha, quite the character, isn't he?" Franklin said, stepping forward to Charlie. He stood there silently for a moment, looking up at the stars.

"Franklin."

"Yes, Charlie."

"Do you think we will ever meet again? Someplace? Somewhere, like back at the trees, where we found Billy?"

"I do not know, Charlie. What's next is a mystery to me that seems cloudier every day."

The Monster knelt down to look Charlie in the eye.

"But as the Prime Minister is fond of saying, we do not have to resolve all that ails us this evening, do we?"

Franklin put his big hand on Charlie's shoulder.

"You going to be all right, Charlie?"

"I think so, Franklin. You?"

"Oh, yes," Franklin said. "Plenty to do to keep me busy. The list is long. And as you know, trouble's always brewing . . ."

Charlie felt tears welling up and saw the Monster wipe away something in the corner of his eye.

"You take care of yourself, Charlie. Keep that chin up . . . you hear me?"

"I will," Charlie said. When he couldn't hold back the tears any longer, he threw his arms around the Monster. "I will."

"Remember who you are, Charlie, and what you can do when you put your mind to it. The possibilities are endless," Franklin said. Those last words seemed to catch in his throat as he said them, but Charlie knew they were true. Franklin Prometheus himself was the proof. He had once lived hidden in bogs and swamps. Nameless, he'd been hunted, lost, and on the run, and now he lived on a mountaintop in a castle, as a statesman, a scholar, and, Charlie thought, his friend.

"Remember, just because you do not see us, Charlie, does not mean we are not there." Franklin tapped Charlie on the chest. "Or here."

Franklin bent down to Ringo and ruffled his long coat. "Good old Ringo."

The Monster stood, hit Charlie softly on the shoulder, and turned to leave.

"Good-bye, Charlie."

"Good-bye, Franklin," Charlie said. He stood with Ringo among the crumbled gravestones, watching as Franklin followed the Prime Minister into the mausoleum and they shut the heavy stone door behind them.

Then the graveyard was quiet, overcome by a stillness that Charlie hadn't felt in a long time.

"Well, Ringo, here we are. Right back where it all started," Charlie said. "But," Charlie began, and then laughed, "I think we're still lost, buddy." Ringo tilted his head quizzically. "Can you believe it?"

After all they had been through, Charlie wasn't so worried about being lost now, though. He was confident they'd find their way eventually, and set off with his best guess for Old Joe's house. They left the graveyard and, avoiding the bog, wandered off through the trees. They walked for what felt like hours, finally coming to sit at the base of a big tree to rest. Bathed in the light of the full moon, Charlie soon fell asleep with Ringo curled up peacefully at his side.

He slept soundly there in the woods, and he did not have any nightmares. He dreamed, though, and his dreams were full of marvelous things. He dreamed of the stories he had heard and the places he had been. He dreamed of snow-covered mountains, clouds of magpies, and forests as deep and mysterious as any cave. In his dreams, he saw faces—Billy and Abigail, Zalika, Dwight York and Ignacio, the Prime Minister, Rohmetall, Oscar and Mrs. Winthrope, even Lester Mortlock still in his stocks, and of course, the Monster of all Monsters, Franklin Prometheus. It was said that when they found Charlie asleep in the woods the next morning, not only was he smiling, but when he woke, he was also well rested. And that Ringo, his fur muddied and matted, was there too, calmly licking an empty pie tin, but still at his side.

Epilogue

——◆✦◆——

*W*HEN THE SEARCH party, led by Old Joe, found Charlie, over forty days had passed since the boy had gone missing. After the first two weeks, the authorities had feared the worst and threatened to stop searching—"a lost cause," they said. But Charlie's family refused to give up, saying that he was a resourceful boy who knew the mountains and these woods and was therefore still alive. They were sure of it. The town was covered in flyers with Charlie's picture, and on the weekends Ms. Hatchet and her fifth-grade class joined the search, shouting Charlie's name as they wandered the woods at the base of the mountains. But despite their best efforts, the boy was still missing, and some began to whisper that wild animals had attacked him or that maybe he had been eaten, possibly by a bear.

Then one day, the numbers of their search party dwindling, Old Joe came across a small clearing. And there, at the base of a big oak, he found his grandson asleep in the morning sun next to his dog, Ringo. Old Joe greeted Ringo and then quietly knelt down.

"You're home, Charlie," Old Joe said softly. "You're home."

Charlie opened his eyes slowly and threw his arms around his grandfather.

"You won't believe where I've been," Charlie said, the excitement of all that had happened washing over him. "You won't believe what I've seen."

But Old Joe stopped him before he could say any more.

"There, there, you've been through a lot. You can tell me all about it when you're ready," Old Joe said, embracing the boy. Then, after a quick glance to Ringo's empty pie tin, he looked over his shoulder and warned, "For now, you watch what you say to these folks. There's going to be a lot of questions."

The small clearing was soon a hive of sheriff's deputies and helicopters and soldiers in uniforms and still others in dark suits. Charlie was flown directly to the big hospital in the city, where he was reunited with his mother and father, who broke down in tears of joy when they saw him and then fainted. Charlie was on the news, a local celebrity, because no one could understand how a boy and a dog could survive that long, at this time of year, all alone in the mountains. But through it all, heeding Old Joe's words, Charlie said little of his experience. He never mentioned Monsterland.

Tests showed that Charlie had suffered a minor concussion, so they kept him in the hospital for observation, which came with a barrage of tests. They examined his shoulder and had little in the way of explanation for the Ranger Ignacio Santos's intricate horsehair stitches. The same went for the mummified crevice in Charlie's arm, which they were forced to conclude was some unidentified fungus that the doctors tried to remove without success. As far as the boy's disappearance, a neurologist surmised that Charlie's head trauma had caused some sort of amnesia, which likely left him disoriented and therefore unable to find his way home. He added that in Charlie's confused state, he had more than likely never been farther than ten miles from the pumpkin patch where he first disappeared. Though the doctor's ten-mile theory was slightly insulting, Charlie still said nothing.

Once the tests were over, Charlie was released from the hospital, and as the days passed and Christmas approached, Charlie's life slowly fell back into its normal routine. With his nightmares gone, Charlie was sleeping better than ever; each morning he woke without a trace of the heaviness he once felt. Back at school, his grades were already improving, and at Birdy Fargus's suggestion, he was thinking about trying out for the cross-country running team in the spring. He had also just recently started to leave his photograph of Billy at home, tucked into the frame of the mirror above his dresser. As time went on, his journey to Monsterland seemed more and more distant, and he wondered if he would ever see the tunnel that cut through the mountain again.

Then one day, when Charlie got home from school, he

found a stack of mail on the kitchen table. And there, among the bills and the magazines, he saw a familiar bundle of letters. Wrapped in rough twine, the letters were worn around the edges and tattered. Charlie pulled them apart and saw that they were addressed to his mother in his own handwriting. Charlie dusted the soot and grime off them and finally understood why Mrs. Winthrope and the Ranger had been so reluctant to guarantee their timeliness.

He thought about leaving the letters for his mother, but remembered Old Joe's warning from the day he was found in the woods. Then again, he had to trust someone . . .

Turning the small bundle of letters in his hands, Charlie decided he would finally break his silence. He decided he would tell Old Joe everything and ran down to the barn to find him. But when he reached the big bay doors, Charlie stopped cold in his tracks. He could hear Old Joe, singing to himself. And while his singing was not unusual, the song he was singing most certainly was.

> "From ghoulies and ghosties and long-legged beasties
> And things that go bump in the night.
> O Lord, won't you save us from the horrors that haunt us
> And give us good dreams till the light.
> For we are the Rangers, the hard-riding Rangers,
> And we'll give all those nasties a fright!
> Those ghoulies and ghosties and long-legged beasties
> And things that go bump in the night.

So step up your horse, and set out your course,

For we Rangers protect what is right!

And be warned, all you ghoulies, you ghosties and beasties,

All you things that go bump in the night!"

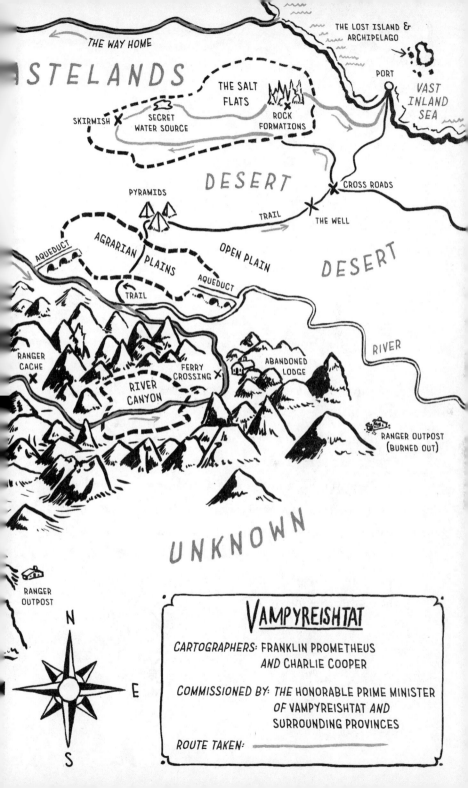

ACKNOWLEDGMENTS

Special thanks to Jennifer Besser and Kate Meltzer, and to Cindy Howle, Christine Ma, Janet Robbins Rosenberg, Eileen Savage, Richard Amari, Morgan Schweitzer, Dana Li, Jennifer Dee, and everyone at G. P. Putnam's Sons and Penguin Young Readers.

Thanks also to Josh Getzler, Danielle Burby, Jonathan Cobb, and the HSG Agency.

To my family and friends for the early reads, and with the utmost respect to Mary Wollstonecraft Shelley, Bram Stoker, and the Brothers Grimm. And, of course, to Doc and Jude for the stories growing up, read at bedtime or told around campfires—my gratitude for the opportunity to travel to all the worlds that may or may not exist.